THE HATCHET MEN

Simmeon Anderson

The Hatchet Men

Copyright 2017 Simmeon Anderson

All rights reserved. The book is protected with the copyright laws of the United States of America. This book may not be copied or reprinted for commercial gains or profit.

This use of occasional page copying for group study is permitted and encourage. Permission will be granted upon request.

For worldwide distribution available in paperback and E Book. Printed in the United States of America

Published by Above Any Odds Entertainment and Publishing LLC

P.O Box 3436
Newark, New Jersey USA

www.aboveanyoddsentertainment.com

Liberty of Congress Control # 2022908581

ISBN 978-0-578-95697-8

ACKNOWLEDGMENTS

First and foremost, I give all praise to God because without Him there would be no me. God gave me a gift and I developed it. Thank you, God.

To my mother: Thank you for always being there through every storm.

To my loving sister: Thank you for being there throughout my journey in life that I am still going through. I will always love you because you're not just my sister, you're my best friend. I can remember when we were kids and the two of us were flipping on mom's couch. My head got stuck between the cushions of the couch and my body was up against the wall. I was screaming for help but you took off, running for cover. Because mom was coming with a belt, somehow and someway with the help of mom whipping my ass, I was able to get free. LOL!

To my kids and my niece Chanell, Tytianna, Simmeon Jr., Aniyah, Shaniya and Ashanti - daddy's little Muffin Top: I love all of you very much and to my two grandchildren Payton and Amir, Pop-Pop loves you!

To Michael and Anthony at Minuteman Press in Newark, New Jersey for the graphic art on the book cover.

To everybody that supported me with my books, *Cartel King and Gangster Chitty, Chitty, Bang, Bang, Queen Cartel Gangster Blooded,* and *I'm My Own Hero*, thank you for your support. I hope to be able to continue to bring you more good entertainment. To my editor, Louise Sanders, for doing tremendous work on this book as well as *Queen Cartel Gangster Blooded,* may God continue to bless you and may we continue to work together. Thank you. We're not going to let either one of these pandemics stop what we do; the one (racism) that's been going on for almost five centuries and the other (COVID-19 aka Coronavirus) that started in early 2020.

Nevertheless, I want to give a very big special shout-out to the people in my nation and people from around the globe for coming together as one voice for those who can't speak for themselves. Thank you more than you could ever understand because I myself am a victim of police brutality. So, I wish to speak for those who can't…

INTRODUCTION

I will never forget that night in Brooklyn, New York in Bedford-Stuyvesant on Lafayette Street. I was working in a crack house and I believe I was no older than 13 years of age. At that time in New York there was a special task force called TNT (Technical Narcotic Task force). That night, they were looking for a police radio that I didn't have. I used to hear them on a police scanner being called to a fake location by whoever had stolen their radio. I remember sitting in the crack house with a few of my friends, smoking weed. On the scanner we heard police shouting out to the guy who had stolen their radio what they were going to do to him when they found him. I would have never in a million years thought the guy they would find would be me.

The police came to the crack house with their battering ram and knocked down the steel door. That night I was working alone. I was able to make it out a window and down the fire escape before the door came down. I climbed up to the roof, but the police were there waiting for me. I jumped off the fire escape's ladder and back onto the fire escape steps, running past the window I'd escaped out of just as the police knocked the door down and crowded into the room. At the bottom of the fire escape I jumped to the ground, running like a bat out of hell. The only thing I had on me was a gun and some drugs in a book bag. I threw it in the doghouse of a pit bull that came running toward me. I stopped and was in a face-off with this pit because at the time I was more afraid of the police than that pit bull.

I started flexing and screaming like I was the Incredible Hulk. I kid you not, the dog took off running into its house. I don't know if it was because of me or because of the police coming behind me. I ran toward the doghouse, scaling the wall and grabbing ahold of the fire escape and making my way up to the rooftop. I tried to hide up there but I felt very unsafe. Plus, they had a police helicopter. I peered a little over the edge and the block was surrounded by police. I ran back across the roof and opened a hatch, climbed down a ladder and started banging on a resident's door for them to let me in. The residents did the opposite. They called the police. And to that family, I am so sorry and please forgive me. I was just a scared little boy.

A police officer came with his rifle and a flashlight, pointing it at me. I put my hands up as high as I could so they could see them. He made me climb back up the ladder and I did it slowly. Once he got close enough that's when he grabbed me, throwing me down to the ground, asking me for a radio I didn't have. More police came and that's when the torture started. Two officers grabbed my arms, almost pulling me apart, and started placing pens and pencils between my fingers. When they asked about their radio and I told them I didn't have it, they would squeeze my fingers together until the pencils and pens broke.

That was a walk in the park compared to what would happen next. Two more officers grabbed my legs and spread them apart. One officer began to beat me with his rife in my chest and ribs and the other officer started kicking me in the scrotum. He acted like my scrotum was a football and he was kicking for the winning score. He did this to me over and over again. I don't remember how many times he kicked me but I cried like I never cried before. I cried out so loud that the people in the neighborhood started yelling for them to stop. They wanted to throw me off the roof top, but the people made sure that didn't happen. As I was barely walking through the same apartment building where I sold crack, one of the cops hit me in my jaw with the butt of his rifle, breaking my jaw. I was taken to the 81st Precinct and one of the head detectives started asking me some questions. He asked me what color was my mom? I mumbled around a broken jaw and told him she was black and asked, why? Then he asked me what color was my father. I told him he was white and again asked, why? He started to smile and his actual words were, "I knew I saw something good in you." I was in so much physical pain from the severe beating; a broken jaw and my testicles being almost crushed, but I still hawked up as much spit as I could and did my very best to spit on him. And at that time I became a nigger to him again and in his own words he said, "y'all nigger's don't know what we got in store for y'all!" At that moment my mom rushed through the precinct's doors and I'd never felt so safe in my life. She made them take me to the hospital where I was hospitalized for more than a few weeks.

I'm a survivor of the continuing injustices that are happening today. This incident that happened to me wasn't the last occasion either. It happened a few more times to me, but as I got older I made it stop. I'd had enough and I wasn't going down without a fight. If a policeman tried to touch me I would stand up for myself. I know when some people read all I've had to say they are going to say, "He shouldn't have run from the police," or "He should've been home," or even, "What is he doing selling drugs?" Yes, all of that is true but as a human being I still deserve the right to be treated with humanity, with equality, with respect and with some goddamn dignity!

I say all of this because of what happened to those that didn't do anything as bad as I did: George Floyd, Michael Brown, Sandra Bland, Jamar Clark, Eric Gardner, Ahmaud Arbery, Stephon Clark, Philando Castile, Freddie Gray, Walter Scott, Tamir Rice, John Crawford III, and Christian Lopez in Mexico. Oh, and the list doesn't begin or end there. You can go back to the year 1615 and trace 405 years of injustices. Just think about all of the undocumented humans that were murdered on the voyages over to this country on slave ships. And some of those that did make it to this country were killed for sport at picnics. Please understand the meaning behind the word picnic ("pick a nigger" to lynch while white churchgoers brought their lunch and children to sit out under the trees after church and watch the lynching for entertainment = picnic). Martin Luther King, Jr. fought peacefully, marching to establish equality for all men and women to be treated equally. Only after his death was the Civil Rights Act passed for African-Americans in the United States. In 1968 Martin Luther King, Jr. died for equal rights and only then was it established. I would like to know why in the hell bother to establish the Civil Rights Act if some people are not allowed to live it? What sense does it make if your own officers who are sworn to serve and protect the people of this great nation aren't doing what they swore to do? Are you really telling me that Martin Luther King, Jr. died for nothing?

When I see true justice, only then will I see this nation as great again. When I see equality, only will I love what I used to hate. When I see humanity for all my brothers and sisters will I not feel fear in my body that makes me want to fight not flight. Only then will I believe. When I see black families no longer having to have "the talk" with their children about what to do if they're pulled over by the police to insure their very survival to come home afterwards is preserved, only then will I believe. When I see mothers of all races and creeds come together, not to march over another black life being taken from hate, but to celebrate the life of a new era of justice in this nation we call home, will I believe.

When I no longer hear the word nigger being called out in a derogatory fashion because of hate, only then will I believe. When I see white men, women and children having the right to pick and choose to have a person of color as a friend, lover or partner in everything that is America, only then will I believe. When I no longer see people of this great nation having to take a knee for injustice and inequality, only then will I believe. When I no longer hear Jay-Z, Meek Mill, Killer Mic, T.I. and Kim Kardashian talking about the injustices in prisons that have been going on in this country for years, only then will I believe. When I see Colin Kaepernick playing on a NFL football field again; a sport he loved but was forced to give up because he couldn't stand seeing the social injustices and unfair treatment of black people in America because of the color of their skin, only then will I believe. When I see 32 of the football franchises have some black owners, and I mean "Jay-Z black," only then will I believe. When I hear the black people who are surviving family members of the 1921 burning of Tulsa, Oklahoma's Black Wall Street get what rightfully belongs to them, will I believe. When I no longer see women like Amy Cooper calling the police because a black man is asking her to do something simple for everybody's sake, only then will I believe. When I see Benjamin Crump no longer have to represent those who can't represent themselves, I will believe. When I no longer see Rev. Al Sharpton on TV speaking for those who can't speak for themselves, I will believe. When I no longer fear that my black children and grandchildren will become a victim of police brutality and instead all colors of children can get stopped by the police and instead of stop and frisk, the police will make sure they get home safe. Only then will I breathe because right now I can't breathe.

To the police that are sworn to protect and serve the people of this great nation: I feel a new system needs to be put in place when recruiting and hiring police officers. They should be required to learn and get to know the communities they are going to police. They need to attend community meetings and meet some of the people they will be protecting so they won't have to be afraid. All officers should take a lie detector test and asked the following simple questions:

"Will you practice racism on people who don't look like you?"

"Will you treat all people you encounter with humanity and respect?"

"Should you have to chase someone down, would you use unnecessary force to stop them?"

White people! Get woke! Black people! Stay woke! I'm out. I can't breathe!

WHEN BLACK LIVES MATTER ONLY THEN WILL ALL LIVES MATTER.

PROLOGUE

It was the year 218 B.C. when a Watcher crash-landed on Earth not too far from one of the world's greatest warriors of all time. It was right before his more than 35,000 men crossed the Alps. His name was Hannibal Carthaginian, General. He'd routed Roman armies at Lake Trasimeno; and after the battle with the Romans, the Watchers that he'd just saved saw that Hannibal was worth receiving a great gift to become the first of the first and best of the best: a Hatchet Man. As Hannibal watched the shining light falling from the sky, and even though he was cold and tired from the long journey, he ran to the crash site and helped the Watcher from the crash. He continued his march on to Lake Trasimeno, defeating the Romans, and the Watcher bore witness. In return, the Watcher blessed him with the power of the "Hatchet Man first born."

Since that battle the Barbarians continued to fight. Just like Hannibal was able to rise to power by a Watcher, so was another named Romulus. However, these Watchers were evil and were going to be the ones behind all the wars, terrorist attacks and any other attacks on Earth. Hatchet Men never got old, or died unless they were killed in battle by another Hatchet Man; that would become Hannibal's fate. He was the first of the Shadows. Shadows were the ones to protect Earth and Romulus was the first of the first to become a Hatchet Man Ghost. The wars between the Shadows and Ghosts would carry on for centuries to come. Also, Watchers started to have sexual encounters with some of the women and men on Earth, making a new breed of humans with the blood type Rh-Negative. Therefore, the Watchers could keep a close eye on them to make sure they would only breed with one another. Attila the Hun rose to power in 372 A.D. Invaders from Asia entered Europe in 372 A.D., driving more and more Germans into the empire. The Celts invaded Europe during the 4th and 5th centuries A.D. and were defeated in 455 A.D. Attila the Hun was a Hatchet Man Shadow who was also killed by a Hatchet Man Ghost in battle. The battles between the Hatchet Men Shadows and Hatchet Men Ghosts continued to occur. Therefore, they were able to stay within the shadows of what was happening on Earth.

PREQUEL

Fourteen hundred and eighteen years had passed since the battle between Attila the Hun and the Hatchet Men Ghosts. A new evil had emerged in Egypt. A princess by the name of Cynthia had made a pact with one of the Watchers by the name of Seth aka "Red God." She'd killed several men that had made her a sex drudge. She'd broken free and ran through their kingdom in Suez, killing the king. With her last breath she yelled, "Red God! I, Cynthia, ask of you to let me walk this Earth, shouting your name and your name only! I am not ready to leave this place. My vengeance on man is not done yet!" Then she dropped to her knees, covered mostly in the blood of her enemies.

Cynthia saw a light from the sky and from the look of things it was a spaceship that looked like a shooting star. Seth, the God of death, appeared before her eyes. He stood 12 feet tall and was 350 pounds of muscle. His skin was grayish-blue and his eyes were red like fire. There were several breathing holes along his spinal cord from top to bottom. Each arm had six breathing holes a piece: one on each of his deltoids, one on each bicep, one on each tricep and one on each forearm. His legs had two large breathing holes: one on each of his outer upper thighs. He had breathing holes on each calf muscle, two on the left and right side of his chest, one on each hand and one on the back of his head.

"Cynthia, my child, you called me. Why…?" Seth asked as he snarled at her.

Cynthia wasn't afraid of his razor-sharp one-inch fangs. She was ready to submit her will totally to him. No more running. She'd been running from her destiny for years, almost a century. She took a deep breath and her head drooped. Her vision had become blurry from all the blood she'd lost. If she were completely human she would be dead by now, but she was born with Rh-Negative blood, born to a Hatchet Man. She had gone to Zenny the witch for help, keeping her powers dormant for years so she wouldn't have to participate in the evil that the Watchers wanted her to do.

Her frame of mind was broken, and her heart was not the same because of evil men. She felt she needed to step-up and put an end to mankind for good. As she spoke to Seth, he gently lifted her head with his index finger so that he could look into her dying eyes. "My Lord, I finally see what you have been trying to make me see for years. I will no longer fight with you. All I ask of you is to give me a chance to show you. Please?"

Seth looked into her soul and saw that she was now ready. But before he helped her to be what she was meant to be, he asked her, "If I do this for you and once you become Queen here in Egypt, I want you to travel to Italy to an ancient country in west-central Italy to Tuscany and parts of Umbria, the center of the Etruscan civilization, and crash the king." Cynthia nodded her head in a yes motion, but Seth was not done just yet. "I also want you to bear my offspring but it has to be of your freewill. Do you agree?"

Cynthia started to cry because after all she'd endured from men on Earth — the rapes, torture, being sodomized and all other types of abuse to her body — somebody still wanted to love her. She found that Seth had great empathy, sympathy and passion towards her. Cynthia looked into his red eyes and saw something different in them this time and replied, "Yes, I will bear as many children as you ask of me."

"Now I will free you and you shall be my Queen here on Earth." Seth helped her to her feet. He passionately kissed her, breathing Hatchet Man life into her body, getting rid of the poison from Zenny the witch. Cynthia fell to the ground in a fetal position, screaming from pain because she had been taking the witch's potion for over fifty years. Seth kneeled down beside her, whispering into her ear, "I didn't say it wasn't going to hurt, but I know you can take it my love." By the time Cynthia's transformation was complete, hieroglyphic writings were appearing simultaneously all over her body. Breathing holes that released gases had developed all along her spine, legs, arms and her right hand. Her eyes started turning yellow with red pupils and her nucleus became that of a Watcher with night vision, long range sight, infrared vision, x-ray vision and precise target vision. Cynthia's brain was now like a video camera. She was able to watch whatever event she saw, over and over again in her mind from different angles, allowing her to catch anything that she'd missed during a battle; from explosions to missed items and clues that she didn't pay much attention to at the time in the heat of battle. She could project the scene from her eyes onto a surface or in the air so others could see.

"Now, you are almost like me," Seth said. "Go get what your heart desires, my love."

"My heart's appetite is for you and only you. The world can wait." Cynthia leaped up, grabbing Seth's neck as she tried to wrap her hands and legs around his body, kissing Seth passionately. Both of their hieroglyphic writings began to glow as they continued to climax together.

Hatchet Men

Seth wrapped his arms underneath her back and placed Cynthia onto the ground, gently spreading her legs. He began kissing her intimately on her inner thighs, making his way to her precious prize between her legs. He knew all the areas he could arouse on her body, giving her the best oral sex of her life. Every time she climaxed her breathing holes would emit gases, making a whistling sound as her pleasure became more intense, causing her body to quiver all over. Seth stopped after 15 minutes of pleasuring her orally to give her his manhood that looked like a man's arm with biceps. He had to release air through the breathing holes on his penis to make it a little smaller so that he could gently enter her rose petal. It would still hurt but not as badly as it would if he were at full size. But regardless of the size, it would not kill her. He slowly worked his way inside of her wetness. Cynthia grabbed his broad back as he slowly made sweet love to her body. Her head tilted backward as she arched back over a dead body on the ground. Both of their hips were moving in rhythm together. Seth's hands and mouth were all over her firm breasts. He could feel his army of soldiers running down his back and his muscles started to tighten up as if he was in battle. He quickly regained control, snarling and showing his razor-sharp fangs. Cynthia rubbed them, lost in thought with him and he felt the same. As Seth's army of soldiers shot inside of Cynthia she felt something she had never felt before — true love and it was like ecstasy. Seth caressed every part of her beautiful body, making her feel loved and it was very real for her and for him.

"Tomorrow, you go claim what is rightfully yours, my love," Seth told her then passionately kissed her.

Cynthia lay beside his warm body with her back up against his warm chest, thinking of all that was going to be done tomorrow. But for now, to her, there was nothing better than this moment with Seth.

* * * * * * * * *

The next day Cynthia got up and awoke the dead, turning them into her new army called "Ghost-like." They started building ships that would be able to take them across the Mediterranean Sea and straight into Italy to the ancient country of west-central Italy to Tuscany and parts of Umbria, center of the Etruscan civilization. Her plan was to take over the world, starting with Tuscany. Some of the people not killed by Seth and her were their slaves. There was one by the name of Zenny. She was not a slave but the very witch who had helped to keep Princess Cynthia's powers dormant for years. She knew what would become of Cynthia if she was to become who she was supposed to become: Evil.

To the naked eye Zenny looks like a tarot card reader. But those who know of her knew that she was a witch in touch with the Watchers through telepathy. Seth had a bounty on her head so she was at her house gathering all of her things. She knew it would only be a matter of time before they came for her. At that same moment Cynthia was telling her army of Ghost-likes where to look for Zenny. She didn't want to expose Zenny because she'd been so good to Cynthia over the years, but she wanted to prove her love to Seth.

Seth was about to leave to go back to Tripueler, the planet of the Watchers. He kissed his love and she walked him to his spacecraft which hovered above the land, using a maglev system to help with zooming back and forth into space. The spacecraft had a trapezoid front and triangular back with short wings on both sides of the craft. Whenever a Watcher was outside of the spaceship a force-field protected it from any intruder trying to board the craft. It used the absence of space to transform it into a flying projectile with three chambers to help it fly faster than anything known to man. The first chamber was used for the absence of space mixed with oxygen and combined into one chamber compressed into one. The second chamber contained different gases with saltwater, and the third chamber held a small star which never burned out. The three chambers release five different chemicals almost simultaneously, one after another. Starting with the first chamber which holds the absence of space, oxygen passes through small air valves which open, pulling in more air, forcing the absence of space and the oxygen to pass through the second chamber like a projectile. It quickly mixes with the different gases and saltwater which causes combustion that shoots through the third chamber to the star. All elements are combined into one causing it to combust, making the third chamber open for exit. On the very end of the ship were three rockets with three circles of rings that shot small lasers around the combustion coming out of the ship, giving it an amazing thrust that was faster than anything. The Watcher's spacecraft's body is made out of magnesium and titanium. The wiring is made from gold, grapheme soft metal, and inside the bottom floor of the spacecraft is made from a magnet called alnico. It's used to help the ship maglev. The door flaps, weapons, chairs and anything that moves run on a bevel gear system made out of magnesium. The spacecraft is driven by a hologram joystick which appears once the driver sits in the driver's seat made from soft gold, grapheme soft metal and samarium cobalt used to magnetically levitate the seat so it can move around quickly to any part of the ship. The driver places their hand around the joystick to control the spacecraft and within their hand are small computer-like chips that allow them to drive the craft and control all weaponry aboard it as well. It's equipped with four laser guns in the front that look like spare bits from a drill. On the back were four more laser guns that looked the same. It can carry twenty magnesium nuclear weapons that can scorch their very own planet the size of the sun in Earth's galaxy. For Seth to get back home, it would take him several days and nights, shooting through millions of galaxies.

Seth and Princess Cynthia walked toward the ship and as they got closer the doors opened. Before Seth entered he passionately kissed Cynthia and said, "I shall return soon. I expect you will have already conquered most of this place, starting with Tuscany."

"Yes, my love, and I will not stop there." Seth rubbed her head and turned his back to her, walking aboard his ship.

Princess Cynthia watched as the doors closed and his spaceship zoomed away. It was now time for her to put their plan into action. Her Ghost-like army started running through every house, looking for Zenny. The army looked like half-eaten people with no eye sockets just flames. Their bodies were mangled by maggots running in and out of their muscle tissues: the biceps, triceps, rectus abdominis, pectoralis major, gastrocnemius, frontalis and the semispinalis capitis on the face that is just a few spots on their bodies. The maggots would eat on their flesh and they would have to drink blood to feed them. The Ghost-like army carried swords covered in flames and bows and arrows. The people had never been this afraid in their lives.

* * * * * * * * *

Zenny had just finished gathering up all the things in her house. As she was about to walk out the front door she saw the Ghost-like soldier coming to her door. Zenny knew the gig was up and that Cynthia had given her up. "That bitch! And after all that I've done for her!" she yelled. But she had to think fast. She ran out her back door, putting her Kimar over her down bent head, walking quickly away. She walked down some steps and as she made a right turn she almost walked right into some of the undead Ghost-like soldiers that were stopping people as they looked for her. She came to a halt and turned back around, placing her back against the wall. She took a deep breath, thinking about her next move.

"Zenny, come quickly, come!" shouted a little boy she knew so she ran toward his house, going inside just as several guards walked around the corner.

"Thank you, Timtim," Zenny said, giving the boy a big hug.

Zenny was very beautiful and even though she was a witch, people loved her and some were willing to help her. She had brown skin, pretty green eyes and long, black, silky hair with white streaks in it. She stood at a petite 5'5" in height and build with white beautiful teeth and a belly ring, dressing in silk. She lived in Italy in Tuscany. Zenny performed most of her magic in a cauldron but she had to leave it behind. The only thing she had with her was her Athame, a witch's knife that had a black handle she used to create a magical circle to direct energy. It is never used for cutting but she kept a boline to fight evil. The point of the Athame knife is the element of fire and a chalice represents water.

At first Zenny was going to communicate with her Watcher through telepathy, but she remembered what he'd told her to say and said, "Oh Isis, deliver me from the hands of bad evil, red thing!" She repeated it over and over, whispering it to herself. The Ghost-like evil soldier didn't stop at the house. Now her next move was to leave Egypt as quickly as possible before Cynthia did.

"Timtim, I need you to help me get out of here. Are you up to it?" Zenny asked him.

He started smiling at her and said, "I'll do anything for you, my lady." Timtim was 12 years old and knew all of the shortcuts around Suez. He also knew how to get to the Suez Canal, and from there Zenny would be able to get on a boat and go to Rome in Italy.

"Timtim, I'm going to need you to distract Cynthia's Ghost-like soldiers. But first, I need you to show me the best route to take where I can get a ride to Rome in Italy."

Timtim smiled again and ran over to a wooden stool. He dragged it across the floor to a wooden bookshelf where he kept all of his homemade routes that he and his crew used to get around the City of Suez. Timtim climbed up the bookshelf, reaching for his homemade maps of the streets in Suez.

"I got it!" Timtim shouted, jumping down to the ground, making Zenny glance back at him. She was peeking around the blanket that was covering the front window as she watched the Ghost-like soldiers interrogate some of the people outside. As bad as she wanted to help them out, she knew she had a greater mission to perform.

"What are you looking at?" Timtim asked Zenny as he came over to the window to look himself.

Zenny glanced at him rubbing his head and asked, "Timtim, do you want to come with me?"

"Then who is going to help the people, Zenny? Somebody has to stay behind."

Zenny smiled, knowing he was a very brave little boy. She bent down and gave him a kiss on his forehead. Timtim started blushing and grabbed her hand, walking her over to a table. He picked up his crude lantern, placing it on the map so he could get better lighting. He pointed at the map.

"This is where you need to go so you can get to here and I will make sure that my boy is waiting for you to take you where you need to go."

Timtim was an orphan child who lived in a crude, small mud and brick house that had a wooden, mud and hay rooftop. He lived there with other orphan children. He was only 5'1" tall with a slim build. He had brown skin with short black, straight hair and brown eyes. His teeth were slightly dirty as were his clothing and he wore sandals on his feet. He kept a dagger on him at all times just in case someone tried to stop him for stealing because he was hungry. His house was basically two rooms. One room was a combined kitchen-living room. The kitchen was just a fireplace where the children would cook their food and share it with each other. They only had two plates to eat off of, three cups to drink from and three spoons to eat with. Timtim would let the younger kids eat first and most nights it would be soup, and on a real good night fish he would have stolen from a fisherman that day. In the same room was an old wooden book shelf with books Timtim used to read stories at night to the rest of the kids in the house before bedtime. There was also a small wooden table with three old wooden stools. The walls and floors were badly run down and in need of a makeover. The ceiling was falling apart. When it rained the roof would leak all over the house. The door was an old wooden one with a small hole in it. There were no real good windows in the house; just some blankets covering them to stop the wind from blowing inside at night.

And the second room was the bedroom with seven beds made out of hay where fourteen children slept. There was a small wooden table by the window with a candle on it that he would light at night to keep the kids safe and sometimes he would read to himself. He kept his graphite rock and paper on the table to write about his everyday adventures. And right before he would go to bed, he would say a prayer out loud.

* * * * * * * * *

"Barkeep, let me get another drink, please, and Barrin we don't have all day so make it quick!" Backgril shouted to his longtime friend.

"Here you go, sir," the barkeep said, giving Backgril his drink of mead.

As he was about to take a drink a petite and beautiful young Egyptian tart had her eyes on him and she decided to walk over to Backgril. "Would you like to take me upstairs?" she asked him, placing her hand on his inner thigh then right on his manhood, making it come to life.

Even though Backgril had just come from out of a room with two tarts already, he smiled and quickly drank his drink. "Let's go," he said, grabbing her hand and walking with her towards the steps to go to his room he'd gotten in the brothel. But just as he was about to go up the steps he heard something outside. It sounded like the voices of soldiers and people screaming.

"What's wrong?" the tart asked Backgril as he let go of her hand to go to the brothel doors and check things out.

He was very surprised when he saw Ghost-like soldiers marching down the streets of Suez City. Backgril quickly turned around and told the tart to tell everybody what was going on. She took off running like a bat out of hell, running from room to room warning the other tarts and men.

Backgril knew something was wrong as he rushed upstairs to get his weapons from his room. He pushed the door open, running to the chest by his bed and opening it. He grabbed his double-headed axe and his bow and a full quiver of arrows. He strapped his axe to his back. The axe was made from the strongest metal from Tripueler and some of the strongest metals from Earth called titanium and magnesium. His axe had a hieroglyphic writing on it which read: *"If this is in your hands you have been chosen to battle, by something less than you. You are a Shadow and Shadows never die or run."* He heard screaming from outside again and when he looked out the window he saw several people being killed by the Ghost-like soldiers of Queen Cynthia.

Backgril ran down the long hallway to warn his friend, Barrin. He started banging on his door and shouting, "Barrin, we have to go now!"

But Barrin was deep inside both tarts that he had in his room. One was sitting on his face and the other one was riding him as they both climaxed together. Both tarts were kissing each other as he was holding the one down sitting on his face, giving her oral sex. "Ummm…"

"Yesss…wooo…!" the two tarts said seconds apart. Barrin made them stop because he started hearing people yelling outside. By this time Backgril was pushing his way through the door.

"Ladies, go to your friends now!" Backgril shouted as he went over to the window with Barrin who was quickly dressing.

"They're everywhere," Barrin said, glancing out the window and pulling on his boots.

As soon as you walk inside the brothel's double doors there is a large bar to the right where a barkeep served the mead. The bar was shaped like a horseshoe with wooden cups of mead behind the barkeep. There were a few wooden tables and chairs in the room for people to sit on. But, there was a hidden room some of the tarts would look from so they could peep at the men who walked in, looking for some pleasure with a tart.

There were three rooms downstairs with several rooms on the upper level the barkeep would rent out to men who wanted to party with a tart or sleep over for the night, usually with a tart. The brothel was made out of mud, brick with a hay rooftop and a window in each room. There was also a kitchen where a cook could make food for the guests. For entertainment they had rattle snakes inside straw-like baskets where they were kept by the snake trainer until show time. There were ten stools for people to sit on and most men would buy a tart some mead and pay the barkeep for the tart to give them some type of pleasure. The inside of the brothel had wooden floors and two sets of steps, one on each side that led upstairs.

"Aaaah!" Backgril and Barrin heard one of the tarts scream and both ran to the door to see what was happening.

Backgril ran from the room to see what was going on while Barrin quickly grabbed his weapons, getting ready. He grabbed his sword that had been passed down to him from his great-grandfather. It was specially made by an ancient Watcher named Isis, a female Goddess of Fertility who was the sister and wife of Osiris. His great-great-grandfather was the one to get the sword. Hieroglyphics were written on it which read: *"You are the first of many to come, and in Shadows you shall become powerful and one with your sword that was forged in fire and steel from Tripueler. You're God-like."* The sword was passed down to Barrin but he, too, kept his powers dormant because he didn't want to face the truth. His great-grandfather was killed by the Watcher Seth. Before he passed away he told Barrin that one day he will rise to become a great Hatchet Man to help people on Earth. Barrin was born in Italy and was trained by one of his father's friends because his father was also killed in battle, but by a Ghost. Barrin became one of Italy's best sword fighters serving the Emperor, but later on left to join his brothers in arms. He was a Barbarian rebel. Once he found out who he was, a descendant of Attila the Hun, he had to go out and find himself, but he didn't want his powers. So he started searching for a witch he had heard about who could help him keep his powers dormant. He'd heard of a place in Egypt that could help people like him. So he went there and that is where he found Zenny. She was the one who could help him just like others before him. Barrin was 6 feet, 235 pounds of muscle with long, silky hair he wore in a ponytail and wore a tunic. He had white teeth, brown eyes, a full beard and he also had the Rh-Negative blood type. He spent most of his time working on his fishing boat with Backgril and with tarts. Out in the hallway, Backgril was the first one running toward the screaming. A Ghost-like soldier was about to cut a tart's head off with his sword of fire. While on her knees, two more soldiers held her down, one on each side of her, holding her arms as they pushed down on her shoulders, making her head push forward as she begged them not to kill her. Backgril grabbed his bow and three arrows out of his quiver. He leaped over the top of a wooden rail, simultaneously taking aim and releasing the three arrows, killing the Ghost-soldiers. He ran over to the tart, helping her off the ground and to his surprise it was the tart who earlier agreed to go to his room with him. "I told you to go! Why are you still here? Now go before you get hurt. Go!" She nodded her head and took off running to the secret room with the rest of the girls.

Backgril stood at the bar, holding two arrows he'd pulled from one of his nonstop reloading quivers. He had two quivers filled with arrows that never ran out. He looked around for Barrin. He'd known Barrin for years and both of them had lost their parents by Seth in battles; he'd lost his father in Africa by Seth's hands. Backgril was a descendant of Hannibal, a long Rh-Negative bloodline of Hatchet Men. He was 6'2" in height, 230 pounds of muscle with gray eyes and also wore a tunic. He was very handsome with dark skin, a bald head with one gold hook earring in his left ear, white teeth with a full beard.

Backgril had also come from Africa, running for his life. He had met Barrin in Italy when they were kids and they had been inseparable since. His father had trained him how to use his bow and arrow. And just like Barrin, his bow and arrows were very special. The flexible black ivory bow with gold stripes had a string made from gold and some type of metal from Tripueler. It came from the God Osiris. It also had hieroglyphic writings on it which read: *"He or she that possess this weapon shall become great and powerful. Hannibal was the first face of many Hatchet Men, and many more shall come as Shadow Hatchet Men, son or daughter of Osiris."*

Barrin ran down the steps to help his friend Backgril. "What the hell are those things?" he asked Backgril as he stood ready beside him.

"Those things are Ghost-like creatures of Seth. Somebody must have awakened their powers for the wrong reason," Backgril replied, walking quickly toward the door and peeking outside.

"Who could it be, Backgril?" Barrin asked.

"I don't know because there are 1,000 of us here with the blood of the Gods so it could be anyone of us. But what I do know, it's not you or me." And as soon as Backgril spoke those words, 10 Ghost-like creatures came through the door and the battle was on.

* * * * * * * * *

Carnage was being wreaked all over the City of Suez. People's homes were on fire and they were starting to become deranged from the presence of these hideous creatures. Timtim had still managed to get Zenny to where she needed to go. She made sure to keep her head down and her hijab and veil over her face. "Okay, we're here," Timtim said, stopping Zenny so he could look around the corner to make sure the coast was clear. "Zenny, here, take the map with you and follow it."

"Are you sure you're not going to need it, Timtim?" Zenny asked as she gave him a big hug.

"I don't need it I made it."

They heard soldiers coming so Zenny told him one more thing. "I need you to go find Backgril and Barrin and bring them to the ship. Can you find them?"

Timtim smiled and chuckled slightly. "Yeah, that won't be a big problem."

Zenny looked at Timtim and wanted to ask him what was funny, but there was really no time for that. She told him to be careful and took off walking quickly. It started raining hard and people were in such chaos that some didn't stop to help others. Zenny did what she could but she knew she had to get to the ships first, so she could warn the Emperor in Rome. She had to pass the castle and a lot of debris was falling down. She had to zigzag through the falling debris and once past the castle she took a deep breath because she knew she wasn't far from her destination. Quickly turning a corner she stopped to catch her breath. Zenny's hair on her back stood up and goose bumps appeared on her body as fear slightly took over. She had walked right upon some Ghost-like soldiers about to execute some children. She knew if she stopped she would not be able to leave the city before Cynthia and her Ghost-like army, but that was a chance she was willing to take.

Zenny closed her eyes, took a deep breath and whispered, "Isis, please help me at this time of need." She opened her eyes, walking swiftly toward the Ghost-like soldiers as she pulled out her boline. There were five creatures surrounding the children. Zenny was a Hatchet Man Shadow who was running from what she really was, until now. One of the Ghost-like creatures raised his sword to kill one of the kids. Zenny became furious and with fire in her eyes she leaped up into the air, squinting her face and yelled, "Aaarrr!" as she came down, swinging her boline downward into the skull of the creature. She ran her boline down its spine, splitting the creature in half. She leaped up into the air again with a boline in each hand, flipping backwards, kicking another Ghost-like in the head, using her bolines to slice two more Ghost-likes. Four of the five were down and before the last Ghost-like could react, Zenny landed right in front of it on one knee then stabbing the creature in the chest with both bolines, running the blades up and down until the Ghost-like was in pieces.

Even though she had kept her gift in abeyance, she was still able to bring some powers to the surface. Her eyes glowed intensely as she continued to kneel on one knee, a boline in each hand dripping with blood as she gritted her teeth. One of the children walked over to her and grabbed her hand. She looked at him, startling him and causing him to jump back because her eyes were completely black, but she hastily returned them to green. "I'm sorry my child." And as soon as she spoke the apology, twenty more Ghost-like soldiers came around the corner. "Come! We've got to go. Now run this way!" Zenny shouted, showing them which way to go. Some of the soldiers started shooting fire arrows into the air. There were so many arrows the sky turned black. Zenny leaped into the air, destroying as many arrows as possible. She even took two in the right arm. Meanwhile, Timtim was sneaking his way around Suez and doing his best not to be seen. The rain was coming down very hard, making it hard for him to see. He managed his way through the streets without being noticed. He was almost at the brothel just a few streets away. Timtim tried to be invisible among the shadows but it started lightning and that made it a little bit harder to do so. Then he heard screaming and it sounded very terrified to him. His heart started to race as he ran toward the voice. To his surprise it was one of the kids who lived with him. A Ghost-like was dragging him on the ground then flung him into the side of a house, hitting his head. The little boy was no older than ten and was knocked out on the ground.

"Hey! You ugly mangled beast, leave him alone!"

The Ghost-like swiftly turned around, growling at Timtim. Timtim clutched his razor-sharp boomerang that he got from Isis himself. He was the first of his bloodline to get his weapons from the Watcher Isis. Timtim never liked taking the potion that Zenny would make for him. He didn't like the potion. He would pretend he took it every time but most times he didn't. When he would take it some of the older orphan kids would pick on him. So he completely stopped taking it and would go train out in the desert with his boomerang and slingshot. Most of the time, he would hide his hieroglyphic under his tunic. It read, "The first of many brave Hatchet Men warriors to come to defend the Earth, so small but very powerful."

Isis would watch him from Tripueler at The Fountain of Eyes. It was used by Watchers to look at their Hatchet Men on Earth. She loved Timtim's drive to succeed, to become better. So she would come down to train him, using the disguise of a homeless woman begging in Suez. Their very relationship started with him bringing her food, not knowing she was his Watcher. Sometimes she would train him night and day.

The Ghost-like soldier started to run toward him. "Yaaaaa!" Timtim shouted, leaping into the air like a bolt of lightning, spinning around and throwing his boomerang at the creature, killing it. He quickly caught his boomerang and ran to his friend. The young boy was bleeding out from his head wound, slowly slipping away from Earth to the next life. "Tokey, stay with me, please," Timtim cried as he dropped to his knees and gently lifted the young boy's head, placing his shirt underneath it.

With his last breath, Tokey smiled as he touched Timtim's tattoos, looking at Timtim's hieroglyphic writing and whispered, "I knew you were always one of them, Timtim."

"Tokey, save your breath; please hold on," Timtim pleaded. Tokey smiled, rubbed Timtim's tattoos again and passed on to the next life. Timtim looked up at the sky shouting, "Nooo!! Why? Nooo…!" he cried as he held his friend's body in his arms. He closed his eyes, saying a prayer to Isis. "Mother of me please protect Tokey as he enters his new life with you from his old life with me."

* * * * * * * * *

Barrin and Backgril were coming around the corner, killing every Ghost-like soldier they saw when Barrin saw Timtim on the ground holding his friend's lifeless body. He slowly walked over to him because Timtim was glowing. "Timtim, are you okay?" Barrin asked as he slowly knelt down beside him. Barrin put his hand on Timtim's shoulder looking just as sad because he and Backgril both knew Tokey. Backgril was still killing Ghost-like soldiers with his arrows and when he was done he ran to where Barrin had found Timtim. It caught him by surprise to see them praying so he dropped to his knees and prayed too.

"We have to continue the fight," Timtim said, looking at the both of them with tears running down his face.

Other kids from Timtim's house who were hiding at another house came outside. Barrin and Backgril stood up and Timtim told them about Zenny's plan for them to get to Rome, before Cynthia and her Ghost-like army get there, and stop her. Timtim told them to get the rest of the Hatchet Men and their soldiers to the shipping pier in Suez Canal. There would be ships waiting for them there.

"Timtim, you and your friends must come with us," Barrin told him.

But Timtim knew it would just slow them down. "No, y'all go. I'm staying here with the people of Suez. Someone's got to keep them safe, right?" He smiled through the tears still running down his little face, holding his friend Tokey.

"Timtim, you and your friends get to the brothel. Y'all will be safe there. Now go!" Backgril ordered as dozens of Ghost-likes could be seen coming toward them in the distance. Timtim nodded his head and took off running, carrying his dead friend as the rest of the children ran with him.

Barrin watched Timtim and his friends reach safety then turned around to help Backgril. He pulled out his sword, shouting in rage. Backgril felt the same way as the two of them battled through dozens of Ghost-likes together. Backgril was shooting his arrows and Barrin was using his sword, spinning around like a tornado, slicing the Ghost-likes into debris. Once they were done, Backgril turned to Barrin and said, "That little boy is one of the bravest kids I've ever met."

"Yeah, and he's much smarter than us because he still has his powers."

Suez was a refugee city for Hatchet Men who didn't want to use their gifts. Most of them just wanted to be normal. But there was no such thing as being normal for a Hatchet Man because once people find out who they were, they would run them away or try to kill them because of misconceptions they'd heard. Suez was a place where all Hatchet Men could come and be whoever they wanted to be, or who they didn't want to be, like Cynthia.

Zenny reached the shipping yard but she was too late. Cynthia was already leaving and she had with her 2,000 ships with over 50,000 Ghost-like soldiers. The only thing Zenny could do was yell out to Cynthia, hoping it would make her stop and turn around. And Cynthia did turn around just to look at Zenny and then she sent one ship back. It had five hundred Ghost-like soldiers on it. Zenny knew she was not going to be able to take them on by herself. She took off running but Ghost-likes were everywhere. There was nowhere for Zenny to run. She would have to stand and fight her way through them because she was surrounded.

Cynthia looked back at Zenny about to fight for her life and blew her a kiss, laughing at her. "I would come kill you myself but I have a country to conquer. It's not like you're fighting for your life!" she yelled.

Zenny zoomed in on Cynthia, shouting back at her. "It's far from over! I will see you again, Cynthia!" Zenny took off running, fighting her way through some of the Ghost-likes. The ship which Cynthia had turned around was just reaching land. The soldiers aboard ran toward where the rest of the Ghost-likes were chasing Zenny.

* * * * * * * * *

Timtim was hiding with some of the tarts in the secret room at the brothel. Some of the children were very afraid and crying. A tart by the name of Tara walked by one of the little girls and stooped to hold her tightly, telling her that it was going to be okay. They could hear some of the Ghost-likes enter the brothel, looking for anybody to kill. They looked all over the brothel but found no one. They were leaving when one of the little kids sneezed. A Ghost-like stopped and called for the rest to come back inside.

"Shit," Tara whispered, hoping they wouldn't have to fight, but it was looking like they'd have no choice. Tara was from Suez. Her parents were the first Hatchet Men to seek refuge in Suez. However, they were killed defending Suez after they'd had Tara who almost died with them. A tart by the name of Lilly was also killed by some men that tried to rape Tara at the brothel and take her from Lilly for their own devices. Tara was petite at 5'2" in height with brown skin, hazel eyes, short black hair with a white streak and white teeth. She was very beautiful facially and loving to whomever she came across. She was the child of Odin. His name meant "The Unwavering One." He was the Norse God of Wisdom and War who created the cosmos. Tara kept her gifts hidden because she felt that her powers were the cause of everybody she loved deaths. Her powers had been dormant for so long that her breathing holes and hieroglyphics didn't show on her body anymore.

The weapon given to her by her mother Lilly had it and she gave it to Tara before she died. The Gungnir was a very powerful weapon and whoever possessed it had great strength. The Gungnir could hit its mark hundreds, if not thousands, of yards away from where it was thrown. The Gungnir would hit its target and return to its thrower. It operated just like a boomerang. Tara hadn't touched it in years and it was upstairs in one of the rooms.

"They're coming, aren't they?" one of the children asked in a fear-filled voice.

Tara looked at Timtim, shaking her head because she had no weapon. Timtim was not afraid. He was ready to fight until death. He had trained all his life for this. It was just a matter of time before they found them. He walked over to Tara, holding her hand and whispered to her, "Tara, it is time you show them who you really are because I'm not going to be able to hold them off forever. I'm going to need you, okay?"

Tears ran down Tara's face because she knew all the tarts and children were depending on her to pull them though. Even though Timtim was very strong, and more than likely could take them out on his own, he would still need her to help keep everybody safe. Timtim grabbed his titanium and magnesium slingshot which could shoot razor-sharp magnesium balls. He could shoot two to three of them and they would kill the enemy and return to their owner. Tara looked at everybody in the room. She remembered the trap door underneath the floor. She quickly opened it and told one of the tarts to get everybody down there and stay there until she returned for them. Her next move was to get to her weapon from upstairs.

"Timtim, I need you to help me get my Gungnir, so..." But before she could finish her sentence a Ghost-like heard them and took its sword and started chopping down the door.

"I'll do what I can. "Arrrr!" Timtim shouted, shooting his slingshot and killing the Ghost-like soldier on the other side of the door. Another Ghost-like started calling for more soldiers. They started arriving like ants coming for sugar. "Tara, go!" Timtim shouted as he leaped into the air, throwing his boomerang at the soldiers coming through the brothel doors.

Tara ran for the stairs but was stopped by a Ghost-like who punched her in the face and threw her across the room. Tara fell to the ground but quickly flipped to her feet. She crouched down, sweeping the Ghost-like's feet, making it drop. She punched it several times and swiftly got up, running up the stairs and to the room where her Gungnir was.

Timtim was outside trying to maneuver the Ghost-likes away from the brothel. But there were just too many of them coming. He had to run a little bit. "Come on, I live for this," he taunted them. "Arrrr!" Timtim shouted, fighting the Ghost-likes with all his might.

* * * * * * * * *

Zenny was also in a battle with some Ghost-likes, and there were a lot of them coming after her. With a boline in each hand, she was surrounded with nowhere to run; flipping them around to be ready for whatever was coming next. "Come on in the name of Isis!" she shouted. Zenny's eyes began to glow but before she could strike even one Ghost-like soldier, Barrin and Backgril were making their way through the army of Ghost-likes to help her. She was never happier to see them both. The three of them started fighting together, clearing a path.

"Zenny, what is going on?"

"Cynthia has given herself to Seth and now she's on a warpath, heading for Italy. We've got to stop her before she takes over the world."

"What can we do?" Backgril asked her.

"We need to get every Hatchet Man and Hatchet Woman she didn't kill and go after her."

"How many ships did she take?" Barrin asked.

"About 2,000 ships and at least 50,000 Ghost-like creatures," she replied.

Barrin and Backgril knew that they were going to have a fight on their hands and they were ready for it. Some of the Hatchet Men started to show up at Suez Canal. They'd already heard the news and were willing to die for Zenny's fight.

"Well, you got what you wanted," Barrin said to Zenny, smiling.

Zenny looked at everyone who was there and saw that she didn't even have a quarter of the men and women that Cynthia had with her, but she was going to make it work. The only advantage that Zenny, Barrin and Backgril had against Cynthia was their soldiers were Hatchet Men and Hatchet Women and not Ghost-like creatures. Hatchet Men were stronger than 20 Ghost-likes put together. And some of the men in Suez also wanted to come and fight. Their army was beginning to look a lot bigger, but still not half as large as Cynthia's army of Ghost-likes. But Barrin had a plan.

"We still don't have enough men and women to win this fight," Zenny said, feeling hopeless because she had to stop Cynthia. Barrin saw the look on her face and smiled. "Barrin, what the hell you find so funny?" Zenny asked, looking at him with a confused look on her face.

Barrin walked in front of Zenny and Backgril, pulling out his sword and said, "This will kill half of them." He started swinging his sword which was making a whistling sound and added, "My sword will kill all of them. All we have to do is get them running toward me and I'll hit the ground, sending a sonic boom that will break the Ghost-likes into pieces."

Zenny smiled and said, "I'll be the one to lure the Ghost-likes to you."

But Backgril wasn't having that and said she needed to focus on Cynthia. He wasn't taking no for an answer either. "Very well then, let's go because we don't have a lot of time," Backgril said.

But before they boarded the ship Zenny asked, "Where's Timtim?"

Barrin and Backgril looked at one another which made Zenny think something had happened to him. Backgril let her know he was safe, but Tokey was killed by a Ghost-like and Timtim had taken it hard. Zenny cried because she knew Tokey and liked his company. Tokey would come to see her every day and help her pack up her stuff each night and walk Zenny home.

Backgril gently placed his hand on Zenny's shoulder and said, "I know he used to walk you home every night. We will succeed for Tokey." She nodded her head and got on the ship.

Barrin climbed up to the crow's nest and shouted down to their makeshift army. "Today, our City Suez has been attacked by Cynthia and her Ghost-like creatures. She was one of us but she chose to become a Ghost!" Barrin looked down at Zenny, lifting his sword and holding it high toward the sky and continued, "Cynthia made up her mind to walk with the God Seth so that she can become a Queen of Darkness! I choose Zenny to be our Queen of Light in the name of Shadow Hatchet Men and Hatchet Women!"

Women and men started cheering Barrin on as Zenny listened with a surprised look on her face. Smiling, Backgril looked at Zenny and dropped to one knee. Everybody on their 500 ships followed, dropping to one knee. Zenny started crying and the Hatchet Men and Hatchet Women started cheering and chanting Zenny's name.

Backgril looked up at Zenny and said, "Do not cry, my lady. We might not be many, but we are here with you until death." Smiling, Zenny gently placed her hand on Backgril's shoulder as she continued to listen to Barrin.

"Our numbers are not as big as Cynthia's Ghost-like army of 50,000, but what we lack in numbers we're mightier in strength! We're smarter, faster and we're very loyal to our Queen!" The men and women cheered Barrin on as he looked down into Zenny's eyes, shouting, "I've never served anybody before you, my lady, not even my God Isis, like I'm about to serve you. I, Barrin, name Zenny, Shadow Queen. I, Barrin, born as to Isis, son of the Queen Isis, Egyptian goddess Eset. She breathed life into me and I give my life to Zenny from this day forward until death!!" All 500 ships of Hatchet Men and Hatchet Women were cheering so loud and screaming Zenny's name that the Gods heard it themselves.

"Sister, do you hear them chanting your creation, Zenny's, name? How dare they do so! I'll go down there and strike all of them in your name!" Osiris offered, upset about what he'd heard.

But Isis thought it was lovely and said, "You will do no such thing to any of them because they need somebody other than me or you to follow. And right now, Zenny needs to become what she is supposed to become. She needs to lead the Shadows."

Osiris didn't like what his sister was doing, but he knew not to go against her wishes. He'd done that before and was in pain for two eons behind it. He squeezed his fist, scrunched up his face, and looked at his sister and just took off into the air. He landed on a mountain. Isis glanced at her brother then turned back to watch Zenny from The Fountain of Eyes. She whispered to herself, "Show my foolish brother why I said what I said. It's time to become what I made you to become." And with those final words she closed The Fountain of Eyes.

* * * * * * * * *

Cynthia didn't sail straight to Italy until the 13th Century because Seth told her about another Hatchet Man Ghost by the name of Behram. He lived in India. He was the leader of a cult named The Thuggee. It's the first cult to be formed in the 13th Century in India. Behram had killed over 900 people single-handedly before he became a Hatchet Man Ghost and amassed a following of 200 Hatchet Men and Hatchet Women along with 20,000 Ghost-like soldiers. Kali had spoken to him and made him her Ghost. He was already waiting for Cynthia to welcome her with open arms.

Behram was handsome. He was brown-skinned, 6 feet tall, weighed 225 pounds with brown eyes and white teeth. He had short silky hair and a full beard and was leader of The Thuggee cult, the first cult known to man. He's one of the most famous killers in the world, even still today. He carried two swords that had a hieroglyphic writing which read: *"Son of Kali, killer of Man, God-like Ghost. Born to be a Shadow killer."* He also had two golden daggers that read the same thing.

So, Cynthia traveled the Red Sea to the Gulf of Aden and then to the Arabian Sea to Kochi where Behram was waiting for her. Once they got together, they were going to travel to Italy. It would take them at least six months to travel approximately 5,400 miles on land. They would have to travel in a caravan of horses, camels and on foot straight through India to Pakistan up to Kazakhstan to Europe and then to Italy.

* * * * * * * * *

Isis called Zenny to Tripueler, and to Zenny's surprise Tripueler was very beautiful. Tripueler cities were all on maglev, floating above ground. But there were cities on the ground as well. The architecture of the buildings were like nothing Zenny had ever seen before. The bridge she was walking on to get to Isis was on maglev and made out of Tripueler marble and gold. The bridge was flanked on both sides by several Hatchet Men and Hatchet Women every hundred yards dressed in army attire, standing like royal guards. One of them was escorting Zenny. She just couldn't stop looking around because she'd never seen anything like this.

"Where am I?" Zenny asked the Hatchet Woman that was escorting her to Isis.

"You're what we call 'dreaming,' but you have been called." That was all she was willing to tell Zenny.

Zenny got into a hover chariot that took her to a pyramid in another part of Tripueler. The pyramids on Tripueler were three times the size of the pyramids on Earth. The doors were 100 feet tall and made out of gold with hieroglyphic writings all over them. Guards stood in front of the doors with staffs that released lava lasers that could quickly disintegrate anything. The golden door opened slowly and Zenny walked cautiously inside, looking at all the hieroglyphics on the walls and vaulted ceiling. Most of the rooms were made out of white limestone, gold and marble. The rooms were at least 1,000 feet in height and 1,000 square feet in length. Each pyramid covered over 25 acres of land. It was just a pinch of the land mass on Tripueler. Isis and Osiris were sitting high on two of the twelve golden chairs. Rose-colored windows in the ceiling shone the most beautiful light from the stars in the universe down onto the twelve statues of the Gods, both good and bad ones: Hera the Mother Queen of Gods; Isis is also the Supreme Mother Goddess of all the other deities; Seth the "Red God" leader of Ghost; Osiris a God of the dead; Lugh was one of the major Celtic Gods; Zeus the Father God of Thunder, King of Gods; Eurus the God of Southeast Wind; Anubis is very evil and not to play with; Ra the Sun God that forges all weapons for Gods; Hatchet Men and Hatchet Women weapons in fire; from the sun, Lu Tung-Pin loved to walk the Earth, looking ordinary, one of the newer Gods made from evil Gods; and last but not the weakest, maybe the smallest, Sorey fights for equality. These are the twelve Gods of Tripueler.

Once Zenny saw Isis and Osiris she quickly kneeled down on one knee with her head down. Isis was very beautiful, even though she had several breathing holes all over her body. She was 10 feet tall with a petite build and long blonde hair with several black and pink streaks running down her back. Her eyes were a bright ocean blue, her skin was a golden brown and she had full lips with white teeth. She was still something to die for. She was dressed in a white robe with gold trimmings, a belt around her waist and her sword right beside her. It was made out of unbreakable steel from Tripueler with gems embedded in the handle meant for her hands only, and was forged in fire from the sun by Ra himself. The sword was handed down to her and the hieroglyphic read, "Supreme Mother Goddess, of all other deities, Hatchet Men, and Hatchet Women."

Zenny did not rise until she heard, "My child, you may rise." Zenny stood up and just looked at Isis and glanced at Osiris. He did not say a word because he did not like the fact that Zenny was there and was going to be able to go back to Earth, remembering everything she saw. But Isis knew what was best for Zenny to know.

"Zenny, I called you because your role on Earth is very important and you shall see why and know what to do. I want you to lead the people on Earth as well as the Hatchet Men and Hatchet Women. I've known you've been running from your true destiny for a while now. But the time has come for you to become rightfully who you truly are. Can you do that?"

"Yes, Mother of Mothers."

Isis smiled and started telling her everything that she must do on Earth. Zenny took it all in and before she left she asked Isis to help Timtim. Isis smiled and told her not to worry because he was going to be fine.

* * * * * * * * *

"Zenny, my Queen, we need you up top!" Backgril yelled from the other side of her door. Zenny woke up and to her surprise Barrin was lying beside her, sound asleep. She quickly got up and rushed to see what the problem was. Zenny hoped she hadn't done anything she would regret later. Once on deck she saw they were about to enter a storm.

"My Queen, what do you want us to do?" Backgril asked.

Zenny knew if they were to go around the storm it would take them longer to get to India. So she told them to ride through it and that Isis was protecting them.

Backgril smiled and nodded. The rain was coming down hard on his head as he ran up to the crow's nest. He shouted as loud as he could, "We keep going through the storm! In the name of Isis!" He stood up there bravely through the entire storm, riding it out. It would take five months to get to India. That would put them two months behind Cynthia.

Now back in Suez, Timtim and Tara were still fighting with the Ghost-likes. There were so many coming after them and Tara was still trying to retrieve her Gungnir but hadn't been able to get to it yet. She fought hard and long trying to get up the stairs to her room but she couldn't. If she hadn't kept her powers dormant for so long she would have been able to call for her Gungnir to come to her. Suddenly, one of the Ghost-likes grabbed Tara and was about to throw her over the railing. However, Timtim saw them and leaped into the air, throwing his boomerang and killing the creature. Then a Ghost-like stabbed Timtim in the back with its sword, lifting his body up off the ground.

"Timtim!!" Tara shouted, gripping onto the railing so hard she crushed it. Timtim fell to the ground. A Ghostlike stood over him about to kill him.

"Leave him alone!" one of the tarts yelled, quickly stabbing the Ghost-like with her dagger. But just as swiftly another Ghost-like killed the tart.

Tara was now becoming very furious and her powers were starting to wake up. She screamed as loud as she could, causing the sound to rumble and crash throughout Egypt. She started pounding her fist on seven Ghost-likes running to her room. There were some behind her but once she reached her room and grabbed her Gungnir, a lightning bolt struck the Gungnir, killing all of the Ghost-likes within a hundred yards of the brothel. Tara ran to Timtim, helping him to his feet. "I must get you to a healing chamber, now!" Tara said to Timtim, looking at his wound.

"There's no time for that," he said, "just cauterize it with your Gungnir."

"Are you sure you want to do that?"

"Just do it now!" So Tara did as he asked.

"Arrrh!!" Timtim yelled and passed out.

Tara told one of the tarts to stay with Timtim and get him in the secret room while she went outside to fight off the Ghost-like soldiers that were still coming. She fought hard, throwing her Gungnir through dozens of Ghost-likes, killing them. The Gungnir made its way back to her every time she threw it. She continued to fight hard, leaping into the air and coming down heavily onto dozens of Ghost-likes coming from miles away. The Ghost-likes just kept coming and coming and she was starting to get tired. Timtim was still out of it but Tara was not about to stop no matter what.

Suddenly, the sky started to turn black. Thunder and lightning started to strike down, killing some of the Ghost-likes. Tara didn't know who was helping her from the sky until Isis and Odin came hurtling down like a bolt of lightning, hitting the ground hard and creating two craters underneath them. They hit the ground so hard that all of the Ghost-likes, and Tara, flew off the ground about five feet into the air. Tara looked and realized it was her God Odin and Isis Mother of all Gods; to her surprise they killed all the Ghost-likes until there were no more left. Tara's ears were ringing from Isis and Odin's crashing down to Earth. She slowly got to her feet and kneeled before them. Tara couldn't believe it was really them.

Isis nodded her head to Odin so he could talk with his child, Tara. Isis kept her eyes on anything that was not friendly. "You may rise, my child," Odin told Tara.

Tara rose up slowly, looking into Odin's black eyes. He stood 12 feet tall 325 pounds of muscle with long, white hair which he kept in a ponytail. Odin and Isis were covered in full body armor made of several metals from their planet Tripueler. The armor could take a blow from a rocket up to a lightning bolt from another God. Their armor is black with gold stripes with gun mounts on their shoulders and over 20 different options of defense built within the armor. One of the options to protect them is that if any creature tried to eat them alive, spikes would be released to cover the suit to protect them.

Odin stood in front of Tara, taking off his helmet. You could hear the air being released from the helmet when he took it off. Much to Tara's surprise, Odin was very handsome. Isis took off her helmet once she sensed there were no more Ghost-likes around. "Tara, why have you been hiding?" he asked.

Tara started crying as she replied, "Because everybody that I come into contact with dies, and I just…"

But, before she could continue, Odin told her, "They died trying to save you because you're more to them than themselves. If they hadn't felt that way, they wouldn't have died for you. So you must fight for them, my child!" Fight!" Tara nodded her head several times and Odin smiled quickly, taking off into the air.

Isis walked over to her and said, "Tell Timtim I'm always around and to keep working on his style of fighting because he almost has it." Then Isis took off as fast as they had come.

Tara started panting as she fell to the ground. She couldn't believe that two of the Gods came to help Timtim and her. She got up and walked back inside the brothel and saw one of the tarts and Timtim walking toward her. He was ready to fight. He saw Tara walking towards them, looking pale in the face as if she'd seen a ghost.

"Tara, what's wrong?"

She stopped and slowly looked up towards the sky and said, "I was just with Isis and Odin. We are able to live another day on Earth because of them."

Timtim didn't know what to say but he wanted to meet his Goddess Isis. If only he knew that unknown to him he had already been meeting with her for years. She was the one who had been training him in the desert for all those years.

Tara looked at Timtim and asked, "Isis told me to tell you to keep fighting and don't stop. You're almost there." Timtim smiled and felt good that Isis had mentioned him and had something for Tara to tell him.

"So Timtim, me and you will train together every day from now on."

Timtim smiled and remembered the old lady he used to train with in the desert who would tell him the women of his dreams will be the women to work with him; and Isis was that woman.

"Why are you smiling Timtim?" Tara asked, walking past him and picking up a chair to sit on. She started rubbing her head because she still couldn't believe what just happened.

"Oh, no reason. We're going to have to work hard, that's all," he replied, still smiling.

"Timtim, would you stop smiling. You're being weird right now. Come on. Let's get the kids and everybody else."

Timtim walked over to Tara, extending his hand to help her up. However, at the same time in his mind he was extending his hand for her to become his Queen. She didn't know that part yet.

* * * * * * * * *

Cynthia and her Ghost-likes finally reached India. Behram was waiting for her with his army of Ghosts and Ghost-likes. Now they were ready to continue their journey on to Italy to conquer it. Behram and Cynthia gave each other a hug even though they'd just met. They were one from the same Ghost. The two of them walked through the bloodied streets of Kochi. Behram had just killed everybody in the city who was not willing to submit to him.

"I like how you do things, Behram," Cynthia said in a sinister voice, looking into his immoral eyes. She saw they were two peas from the same pot.

"I like your look," Behram told Cynthia with a devilish smile on his face.

Cynthia liked the compliment, but more than anything she had taking over the world on her mind. Cynthia was very good at the art of seduction. She knew what was on his mind, just like many men before him had on their minds. She placed her hand on his chest, running it down to his stomach, saying, "If you help me take over the world, only then can you get this." She looked into his eyes and kissed him passionately. She could feel the lust flare within his body. She slowly walked away, telling her Ghost-likes and Behram's men to move out.

* * * * * * * * *

Zenny, Barrin and Backgril were still at sea with their fleet of 500 ships. They were sailing the Arabian Sea, not too far from where Cynthia and Behram were. Zenny was watching Barrin fish and saw that he had a skill for what he was doing. Backgril saw Zenny watching Barrin and walked over to her. "Would you like to learn how he does that?"

"Why? You're going to teach me?" Zenny asked, smiling at Backgril.

"No, but I'm sure he will."

Zenny didn't want Barrin showing her anything because they used to deal with each other. They'd fallen out a few years ago. Barrin saw her watching him and slightly smiled. Zenny looked at Backgril and rolled her eyes, walking over to where Barrin was showing some of their men how to fish. She grabbed a fishing rod which was made out of wood and tried to throw it. But the hook caught on the railing of the ship, causing the men and women on the ship to laugh. Zenny kept pulling on it until Barrin came to help her.

He gently grabbed her hand and whispered, "Let me help you, my lady." Zenny really didn't want his help because she didn't like what he'd done to her fifty years ago.

"I can do this on my own!" Backgril started laughing at the two of them because they were both stubborn.

"Why don't you let me help you?"

"Just like you helped me years ago, right?" Zenny asked, waiting for his answer.

"Zenny, I never meant to hurt you, but I had to do it or she would have killed you."

She became furious because she'd loved Barrin with all of her heart and after the way he'd treated her she would have rather fought the Queen for the man she loved. "Please! You were in love with that bitch! Don't tell me anything different Barrin!" Zenny shouted, looking into Barrin's eyes.

Barrin saw that her eyes were getting watery so he passionately, but gently grabbed her arms and pleaded, "I love you more than you will ever know. What I did back then was so you could live in peace without that bitch coming after you. I believe that if you love somebody there is nothing you will not do for them, and that is one of the things I was willing to do for you. I'm sorry if you don't see it that way but that's the truth so help me, that's the truth."

Zenny looked into his eyes and knew he was telling the truth. Still, she pulled herself away from him and walked away toward the front of the ship.

Backgril walked up to his longtime friend, placing his hand on his shoulder and said, "Just give her some time my friend."

"How much more time do I have to wait for her to come around, Backgril?" It has been 50 years already."

Backgril started laughing, patting Barrin on the shoulder. "Well, it's a good thing you're a Hatchet Man because you have all the time in the world my friend." Backgril started walking away from him.

Barrin yelled, "What if I die in battle, then what?"

"Then don't die!" Backgril shouted back, laughing.

Barrin looked at Zenny as she stood up front, looking out over the ocean. She glanced at him and turned back around. Zenny still loved Barrin, but she was not going to let him just walk back into her life so easy.

Later on that night as they were sailing the sea, Zenny, Backgril, Barrin as well as some of their Hatchet Men and Women were sitting around and drinking some mead. One of the Hatchet Men started telling some stories about how Barrin saved his life years ago. Zenny was listening but acted like she wasn't until he said, "Barrin had to act like he was going to kill me just so I could live. And when the time came for him to do so, he freed me from my masters and we killed them all." The man raised his cup to Barrin saying, "To you Barrin, to you." Barrin smiled and glanced at Zenny as she got up and headed to her chamber down below.

Backgril walked up on Barrin and whispered, "You better go after her. What are you waiting for? Go already, go!"

Barrin took a deep breath and started walking towards Zenny's room. He walked past some of their men and women who were drunk as hell, kissing and making out. He started to think about the good times he and Zenny used to have together.

Zenny was in her room, crying to herself because she really loved Barrin. She stood by her window, looking up at the stars. She turned on her crude lantern and Barrin knocked on the door, opening it at the same time. "Did I tell you to enter, Barrin?" Zenny asked, looking at him and waiting for his answer. The two of them just stood there for a few seconds. You could feel the love in the room and the energy generated from their bodies wanting each other. She took a deep breath preparing to say something but Barrin shut the door and walked quickly across the room.

Barrin took her into his arms and kissed her fervently. Zenny wanted to push him away but her eyes and body were telling another story. She squint her eyes slightly, pushing him off her, but her pushing turned into grabbing him. She pulled his face down to her soft lips, locking tongues with him. They playfully kissed each other with small pecks on the lips. Barrin put an arm underneath her legs, picking her up and used both arms to lift her up into the air. Zenny wrapped both her legs around his waist and her arms around his neck. He carried her over to a sheet on the floor and gently placed her on it as he continued to kiss her. They started undressing one another until they were completely naked. Both of them began to feel a sexual desire for each other that they hadn't felt in 50 years. Barrin kissed her lips, neck and chin and made his way slowly down between her breasts and began to lightly suck on her right nipple. Without haste he worked his way down to her stomach then slithered down to her thighs and stopped, building up a sexual drive in Zenny that made her remember what they used to do. She couldn't take it anymore and pushed his head between her legs. He started kissing her outer vaginal lips, stopping to examine her pretty wet peach between her legs. It still looked the way he remembered. It made him smile as he kissed, licked, flicked with slight nibbles to her clitoris head.

"Ahhhh! Yessss!" Zenny shouted with both hands holding his head. She arched her back, lifting her head to look at what Barrin was doing to her. She started moaning nonstop, working her hips in a rhythm over Barrin's mouth. Zenny started to climax which caused her breathing holes to whistle as she bit down on her bottom lip. She tilted her head backward and with her eyes closed, Zenny started humping Barrin's face, pushing his lips and tongue against her lovely, soft clitoris. Her vagina squirted over and over again as she climaxed. When she lifted her head again, her eyes were the eyes of her inner Hatchet Woman. She pulled Barrin's face up to her lips, kissing him ferociously which caused him to push himself inside of her wet, pretty prize.

"Yessss…hhhmm…ummm…" Zenny whispered as she kissed Barrin on his ear, working her hands up and down his back, squeezing his ass tightly; pushing him deeper and deeper inside her. The two of them were locked into a world of their very own where there was nothing but lovemaking. Zenny rolled Barrin over onto his back and sat on top, riding him. She placed her hands on his chest, pushing her lower body down onto his manhood, working her hips like nothing Barrin had ever felt before. Even though the two of them hadn't had sex with each other in over fifty years, Zenny still knew how to work him. She squeezed his manhood with her vaginal walls as he slowly made sweet, passionate love to her. She would rise all the way up to the very top of Barrin's penis ring, squeezing her vagina muscles tightly. She would push down just below his penis ring then slide back up to the tip. She did that three times before dripping her vagina amative down until his manhood couldn't go any further inside of her precious, wet prize.

Zenny looked into Barrin's amorous eyes and saw the face of the man that she had loved so very dearly. She started to feel old emotions mixing with her new emotions. She tilted her head and arched her back, pushing on his chest to push downward onto his penis, working her hips in synch with Barrin's. His eyes started to glow as he whispered, "Ummm…I love you…" His breathing holes started making sounds like steam coming from a volcano right before it erupted and then his semen shot out like hot lava. Now, there was another battle going on inside of her: the creation of new life. Barrin was far from being satisfied and was just beginning a long night of lovemaking. Hatchet Men didn't burn out so easy. They could have sex for hours and the women could for days. He touched her firm breast, squeezing her plump nipples with both hands. He rose up, placing his lips erotically over her right nipple, sucking on it like a newborn baby. He flipped Zenny over on her side and pushed her legs up to her chest then gently pushed himself inside of her constricted rose petal. Zenny smiled because she remembered the type of sex they used to have and it felt like yesterday to her. She was thinking to herself that Barrin hadn't missed a beat. He rubbed his hand softly down her back to her waist, holding her as he made love to her.

"Barrin…ummm…you feel…good…" opening her mouth and moaning softly because she didn't want anybody to hear them.

He started to pull on her hair, pushing her down onto her stomach. He reached underneath her with his right hand, placing it on her vagina, spreading her vaginal lips apart with his index finger and ring finger; using his middle finger to push very strongly on her clitoris head, rubbing it in a circular motion. He cupped her left breast with his left hand while pushing her body down onto his finger as he pushed his elongated penis deep inside of her.

"Barrin…you…better…never stop loving me…"

"I never did stop loving you. I've always loved you, my love."

"So why did you stop seeing me for that Queen bitch…?"

"Because she wanted to kill you and Backgril so, I did what she wanted. And when you left me, I couldn't see you anymore so I killed her."

Zenny didn't know all of that had happened. She stopped and turned around; looking into his eyes she saw the sincerity in them. Both of them were breathing hard, looking at one another for a few seconds. Zenny reached up with her hands, pulling his head down and gently kissed him. Barrin continued to tell her everything and by the time he was done, Zenny had officially forgiven him.

Zenny, Barrin, Backgril and the rest of their army finally reached India. The land was covered in blood and the smell of the dead was strongly in the air. Crows circled in the area where most of the dead were. "What the hell did Cynthia do?" Backgril asked as he looked around not seeing one sign of life.

"Spread out and check all of the houses for any sign of life," Zenny shouted to her soldiers of Hatchet Men and Hatchet Women. Zenny called on some crows from the sky to go look for Cynthia and her army of Ghost-likes.

"How long do you think it's going to take them to return with what you're looking for?" Backgril asked Zenny.

"No longer than two weeks; but until then we better keep moving. They knew which way to go because the smell of the dead was in the air.

* * * * * * * * *

Cynthia decided to set up a campsite for the night in Kazakhstan. Behram set up his tent next to hers. She was inside her tent with a few of her attendants, getting ready to leave to see her lover, Seth. She grabbed her Katar sword and as she was about to mount her horse, Behram called out to her. "Princess Cynthia, lady of Seth, where are you going?"

Cynthia got on her horse, pulling in the reins to turn her horse around and replied, "I'm going to talk with my love. I'll be back in a few hours."

"Would you like me to ride with you?"

Cynthia smiled and looked at Behram, saying, "Do I look like I need help? I hope not because I can take care of myself." Cynthia clicked her heel in the stirrups and her horse took off, riding through the City of Oral. Seth was there on the outskirts of the city. As she rode up on him she started smiling because she had thought it would be a while before she saw him again. She leaped off of her horse and right into Seth's arms. Cynthia kissed him three times. "I'm so happy to see you, my love. How is everything in Tripueler?" Cynthia asked, rubbing her hand on his stomach and moving it down to his penis, playing with it.

Seth loved her and wanted to be with her but he knew she would need to be ready for what was ahead of her. "The one you call Zenny, why is she still alive?"

Cynthia was caught off guard because she thought Zenny was already dead. "What do you mean? She's still alive?"

"Yes, she's not too far away from here."

"Where is she? I'll turn around and kill her!" Cynthia replied, becoming furious.

But Seth told her, "No, just keep moving on what needs to be done here. That is more important." Seth didn't want her to stop doing what needed to be done in Italy, but he was concerned about her. "Are you sure you're up to this?" he asked her.

Cynthia felt a little hurt that he would ask her such a thing. "Yes, my love, yes!"

Seth turned and walked away with his back to her and said, "I need you to do something that you might not want to do."

Cynthia walked quickly over to Seth, placing her hand on his chest and looked into her loved one eyes. "There's nothing that I won't do for you. You're the reason I'm still here, so whatever you need to be done shall be done. Just say it."

Seth was happy to see that Cynthia was on board with whatever he needed her to do. He told her his plan that involved her and Behram. Seth told her he needed her to sleep with Behram but not until they had overtaken Italy. Cynthia smiled because she was already on it. "I already have that in motion, my love," she replied with a slight giggle. "If that is all, consider it done, my love. Is there anything else?" Cynthia asked, looking into Seth's eyes, rubbing his chest with her hand, working her brand of seduction.

Seth's manhood started to awaken, calling for Cynthia. But he hadn't come here for that. He was going to see her after their victory battle in Italy. "Yes, that is it for now, he answered. I'll see you after you conquer Italy."

Cynthia kissed him passionately on the lips and turned around, twitching her butt, working her art of seduction as she walked away.

Seth stood there, watching his love ride off when the ground around him began to rumble. It was Kali, shooting down like a falling star, causing a crater to form when she landed in a crouched position with her head hanging down. The travel from Tripueler to Earth by wormhole could be exhausting and dangerous for the Gods. Many times they would travel in their armor when using the wormhole. If they would travel by ship it would be easier but many times they liked to travel in just their suits because it would give them a rush like nothing else in the universe. Kali quickly stood up, smiling slightly as she swiftly whipped off large chunks of flesh and blood.

"Did you have a little problem, my dear?" Seth asked, looking at Kali as she approached him.

"It was noting I couldn't handle. It's no fun if a girl can't kill here and there on her way to Earth," she replied as she took off her helmet. She kissed Seth passionately on his lips. "What about our plan? Is everything in motion?" Kali asked him.

"Yes, Cynthia was already thinking the same way."

That made Kali smile and rub a finger across Seth's lips. "I like…her…"

"She's going to give Behram a little loving once they take over all Rome," Seth said.

"What about your semen?" Kali asked him as she walked around him slowly, checking him out from head to toe.

Seth turned to her and said, "That plan has been in effect ever since the last time I mated with her."

Kali smiled as she stood face-to-face with Seth. "How was it? Was it good?" Kali asked, waiting to hear Seth's answer; and to make things more intense, she started rubbing Seth's chest and kissing him on his lips, down his chest, placing her hand on his manhood. Seth closed his eyes, taking deep breaths and was short on words. Kali loved when she had Seth the way he was right now. "This baby, will it be just like us?"

"Yesss! It will be just like us, but look more human so it will be able to free us," Seth replied, grabbing Kali and lifting her up into the air then laying her gently onto the ground and started slowly taking off her armor.

Kali loved it when Seth handled her the way he did. She loved having sex right after a battle with Red Worms as she traveled through the wormhole. It gave her a rush! And she loved to be in control when it came to making love with her love, Seth. Kali stood at 10 feet tall, 225 pounds and very curvy. She was a beautiful Goddess. Seth got on top of her in the missionary position. He started giving her passionate kisses on her lips and worked his way down to her neck then her breasts, running his tongue from right to left. Seth slithered his tongue down her brawny stomach to her breathing hole on her thigh right beside her vagina. He started blowing inside her breathing hole on her left leg while playing with her clitoris. Kali climaxed very quickly. Seth knew where to touch Kali because they had been making love for eons. He loved making love to her because he didn't have to shrink his manhood. He could actually make it larger by breathing more air into his breathing holes which makes him larger.

"Ummm...Seth...give it...to...me!" Kali whispered urgently, looking into Seth's reddish eyes.

The more air he took into his penis the more it extended in length and width. The Gods were nothing like man had ever known because when it came to sexual feelings they were like lions in the jungle. The same way spikes come out of the male lion when he's having sex, is the same way with male Gods. The more Seth's spikes extended the more Kali loved it. Both of their breathing holes started sounding off as they climaxed together. The more Seth's spikes scraped inside of Kali, the more she squeezed her inner walls tighter, screaming in ecstasy. Her eyes started to glow just as Seth hit her "J" spot. Her fangs extended as she squeezed Seth's broad back. Kali looked up to the stars, working her hips in synch with Seth's. Meanwhile, by the time Cynthia got back to camp, most of her men were sound asleep except for Behram. He'd stayed up, waiting for Cynthia's safe return. He stood up when he saw her coming from a mile away. Cynthia could see him waiting for her and started smiling because she knew she had him right where she wanted him. "How was your trip, my lady?" Behram asked Cynthia, helping her off her horse.

"It was fine but shouldn't you be in bed? We do have a big day ahead of us tomorrow you know."

"I had to make sure you returned safely. I can't have my future Queen and the mother of my child not returning safely."

Cynthia started grinning, thinking to herself how she already knew she was pregnant with Seth's child. She walked toward her tent and told Behram she would see him in the morning. Before she closed her tent she gave him a passionate kiss on the lips then pushed him away. Behram took that as a sign that she wanted him as he walked toward his tent, getting ready for tomorrow. Inside her tent, Cynthia was thinking about how tomorrow wasn't going to be an easy battle because they were going up against Romulus. Although just like them, he was better because he was God-like. The only difference between Cynthia, Behram and Romulus was that Romulus was no longer on their side.

Romulus and Remus' story started somewhere in 735 B.C. in Rome. Seth told his brother, Ares, to go down to Earth. So Ares went down from the heavens to Earth and had a sexual encounter with their mother, giving her demigod children. The Emperor got word of what happened and heard that the people in Italy were treating Romulus and Remus' birth as if they were Gods. The people were no longer worshipping him and that didn't go very well with him. He sent an army to the brother's house in Rome to kill them and their mother in order to send a message to Seth. The soldiers were able to kill the mother but not before she'd singlehandedly killed fifteen of them. She'd told her sister to take both of her newborn sons and leave. But when the sister tried to leave she was shot in the stomach with an arrow and was only able to make it to the Tiber River. The river makes its way from the Italian highland down to the Tyrrhenian Sea. The soldiers didn't even bother to chase her because they felt the wolves would finish her off. They were very wrong because those same wolves were sent by Seth himself from Tripueler.

The wolves raised both boys into men and later on they came back to avenge their mother's death, taking Rome by force. The people began to look up to them as Gods and Romulus and Remus began to like the admiration. This made Ares and Seth very angry with them because now they felt like they were being forgotten by the people. So, Seth told Ares to kill them but the brothers got wind of Seth's plan; and the two of them figured out a way to get to Tripueler where they started wars with the Gods. Some Gods were even killed by Romulus and Remus. This was becoming a very big deal on Tripueler, so big that Earth was on the verge of being destroyed by the Gods. When Romulus and Remus returned to Earth they were bigger than the Gods on Earth. Even after some years had passed, Romulus and Remus were becoming larger than life itself on Earth. Seth talked with Ares and decided to go to Remus to see if he would join him and Ares to get the people back to the way everything once was. Remus was getting tired of the way his brother was acting and decided to work with the Gods. When Romulus found out about his brother's meeting with the Gods, he killed Remus without thinking twice which precipitated the beginning of his downfall. This was what was left for Cynthia and Behram to deal with tomorrow on the battlefield.

Cynthia was lying on her side, sound asleep when she felt a hand touch her. To her surprise it wasn't who she wanted to see. Cynthia leapt to her feet, grabbing her sword.

"If I wanted to kill you I would've done it already," Isis told her.

Cynthia knew who Isis was. "What do you want with me?" Cynthia shouted.

Isis started smiling and said, "Cynthia, be a little smarter than them. You're being used to do Seth and Ares' dirty work they created a long time ago. Stop being a tool for them and come with me. I will protect you and your baby."

Cynthia started laughing but Isis was not. "Do I look like a fool to you, Isis? You think you can just walk in here and talk with me?"

"I just did Cynthia. What you're going to do tomorrow might be the end for your child that you're carrying inside of you."

Cynthia didn't like that kind of talk at all. She started getting defensive, holding her stomach with one hand, but quickly said, "Bitch, you're trying to trick me so I can come with you!" Cynthia started swinging her sword at Isis but Isis didn't swing hers. She just made sure Cynthia didn't hurt herself. Then Cynthia leaped into the air, coming down onto Isis. Isis grabbed her, pinning her down on the ground and placing her dagger at Cynthia's throat to make her stop fighting with her.

"Look, I don't have much time left," Isis said urgently, "so stop fighting with me. You're putting your baby in great danger and it could get greater. Cynthia you must choose before it's too late."

But Cynthia locked her legs around Isis and flipped Isis over onto her back with her feet. Then Cynthia jumped to her feet and started backing away from Isis.

"Cynthia, you're not a fool so stop acting like one because if your child won't do what they want it to do, it will end up like Romulus tomorrow."

Cynthia became furious, charging Isis. Isis grabbed her and put her in a headlock with her right arm then took her left hand and placed it on Cynthia's stomach, rubbing it. Her stomach started glowing and Cynthia started to panic, saying, "What the hell are you doing to my baby?"

"I'm doing what you won't do to protect it!"

Cynthia woke up in a very cold sweat and breathing very hard. She knew her dream was very real and that made her slightly afraid. Cynthia encircled her stomach with her arms, looking at it with a somewhat sad expression on her face. She started thinking what if what Isis said was true?

"Cynthia, may I enter?" Behram asked her from outside the tent.

But she told him she was coming out soon and to just have the men ready to go. She stood up, wiping tears from her face. It was the only thing that made her feel human again.

* * * * * * * * *

Romulus was in Rome, sitting in his chair that was made out of gold. He had several women tending to his every need. Romulus was God-like to the people of Rome. He was 6'5" in height with light-brown eyes, long, silky black hair, a full beard and white teeth. He was a Caucasian male, very strong and muscular. He was the only one who could go up against the Gods and win. He still wore a tunic and sat in the palace most of the time, training with several Ghost-likes. His castle stood on the very top of a mountain. The only way to access it was to climb the tall walls or take it by storm. Seth and Ares were able to turn one of Romulus' tarts into a spy. She was able to give them all types of information about Romulus. She had his time schedule down to a science. She knew when he would want her to come over and how long it would take for him to climax. She knew what time he got up every morning to use the bathroom; what time he would train in the mornings; what time he ate; and the time and days he would drink like a madman and party with over a dozen women. That was the time he was most vulnerable. The tart knew exactly the time of day he would do a number two in the bathroom. She had it down to the second. His schedule was hers and this was one of those nights he had a dozen women in his bed.

The tart was a part of the dozen. Her name was Ash. She stood 5'5" in height and was petite with long, blonde hair, bewitching blue eyes and beautiful lips. She was very good at seduction. She woke up from out of her sleep right next to Romulus with his arms around her neck. He was out cold and drunk as usual. Ash lifted up one of his arms and slipped out of bed just like she always did. She was the only one that Romulus would let use his bathroom because one day she proved her loyalty to him. She warned him about one of his men who wanted to kill him for the Gods. Well, that's what he thought would happen but she was the one that set the guard up in the worse way. She dressed, grabbed her bow and arrows and left to go for a walk. Usually she turned right to go into town but tonight she made a left turn, heading towards the drawbridge. There were four guards on duty. Ash knew she had to get the drawbridge open so Cynthia, Behram and the rest of their army could get inside. Cynthia had some of her Hatchet Men with grappling hooks ready to climb the high wall. Ash stepped into the shadows and readied her bow and arrows, quickly shooting each guard, one-by-one. She swiftly ran over to the drawbridge and just as she was about to lower it an arrow hit her in her back. She turned around and another hit her in her stomach. She started bleeding from her mouth and when she looked up to see where the arrows were coming from, she saw Romulus smiling devilishly at her from one hundred feet away. With her last ounce of strength, she took another arrow and shot the rope that was holding the drawbridge up at the same time Romulus shot her in the chest, causing her to fall. The drawbridge hit the ground the same time Ash did.

Cynthia saw the drawbridge was open and shouted, "Forward!!" She grabbed her Katar sword, clicked her heels in the stirrups against her horse, taking off. She extended her claws as she rode across the drawbridge with her Ghost-likes behind her. Arrows shot through the air, whistling past her head, barely missing her. Cynthia stood up in the saddle on her horse, crouching down with her sword in one hand and her claw on her free hand extended. As her horse rode into Romulus' Ghost-likes, Cynthia leaped into the air right into the center of them, swinging her sword, killing dozens of them. An arrow shot from behind her and she quickly blocked it with her sword. She glanced up at Romulus to see him smiling at her. She rushed over to Ash lying on the ground, and held her head.

"Do…you…think…the Gods…will…forgive…me?" Ash struggled to ask Cynthia.

"Yes my child, all will be forgiven. Go home," Cynthia told her and Ash passed on to the next life. Cynthia closed her eyes and laid her down to rest then went back into battle.

Behram and his Hatchet Men started scaling the wall with their grappling hooks. As a few of Behram's Hatchet Men made it to the top of the wall and started to fight with Romulus' Ghost-likes. Some of Romulus' Ghost-likes started shooting flaming arrows at them as they were making their way up the side of the wall. Behram quickly pushed himself off the wall, swinging himself over to the right and out of the way of the arrows. He pushed and pulled himself up over the wall. Three of Romulus' Ghost-likes were there to meet him. Behram leaped into the air, spinning around and slicing them to pieces. He started to push his Ghost-likes forward toward Romulus' castle doors.

Hatchet Men

Cynthia continued to fight her way through Romulus' Ghost-likes. She leaped into the air, throwing her sword through five Ghost-likes, her sword plunging into the ground. While she was still in the air she extended her claws, coming down and slicing and dicing Ghost-like after Ghost-like. She swiftly grabbed her sword and with a front flip into the air, she came down hard onto two of Romulus' Ghost-likes. Cynthia and Behram had some advantage over Romulus because they had Hatchet Men with them. After Romulus killed his brother he never let another Hatchet Man enter into Rome and it kind of made him weak. But he was still very strong by himself, so strong that the Gods didn't want to take him on. Cynthia and her Ghost-likes started to make their way into town with a battering ram to take down the doors at Romulus' castle. Behind the doors, Romulus was surrounded by Hatchet Men and Hatchet Women, but he was not going out without a fight. He had both his Viking axes made in Tripueler given from Ares himself with the hieroglyphic "Son of Ares God of war, Son of war Romulus the killer." His signature move was to stab his enemy with one axe and while it was embedded in their body, lift them up with the axe then chop off their heads with his other axe. Then he would throw the body with one kick. He had an axe in each hand, swinging like a madman; kicking and punching, leaping into the air and coming down hard on five Hatchet Men, killing them instantly. "My name is Romulus!!" he shouted, swinging his axes into two Hatchet Men chests, making their bodies smash into each other. He quickly pulled the axes out of their bodies and leaped up onto a wall, looking down at all the Hatchet Men that were trying to get to him and shouted, "You will die today and some of you will die slowly!" Several arrows were shot at him but he zigzagged out of the way and took off running toward the main wall.

Cynthia met up with Behram at the main wall with the battering ram. They started trying to take down the doors. Romulus shouted to his Ghost-likes to drop the hot tar from the very large steel pots, behind the wall, onto Cynthia, Behram and their army below. Cynthia was so focused on getting the door open that she didn't see the hot tar about to rain down. "Cynthia!!" Behram yelled, running toward her and grabbed her within seconds of being burned badly by the tar. But some of it hit Behram because he'd used part of his body to shield her. "Arrrr!" Behram shouted, looking at Romulus smiling down at him from on top of the wall.

Cynthia saw what Behram had done for her and became furious at Romulus, running toward the door and kicking it. Then she and a dozen Ghost-likes and Hatchet Men and Women lifted up the battering ram and began hitting the door.

Romulus stood on top of the wall, looking down. "She is very determined to kill me," he whispered to himself right before dozens of arrows shot upward at him. Romulus leaped off the wall with both axes in his hands simultaneously flipping them around. He started walking toward the corridor Cynthia, Behram and the rest of their soldiers would have to enter.

But Cynthia continued to thwack the door with the battering ram. "Arrrr!" Cynthia cried out as she ceaselessly rammed the door trying to make the door open and finally the bolt opened.

"Arrrr!" the soldiers shouted. They ran inside, spreading throughout the castle as they searched for Romulus.

Cynthia grabbed Behram's left arm, placing it around her shoulder, but he told her to go. Cynthia nodded her head and as she took off running he shouted, "Do as we planned. I'm right behind you!" Cynthia stopped for a second, looked at Behram and smiled, blowing him a kiss. Then she took off running down a corridor right into a big battle. She extended her claws, severing the heads of Ghost-likes as she made her way through the crowd, killing them. "This way!" she shouted, pointing down a corridor that would take them to Romulus. Cynthia took off with her fifteen inch daggers whose hieroglyphic read, "Killer of Hatchet Man Shadows, lover of Seth." She was clearing the path as she made her way to where Romulus would be.

Behram was making his way with a dozen Hatchet Men coming from the opposite direction. He was a little bit out of breath as his wounds were healing, but not fast enough. He remembered his God Kali telling him to shout her name when they were around Romulus because it was going to take the five of them to fight him.

Romulus turned the corner in his castle and Cynthia was no more than one hundred feet from him. Cynthia felt his presence and knew he was watching her, smiling. She turned around, locking eyes with him, watching as he stepped into the shadows. She started making her way to the corridor where she'd seen him. "Do not let anything get past you!" Cynthia shouted to one of her Hatchet Women as she ran off after Romulus.

Romulus stood on the edge of the wall with both axes in his hands. He took a look at the long drop to the crevasse below and lifted his head up to the sky, shouting, "You think I will beg forgiveness? Never! I will kill all of you!!" Romulus was not about to stop. He was going to fight until he was dead.

"Romulus!" Cynthia shouted.

Romulus glanced over his shoulder at Cynthia, smiling. He slowly turned around to face her, walking slowly on the edge of the wall. Cynthia was covered in blood from head to toe. She was breathing heavily as she, too, walked slowly toward Romulus with both fifteen inch daggers in her hands. The one in her right hand pointed forward and the other one in her left hand was pointing backward with both hands held face-high.

"So you've come to kill me. Did they tell you that they were going to make you into their God?" Romulus asked Cynthia, smiling at her. Cynthia just kept walking toward him slowly. "Don't tell me you're mute," he asked her, looking into her eyes, still smiling at her. He stood on the edge of the wall, twirling both axes in his hands. Cynthia stopped in the center of the floor, watching Romulus' every move. There was nobody else up there, just the two of them. "So, are you going to come join me on the wall, or are you going to stay down there?" he asked Cynthia, blowing her a kiss. Cynthia squint her eyes and leaped into the air, landing on the other side of Romulus, crouched down and face-to-face with him. "That's what I'm talking about right there," Romulus crowed. "Where's your man?" "That's not my man. You know nothing Romulus, but today you will know death!" Cynthia yelled as she ran toward him. She leaped into the air, trying to strike Romulus with her daggers, but she missed. They started fighting on the edge of the wall. Romulus swung his axe upward, aiming at Cynthia's chest with both of his axes. Cynthia quickly raised both hands, blocking Romulus two axes. However, the blow was so fierce that Cynthia slid backward slightly, digging up the ground.

"I hope you didn't think it was going to be easy?" Romulus asked Cynthia.

"Cynthia said, "You're going to die today and you're going to die badly…" She smiled as she walked slowly toward him.

Elsewhere, Behram was making his way to where Cynthia and Romulus were. It took him some time because he was fighting with quite a few Ghost-likes, and he was still healing. Then he heard Cynthia and Romulus fighting and knew he wasn't too far away from them. Behram fought hard and strong, making his way to Cynthia. Once he got there, Romulus had Cynthia pinned down over the edge of the wall.

Romulus was choking her, shouting, "Did my father send you, bitch?"

Behram quickly went into action, running across the floor and leaping into the air with both swords in his hands. Romulus felt his presence and turned around rapidly, kicking Behram in the chest. Behram went flying across the room, landing on his back, but quickly flipped to his feet. Cynthia saw a window of opportunity and kicked Romulus, stabbing him in the stomach with one of her daggers, making him furious. He leaped into the air, kicking her in the chest which sent her flying across the sky. Behram leaped into the air, grabbing her.

"So this is your man? I think you would be better off with me. So what do you say? You have two seconds to decide or die."

Cynthia and Behram stood back to back. They glanced at one another and leaped onto the wall. They took turns fighting with Romulus. However, it wasn't conducive for them to fight one at a time. Romulus fought with both of them, smiling, and that started to piss Cynthia off. "What the hell is so funny? You're about to die and yet you still smile, why?" she asked, twirling her daggers in her hands. Behram had his two swords and they started to walk deliberately toward him.

Romulus scanned Behram's body and saw he was still healing from the tar poured on him. Then he scanned Cynthia and a very peculiar look appeared on his face which Cynthia noticed. "You're pregnant by one of the Gods!" Romulus accused her.

Behram looked at Cynthia with a confused look on his face. "Cynthia, what is he talking about?" Behram asked.

Romulus started laughing at him, leaping off the wall onto the floor. Cynthia didn't know what to say so she said nothing. She stepped off the edge, landing down onto the ground not too far from Romulus. Behram took a deep breath, leaping down as Romulus pointed one of his axes at Behram and shouted, "I guess you thought you were the father, right? You didn't know, did you?" Cynthia ran toward Romulus and Behram ran around from the top of the wall, coming up behind Romulus. The three of them continued to fight. All you heard was the clash of swords, axes and daggers.

* * * * * * * * *

Zenny, Backgril, Barrin and the rest of their soldiers were just reaching Rome and it was not hard to find where the war was taking place. "It seems like the war is this way!" Zenny yelled. They started moving quickly towards the sound of steel swords clashing in war. It did not take long for them to start fighting. Not only were they fighting Ghost-likes, but other Hatchet Men.

At the castle, Cynthia and Behram continued to fight hard but Romulus was just too strong. Not even the both of them could take him out. "Behram, go back up top now!" Cynthia shouted and they both leaped back up on the wall.

"Now you run from me," Romulus jeered, looking at the both of them.

"No Romulus, not run, just stepped back. Now Behram! Now!" Cynthia yelled and Behram shouted up to the Gods.

Romulus became very irate because he knew that he would need all his strength to fight with the Gods. He hurtled himself into the air, trying to kill Cynthia and Behram. He knew his time was short before the Gods came. When he'd heard Behram yell, "Seth and Kali" he'd felt disrespected. "Father, you don't even have the honor to kill me yourself, your own child!" Romulus blustered. Then he started focusing on Cynthia. He punched Behram in the face and almost kicked him off the wall. Cynthia ran over to help him but Romulus grabbed her by her throat, lifting her up into the air, squeezing her esophagus, making it hard for her to breathe. She started gasping for air. Behram was holding onto the edge of the wall with both hands, but when he saw Cynthia being choked, he quickly grabbed his dagger, stabbing Romulus' foot.

"Arrrr!" Romulus howled in pain, flinging Cynthia to the floor. He turned around and cut off Behram's fingers, causing him to let go of the wall, falling down into the crevasse.

"Nooo!" Cynthia shouted as she watched Behram fall to his death, only his bloody fingers left on the floor as a reminder of him.

"Don't worry; you're going to join him. The Gods are only using you for your child you fool. It doesn't matter because you and your child are going to die!" Romulus said, laughing as he started running towards her. But before he could grab Cynthia, a lightning bolt shot down from the sky and pierced through him. Blood spurted out of Romulus' mouth and both of his axes fell from his hands, hitting the floor. Romulus fell to his knees. Seth, Kali and Ares were now standing on the wall, surrounding Romulus, and the entirety of Rome could see the display of power. The lightning bolt had stabbed Romulus in the back and protruded through his chest. He lifted his head, looking at Cynthia. She stood up and slowly smiled, wiping the blood from her mouth and spitting on him. Romulus looked at her, still smiling. He glanced at his father walking toward him.

"Romulus, you have been very bad for many years. It's time for you to move on, son."

"Don't give me all the long speeches. Just do what you came to do!" Romulus shouted, pulling the lightning bolt out of his body and dropped his head then slowly got up to face his father, Ares. Romulus was bleeding from the mouth, nose, chest and his foot. This was the first time someone had made him bleed.

Seth walked up to Cynthia, asking her, "Are you okay, my love?"

"Yes, I'll be fine. What about Behram?" Cynthia asked as she wiped the blood from her mouth.

"He's dead," Kali told her as she walked towards them.

Romulus started laughing and just before Ares stabbed him again he told Cynthia, "You and your baby are nothing to them. Listen to Isis although I hate her guts!" Ares stabbed him in the chest with a lightning bolt and Kali kicked him over the wall where he fell down into the crevasse with Behram.

Seth turned his attention to Cynthia, questioning her about Isis. "What did Isis come to you about? What did you tell her?"

"I told her nothing!"

Seth knew she was telling the truth, but he wanted to know what Isis wanted from her. "What did she want from you?"

"She wanted me to walk with her, but I fought her off."

"Did she do anything to you?" Kali asked, scanning Cynthia to see if she would tell the truth. Cynthia didn't know what to say because Isis did do something to her so she said, "No, I wouldn't let her."

"Lies!!" Kali screamed and slapped Cynthia, sending her flying into the air where she landed on her back, making an indentation in the floor. Kali turned to Seth telling him to kill Cynthia now as she and Ares shot back into the sky, going back to Tripueler, leaving Seth to kill Cynthia who was unconscious on the floor.

Seth walked over to her and said, "It's a shame because I loved you. Arrrr!!" He grabbed his sword and swung downward over Cynthia's body, but Isis had put a shield around her body the day the two of them were fighting. In a rage, Seth flew into the air but hit his head on the wall of a mountain a few miles away and was rendered unconscious.

Zenny, Backgril, Barrin and the rest of their army made it to where Cynthia was knocked out. "What the hell happened here?" Zenny asked, walking over to Cynthia.

"What do we do with her?" Barrin asked.

But just as Zenny was about to kill her the ground rumbled underneath them. "Zenny stop!" Isis yelled, walking over to them. She looked at Cynthia on the floor and said, "Take her and make her have the baby. Then take it from her. As for Cynthia, keep her locked away. Zenny, can you and Barrin raise the child?"

Barrin looked at Zenny as they looked at Cynthia still unconscious on the floor and said, "Yes, we can, but what is so special about this child?"

"Good. Make sure the child doesn't know what it really is. It's only to know that it's a Shadow. And when you feel the time is right you can tell the child about its mother. Make sure to give the child lots of love because this child is the future."

"What's so special about this child?" Backgril asked, walking toward Isis.

"This child is going to be very powerful, and when raised around the right ones it will become great; more powerful than Romulus and Remus put together." And with those last words, Isis took off into the sky just as fast as she'd arrived.

"Where are we going to keep her locked away" Barrin asked Cynthia and Backgril.

"I don't know, but let's go. Backgril, can you carry her?" Zenny asked. Backgril picked Cynthia up, placing her over his shoulder. Zenny then leaped up onto the wall, looking over the edge, trying to see if she saw any signs of Romulus and Behram. She saw nothing so they all walked back the way they'd come.

A few miles away, Seth regained consciousness beside a mountain. He was slightly disoriented as he stood up. Then it all came back to him. "Isis, you bitch!!" he shouted and quickly took off into the sky and back to Tripueler.

Chapter One

Since that very day Seth tried to kill Cynthia and her baby in Italy, the world had changed dramatically. About seven hundred years had passed. The year is now 2050, the space age and the world is vastly different. The Watchers continue to work with mankind by helping them build a better world on Earth, the Moon and Mars. Most of the cities on Earth are now elevated above ground on a maglev system. The ground is used only for farming, wild life preserves and trees to help with global warming. Magnets the sizes of 100 yards by 50 yards are buried 50 feet underground. Magnets of the same size are placed underneath cities to make them maglev; to help them stay afloat. Some of strongest magnets are used: Neodymium, Alnico, Serrite and Samarium cobalt. Any vehicle—cars, trucks, trains, motorcycles, etc.—on land is now run by an electric system only. They can hover above ground as high as fifty feet in the air.

Some of the wealthiest people still have vehicles from the early 20th Century. Trains are now interconnected all over the world on a maglev system. You could travel the entire world in three days. The future was very promising to those who wanted a future as well as to those who didn't and were still trying to destroy it. That's why it became illegal to practice any type of racism in 2050. You could be imprisoned for 20 years. Hate crimes had gotten so bad that the United Nations put an end to anyone who practiced hate. All computer and handheld devices were run on a virtual reality system. But for the most part the world was a better place. Hatchet Men worked with the CIA (Central Intelligence Agency) in the United States, Mossad in Israel, British Intelligence MI6 (Military Intelligence Service), and SIS (Secret Intelligence Service). The Hatchet Men and Hatchet Women were also friends with Italy AISE (Agenvia Informazioni Sicurezza Esterna) and SISMI (Servivic Informazioni Sicurezza Militare). In Russia it's the FSO (Federal Protective Service) and FSB (Federal Security Service of the Russia Federation). And, The Hatchet Men also dealt with the Middle East ISI (International service Intelligence). And last but not least is the HUWP (Hatchet Men University Watchers Program). Only two to five people in each of the other agencies knew of the HUWP and the information had been passed down from generation to generation. HUWP is the most top secret organization in the world, and the oldest. The United Nations sat at the head of the table amongst all the agencies

The world as we know it had changed since 1418 A.D. We evolved but not fast enough. The ground on Earth still had a few cities on each continent around the world where people lived and went to party. Most of the people lived on the ground and were considered to be poor. But some were very wealthy and lived in these cities. Hatchet Men and Hatchet Women who kept their power dormant lived on the ground. Sometimes they would go to the maglev cities to work or shop, depending on the individual Hatch Man or Hatchet Woman. New York, Baltimore and Los Angeles were some of the cities in the United States that were still functional and up and running normally that people visited. Crime was still at an all-time high in some of the cities above ground as well as on the ground. The biggest crime was sex trafficking; secondary were murder for hire and drug dealing.

Terrorism was at the top of the crime chain among all crimes and that is where the HUWP was most useful. They were responsible for stopping all terrorist activity around the world. The terrorist group that was the most serious threat was HMG (Hatchet Men Ghost). Their goal was to make global warming worse to kill off the human race. The HUWP Shadow team were always on the lookout for HMG's, nonstop. The Hatchet Men Shadows had several bases around the world. One of them was in the Pacific Ocean on a semisubmersible. Catalina Island had an undersea base where the Watchers would come to talk with Hatchet Men Shadow teams.

The Hatchet Men Shadows and Hatchet Men Ghosts had been at war since 222 B.C. Both teams worked for the Watchers from Tripueler. The war between both groups had been able to stay beneath the table of mankind for so many years because Hatchet Men and Hatchet Women are able to change their facial features every century to help keep their true identity a secret. But not all Hatchet Men and Hatchet Women change their identity. Some stay in the shadows and some stay as a Ghost.

* * * * * * * * *

"Jennifer, are you going to take me to school?" Laura asked, as she stood on the other side of Jennifer's closed room door.

Jennifer was not really up to taking her sister Laura anywhere. She had just been released from the hospital a few weeks ago. She was still grieving over the loss of her fiancé. He had died in an appalling way. Jennifer was lucky to have survived the crash. She had been two months pregnant and her baby she had been carrying had not been so lucky either. Jennifer just sat in her room most of the time, looking at pictures of her and her fiancé, crying to herself. "Laura, I don't feel like taking you to school, so ask dad," Jennifer shouted through the door.

Laura was worried about her big sister. She knew how much Jennifer had loved her fiancé, but she didn't want her to slip into a deep depression. "Jennifer, would you open the door, please?" Laura implored. She stood there for a few seconds and when she didn't get an answer she started walking away. As she reached the top of the stairs she heard Jennifer's door open. It made Laura happy because she did not like to see her sister feeling sad. "Jennifer, what's up?" Laura asked as she walked inside of Jennifer's room. Jennifer had walked back to her bed and was now lying on her stomach, looking at some pictures, smiling and laughing to herself. Laura started to wonder if her sister was losing her mind. "Jennifer, are you okay?"

"Yeah Laura, what makes you think I'm not?" But before Laura could answer, Jennifer sat up, showing Laura some pictures of Laura, Jennifer and Eric, her fiancé, saying, "Laura, remember when we went here?"

Laura took a look at the picture, giving Jennifer a slight smile as she glanced at Jennifer. She wanted to just make sure Jennifer was okay. "Yeah, I remember that. We had so much fun that day."

"I know, right? Eric loved this picture of all of us together. You know he loved you like a little sister, right?" Jennifer glanced at Laura then she turned her attention back to the picture and continued to smile.

Laura began rubbing Jennifer on her back as they sat on the bed, hugging her and leaning her head against Jennifer's head. "Jennifer, I'm worried about you. You haven't come out of this room since you've been home." Jennifer just sat there, smiling and looking at the pictures. A car pulled up in the driveway and started blowing the horn. Laura got up and looked out the window. She saw it was her friends. "Jennifer, I want to take you out on Saturday. Please tell me yes."

"Sure, I'll go with you Laura," Jennifer said, glancing at her then quickly turned her attention back to the photo album.

Laura gave Jennifer a kiss and a big hug, telling her sister how much she loved her and walked out of the room. Their father, Chris, had been standing at his room door, listening at their exchange the entire time. He knew it would be a while before Jennifer would return to her old self.

* * * * * * * * *

"Laura, what's up with your sister? Is she going to come with us to the club Saturday?" Tisha asked while she was putting on her lip liner. Laura glanced up at her sister's window as she got into Tisha's 2047 black, twin turbocharged V-12 BMW M5 electric hover car. It could go from zero to sixty in 2.2 seconds. Top speed was 250 mph with 720 horsepower, seven-speed dual automatic clutch and it ran on a maglev system.

"Yeah, she's coming with us."

"Good because she needs to get out," Melissa said from the back seat, hugging Laura from behind her seat. Laura, Tisha and Melissa had been friends since the first grade. They were now seniors in high school.

"Okay, let's go. Everybody looking good?" Tisha teased as they all looked at themselves in their mirrors and then looked at each other and laughed. They took off to Lake Clifton high school in Baltimore. Laura lived in South Baltimore on Elm Tree in an area called Curtis Bay with her sister Jennifer Lin and her father Chris Lin.

Back at the house Chris was getting himself ready for work. But before he left he stopped by his daughter's room. He knocked on her door and then entered. "Hey Buttercup, what's going on?" Chris asked as he stood in the doorway.

Jennifer sat up and turned to her father, smiling, but he knew she was hurting inside. "Just chilling, dad. Are you about to go to work?"

"Yes. Do you need anything?" Chris asked, walking over to her.

"No dad. I'll be okay. If I need anything I know how to get in touch with you."

Chris smiled at his daughter. He kissed her on the forehead and told her, "I love you" and left her room.

After Chris left Jennifer rolled over on her back and said, "Eric, play our song." Jennifer had named her automated response machine after her fiancé Eric. She'd done this after she got home from the hospital. Whenever she found herself home alone she'd start crying. Their song started to play and it was Sade from her "Collection" CD2 track 3, "I'll Be There." Jennifer started to cry softly from the inside, the tears working their way to her pretty green eyes. They ran down her soft, light-skinned complexion face. She was Asian-American. The pain seemed to be to overbearing for her 138-pound body. She grabbed the ends of her long, lush, silky hair, playing with them just like Eric would do when their song played. And even though she stood at only 5'4" in height, Eric's 6'2" height made her feel taller. Jennifer stood up, wiping her tears but they just kept falling. She walked over to her full-length mirror and took off her blouse. She was only 23 years of age but she felt like she was much older in Spirit. She looked at the tattoo that she had of a phoenix on her back with fire wrapped around her upper right arm to remind her of who she was. She'd had it done the way Eric would have done it. He would've made her turn around and tell her how lucky he was to have her. His exact words were, "You're the most beautiful woman in the room and most of all you're mine." Jennifer started to cry some more. She became lost in thought, listening to Sade.

Jennifer was not ready to let go of Eric just yet. She got dressed, grabbed her car keys and headed out the door. She sat in her car, wanting to leave the house but she couldn't find the nerve to drive just yet. She started to think about Eric and their last night together, right before the accident:

It was a very beautiful and luxurious setting at 57 BAR and KITCHEN, a restaurant in Locust Point. What made it so great was the way the design was that of the 20th Century over the years which brought a lot of people to the restaurant. That night, Jennifer and Eric were out on the town. She ordered Queso Fundido. It was a very simple dish where you scooped cheese with tortillas de harina and it was to die for. When she took a bite from her plate and put it into her mouth, her taste buds lit up. "Oh my God...Eric you got to try this!" she said as she chewed the food. She started to feed Eric some of it and his eyes opened so wide it made his eyebrows jump several times. Jennifer couldn't help but laugh at him. That was one of the things she loved about him. "You're so crazy," she told him.

"And that is why you love me."

They kissed and continued to eat their meals. Eric ordered the Veal Tongue Bocadll.l.o. He fed Jennifer some of it from his fork and the two of them melted away after every taste from one another's plates. Jennifer looked into Eric's beautiful brown eyes, smiling, and said, "I hope everything goes okay this time with the baby, Eric."

"Why wouldn't it, baby?"

"Because we've been trying for a while now and this is our third time."

Eric took her left hand, holding it gently and with his other hand he picked up his glass of Salon 1999 Blanc de Blancs Champagne Le Mesnil. It was a special night for them because Eric was going to ask for her hand in marriage. Her father had already given Eric approval to marry his daughter. Jennifer did not know what was about to happen next. Eric told her to close her eyes and she did. When he told her to open her eyes there was a diamond ring sitting where her plate had sat. She was at a loss for words and her heart was beating fast, filled with joy. She started crying and smiling at the same time at him. He told her to pick up her glass so they could make a toast together. He got down on one knee, looked into her eyes and asked, "Jennifer Lin, will you be..."

"Yes! Yes! I will!" she squealed. Eric couldn't even get the words out before she cut him off and bent over, throwing her arms around his neck and kissing him all over his face. He stood up and placed the ring on her finger. People in the restaurant started clapping for them. She admired the ring and gave him another hug. Eric had made her feel special as always.

Jennifer's phone started to ring, bringing her back to the present. She had been sitting in her car for so long that two hours had passed. It was raining and coming down heavily. She answered and a voice asked, "Jennifer, what's going on?" It was one of Jennifer's friends named Jamey.

"I'm still caught up Jamey. I just can't stop thinking about him."

Jamey and Jennifer had been friends for a very long time, since first grade. Jamey didn't live too far from Jennifer. She lived in Brooklyn Park. "Jennifer, just stay strong girl. I can't begin to imagine what you're going through, but I'm here for you. I'll be over there in five minutes."

"Okay, I'll leave the door unlocked for you." Jennifer got off the phone and ran back into the house and to her room. Her phone started ringing again and this time it was her job, asking if she could come in to work today. She told them yes and called Jamey to let her know not to come over. Both of them worked downtown at the World Trade Center as secretaries for a big law firm.

At the high school, Laura, Tisha and Melissa were just arriving. They were considered some of the hottest cool kids in school without acting elitist to others. "Hey Laura..." one of the boys standing with a few of his friends called out. He hoped she would say hi. And not only did she say hi, she called him by his name which really made his day.

"What's up, Tony!" she replied. Then she smiled at him as she walked by. His friends gave him a high five as they watched Laura, Tisha and Melissa strut into school.

The three of them were very popular at school and were always wearing the latest fashions as well as the very best of them all. The young men continued to watch Laura. She was only 5'2" in height and petite but her 120 pound, slightly curved and beautiful body said a lot. Tony was so much in love with her that he would help her with her homework after school sometimes just so he could look into her stunning green eyes. Most of the time he would get lost in thought about her and Laura would have to snap her fingers to bring him back to the present; but only for him to get caught up again in her light complexioned skin which had a glow like nothing he'd ever seen before. Tony loved it when she got on the phone because she would play with the ends of her long hair and it smelled so good. He would imagine running his hands through it. And whenever she smiled at him it made his day because she had a beautiful set of white teeth.

Laura also had a matching tattoo of a phoenix on her back just like her sister Jennifer but with fire coming from just underneath her arm. "She is something to live for," Tony whispered to himself as he walked into the school with his friends.

"Laura, man I hope this weekend at the club will be jumping," Melissa said, making Laura and Tisha laugh in unison. The bell rang and all of them headed to their first class.

Chapter Two

Somewhere deep in the Pacific Ocean on an invisible semisubmersible was a base for HUWP (Hatchet Men University Watcher Program). This base was fully equipped with four HPIG's (High Power Incinerator Guns), each being 12 feet tall and sat on turrets where one person sat inside operating it manually, or operated by remote control from the tower. One HPIG sat on each of the four corners of the semisubmersible. They were used to defend the base. They could shoot shells one foot in length and six inches in width. One shell could take down any aircraft, even if it was on the edge of the Earth's atmosphere. It would be obliterated. Their radar could pick up anything within 2,000 miles coming towards Earth's atmosphere from space.

A helicopter was about to land. You had to have special clearance to fly within fifty miles of the base. This was not just any base. It was also an underwater prison for Hatchet Men and Hatchet Women deep down below sea level at fifty yards. That was 150 feet, making it very difficult for anyone to escape or break inside. There was a heavily armed elevator that took prisoners straight down to their cells. They never leave their cells. Everything they would ever need was inside and whatever they did not have was brought to them. Under no circumstances were they to leave their cells. Only when their time was completed could they leave the semisubmersible and it would be in the manner in which they arrived: knocked out.

A few of the young Hatchet Men were above deck training but they stopped to see who was on the prison transport. Over twenty armed guards ran out of the elevator with fully automatic rifles ready to receive the prisoner. One of the HPIG's was pointing at the helicopter as it was landing. The young Hatchet Men had never seen so many guards come out for just one prisoner. There were five of them training. "So who do we have coming in today?" Terron asked his partner, Carol. She knew just as much as he did. Nothing.

"I don't know compadre. I wonder why they have her strapped down in a chair like that."

"I don't know but it's a first. Whoever she is she must be very dangerous," Terron told Carol. He started walking a little closer as if something was drawing him to the woman.

"Terron!" Tara yelled, making him snap out of it. She was his grandmother/team leader.

Terron quickly turned around and said, "Yes, what's up?"

"I need you and your team in the conference room, now!" Tara replied, glancing at the prisoner being escorted to the heavily armed elevator. Tara turned and started walking toward another elevator to meet with Terron, Carol and the rest of their team. Tara texted Timtim and it said, *"He looked but it was too early to say."*

"Come on, we got to get the rest of the team," Carol said, walking with Terron to get the rest of their team. Carol and Terron had been friends since they were little kids. They both grew up living in the same house and raised by the same adoptive parents before they were drafted to HUWP. Neither knew their real parents but they were like brother and sister. Carol was very good with martial arts and another thing she specialized in was working with poison. She'd attended some of the best schools before being recruited by her adoptive mother to HUWP. What made Carol stand out from the rest was the "way" she fought hard in battle. She was only 5'5" in height and weighed 125 pounds. Most men that went up against her thought she would be easy to take down. But she always showed them that just because she was very petite in size it didn't mean that she couldn't hold her own. Men got caught up in her baby face, brown bedroom eyes, short silky hair and her beauty but she packed a powerful punch. The tattoo of a dragon on her back she'd earned in fight clubs. The dragon's tail ran down her right arm. She would smile at her opponent, showing her pretty white teeth. But as good as this Asian beauty looked she was just as good in the ring. She and Terron used to scam fight clubs by taking side bets on Carol.

When Terron and Carol got downstairs where the rest of their team was, some of them were training in the gun room. The room was filled with holograms of Hatchet Men Ghosts and Ghost-likes. Terron and Carol's team had to take out as many of them as they could without being detected by the holograms. The program is virtual reality but depending what level you set the program, if a Ghost or Ghost-like attack you in training you do feel pain. The program is designed to make Shadow teams better. The only ones who had completed the entire program were Carol, Terron and Ashley.

"I bet she don't complete it. I'm taking all bets!" one of the Hatchet Men shouted as Ashley was about to enter the training room. She stopped in the doorway and turned her head to the left and smiled slightly.

"If I was you I'd stop now because you're going…"

Before she could finish the sentence Terron said, "What's the wager, player?"

The Hatchet Man was with a few of his team members and they started whispering to one another. Then one of them shouted, "Five grand! Can you handle it?" They started laughing and giving each other high fives. Ashley just stood at the door looking at Terron.

"I keep that for blow-away money. You're on," Terron said and Ashley walked inside.

Another dude shouted, "Two more grand if she uses no guns, just her birth weapons."

"You're on!" Ashley shouted, dropping her gun belt from her waist. She kicked it to Carol, smiling.

She walked fully into the room with only her birth weapons. The room was the size of half a football field. All of the other Hatchet Men that were training ran over to watch Ashley from the balcony above the room. She grabbed her two twin knight Templar crusader daggers that were forged in fire on Tripueler by the God Sorey. They had razor-sharp ridges, a chain mail and pearl handles that fit her hands perfectly. On the blades were hieroglyphics which read: *"The art of death can be beautiful when it's in the hands of the beauteous one, child of Sorey."*

"Light!" Ashley yelled, twirling both daggers. She stopped, then sprang into action.

Hoping no one saw him, one of the Hatchet Men walked over to the virtual touch screen, making the level harder for Ashley. But they did. Terron and Carol did not care because Terron's team was the best of the best. The hologram in the room was a street from the 20th Century; a block in Brooklyn, New York in Crown Heights. Two Ghosts leaped out trying to kill her, but Ashley was very light on her feet. "Arrrr!" she yelled as she ran toward the building, running up the wall with tremendous force. She was very petite and 120 pounds of sexy. She worked out a lot. She had several breathing holes over her body which helped her muscles get the oxygen they needed for her to do the things she did.

The two Ghosts ran behind her but Ashley kicked off the wall, performing a backflip over them, stabbing them in the head, killing them. She quickly turned around, leaping into the air and kicking another Ghost in the face. Ashley was far from weak and even though some of the Ghost-likes stood at 7' to her 5'7" she was still better than they were. Ashley was a very beautiful European-American woman with pretty eyes that were usually gray. But right now her gray eyes were black and gray because she was in Hatchet Woman mode. Every time she killed she would smile, showing her white teeth.

One of the Hatchet Men Ghost holograms turned to grab her from behind. Ashley crushed its face with the back of her head then leaped into the air with a roundhouse kick to the chest that smashed it into another Ghost she stabbed in the chest. She took off running down a corridor with a dagger in each hand. Terron could see some of the Hatchet Men who had made the bet getting nervous because they knew they were about to lose the bet. All Ashley had to do was kill twelve more Ghosts and make it successfully out of the room like she had done many times before.

She reached the end of the corridor where two, three feet, razor-sharp blades shot out of the walls. But Ashley, in a lightning-quick move, arched her back low to the ground and slid on her knees underneath the blades as if she was doing the limbo. And right as she passed the blades three Ghost-likes were right there. She leaped into the air, kicking off the wall and grabbing one of the Ghost-likes and jerking it down to the ground and breaking it and in the next second breaking its neck. Ashley leaped to her feet, stabbing the other two Ghost-likes in the chest, killing them. Ashley looked up at the young Hatchet Men that had made the bet, smiling and nodding her head at them.

Then a Ghost leaped down from the roof of a building, swinging its sword at her. Ashley took two steps backward then leaped over the Ghost, putting it in a headlock, stabbing it several times in the back, just like an inmate in battle, quickly and deadly. This was one of the reasons she was a part of the dragon team and why she was able to wear a full dragon skin tattoo on the right side of her body. She killed just like she looked: beautiful. Ashley walked out of the training room smiling.

Terron walked up to the young Hatchet Men and said, "When you thought you were going to win that's the time you were supposed to stop. We're the best for a reason." The young Hatchet Men couldn't say anything. Carol began to fill Ashley, Leyla and Todd in on what was going on as they walked to the conference room to meet with Tara. She was already in the room waiting for them. She was on her iPhone texting her husband and as the team walked inside she got off her phone. "So, you're still taking bets on Ashley and Carol, Terron?" Tara asked him. Terron couldn't do anything but smile. Tara gave a small laugh and started to use the virtual reality board, showing them the target they were after.

"Okay people, these are the Sevdeski brothers. They deal with drugs, but this one over here," she said, pointing at the board, "likes to eat with terrorists that are enemies of the State. They're going to be in the States this weekend at Jay-Z's 4040 club in Brooklyn. This is where y'all will come in to play and neutralize them. Our informant tells us that this one right here," she pointed again, "Joker Sevdeski, is going to be at the club. He's going to try to make a deal with some terrorists that we all know a little bit too well — the HMG (Hatchet Men Ghost)."

When Terron's team heard that, it made them look deeper into the situation because they knew it might not be a walk in the park, especially if it might be some Ghost just lying around. Tara also told them that the Joker always traveled within groups of terrorists and was very heavily armed to the hilt. She said he has to be stopped no matter what. His brother, Emil Sevdeski might not be too far from the club so they needed to be on the lookout for him, too.

"What about casualty damage?" Terron asked, taking notes.

"We're prepared to give Jay-Z over one billion in damages. So make sure that all damages happen outside of the club. If things must happen inside the club, make it quiet." Tara said then dismissed them. But she needed to talk with Terron. "Terron, hold on a minute, please."

Terron told the rest of the team he'd meet them downstairs. Carol told everyone to go with her and Terron stayed in the room. "What's up?" he asked Tara, smiling.

Tara looked at Terron, smiling slightly. "How is everything with you?"

"Everything is as good as it's going to get. Why? What's up?" he asked her again with a kind of puzzled look on his face.

Tara just smiled and told Terron his mother had been worried about him and asked her to ask him, that's all. Terron just smiled and Tara told him he could go.

But before he left he asked, "Aunt Tara, who was that prisoner today?

"Why do you ask?"

"Because since I've been here I've never seen anyone so heavily guarded like that. Why is that?"

Tara had her back to Terron, looking through some papers and turned around to face him. "She is the worse of the worse. She's just as old as I am. She was once a good person but people change, and she changed for the worse." Tara's phone rang and she told Terron he could go.

Terron left, still wondering who the prisoner was until he was around his team. They sat down, putting together a plan about how they were going to implement their plan. Terron already had a plan in the making and he knew that Leyla might not like it, but she was a team player.

****

"Jennifer, please tell me that you're almost ready," Laura pleaded from the hallway.

Jennifer was on the other side of her bedroom door, looking at herself in the mirror, making sure she looked the way she wanted to. But she really didn't feel like going out tonight. She had on a hot-pink lacy Victoria Secret bra and cheeky pantie set that really looked good on her light-skinned body. She had her hair wrapped in a bun. It was waist length and she didn't want anything covering the dragon tattoo on her back that she had proudly earned. Every time she looked into the mirror she would touch her stomach and think about Eric. But Laura was not about to let her big sister stay home tonight. So she banged on the door until Jennifer opened it.

"Laura, I can't seem to find anything to wear," Jennifer said as she opened the door, letting Laura inside. Laura strode straight to the closet and grabbed an outfit.

"This looks fine to me now put it on, Jennifer. I don't care what you say, you're going out tonight."

Laura began to help her sister get dressed and once she was done Jennifer looked absolutely amazing. She had on a black Louis Vuitton sleeveless open-backed dress that hugged her petite body. Her tattoo of a phoenix on her back with fire wrapping around her right arm made her look even more stunning. The outfit was capped off with a Louis Vuitton black evening bag with red stripes and black, red-bottom stilettoes on her small feet. Her fire red lipstick made her look even more exotic. As far as accessories, she had on a diamond Panthere de Cartier necklace with a Cartier diamond watch and the finishing touch was Eric's engagement ring. Jennifer's green eyes made her look like the most beautiful woman in the world.

"Jennifer, you're beautiful," Laura whispered in awe, hugging her sister excitedly as she stood behind her, looking at them in the full length mirror.

"You're just saying that because you want me to go with you." Jennifer walked away from the mirror and over to her bed. She sat on its edge and hung her head.

Laura walked over to her sister and stood behind her, gently holding her by the shoulders. "Jennifer, yes I do want you to come, but you do look beautiful. Nobody can take that away from you. It would be a shame if you never get to wear this beautiful dress you have on. It took you so long to get it so wear it, please?" Laura asked, rubbing her shoulders and hoping she would say yes because she'd bought the dress when she and Eric were going to get married.

Jennifer got up and walked back over to the mirror, taking a good look at herself and said, "Okay, Laura, I'm going to go. But if I feel…"

Before she could say another word Laura ran over and hugged her, but quickly stopped because she didn't want to mess up Jennifer's look. And Jennifer was looking gorgeous. Tonight was going to be her night out on the town in New York City.

Terron and his team were already at Jay-Z's club. "Team leader, come in. System check, give me a yawn and a freaking stretch, please," Ashley said through her microminiaturized microphone on her lips disguised as lipstick; her headset looked like an earring. Ashley and Todd were on a rooftop about a quarter of a mile away from the nightclub. Both of them were marksmen and had black Mark's carbine choice Anderson AR-15 high-powered rifles with special rocket sounds and target tracers. Once the transmitter is placed on its host, it is small enough that it will fit on your fingertip, just like sticky paper, but it dissolves into your skin and it lights up. The scope on the rifles could see through walls with thermal vision that can pick up any body temperature if needed and can stop reflection from light. Those were just a few of the many features on the rifles. They made sure to set the rifles up on turrets.

Terron started to yawn and stretch, saying, "Are you happy now?"

"Now open your mouth just a little bit wider, dude" Todd said, making Ashley chuckle at him.

"Todd, fuck you," Terron responded.

"Now that is too funny. Okay boys, it's time to stop playing and focus on work," Ashley said, looking around the front of the club for any signs of the Sevdeski brothers.

"I love it when you get mad, dude," Todd said to Terron, making him laugh because Todd was a big jokester. Ashley and Todd lay down on the rooftop on their stomachs, eyes on the prize.

"Little Mice, what's going on inside?" Terron asked as he stood outside in line out front with Carol, pretending they were waiting to get inside with everyone else. They could've easily walked inside but they wanted to see the Sevdeski brothers pull up so they would know how many men were with them. Little Mice was Leyla's code name and she was already inside of the club playing the part of a waitress; and she was a showstopper.

Leyla made sure not to overdress for the situation. But it didn't really matter what she wore because she was an African-American beauty and no matter what she wore she would look stunning. She was serving drinks and got a lot of attention. "Yes, this is Little Mice working and all systems are go," Leyla said as she was serving a customer a bottle of Chateau Haut-Brion 2009 Pessac-Leognan. The customer palmed her ass and Leyla did not like it at all. She turned around, grabbing the man's hand, twisting it around, making him drop to his knees.

"Aaaah!" the man yelled.

The rest of the team heard the man's distress over the radio.

"Leyla, would you stop. We're working on the clock," Terron said and smiled because he knew what she was going through.

"Motherfucker don't you ever put your fucking hands on me again!" Leyla said. The man nodded his head in a yes motion, letting her know that he understood her. He had a pained expression on his face.

Leyla was only 5'3" in height and weighed 133 pounds. She was a beauty and very curvy. Her eyes were a deep brown and her skin was brown and silky. She had long, fire-red hair that she wore in cornrows just for tonight. From the way she was handling things you knew she had earned her tattoos, looking at the dragon on her back and the flames from the dragon on her right arm because she was on fire tonight. Leyla let go of the man and she picked up the tip from the table. She looked at him with a frown and said, "You want to touch a woman's ass and this is all you have to give me?" The man quickly went into his pocket, giving her more money.

Chapter Three

It was so funny and although all of them got caught up in the joke on the guy, Ashley noticed a few 2047 black hover Mercedes Benz G63's pulling up. "Okay, food on land. I repeat, food on land," she broadcasted to the team. Food on land meant their target had arrived. Terron and Carol saw the five G63's pull in right up front, two men in each car. Ashley and Todd had their scopes locked on them.

"Computer scan," Terron requested.

Back at headquarters on the semisubmersible, the computer started to perform facial recognition on all 10 men. "Joker Sevdeski is one of the men with his heavily armed guards. Emil Sevdeski is not with them. Each man has a fully automatic rifle, fully loaded, and each has a side arm," the computer reported to Terron and the rest of the team.

"Little Mice, you know what to do," Terron said, but Leyla was already on it. She had two tables set up just for the Sevdeski brothers.

"I'm already on it, Blue Dragon."

Blue Dragon was Terron's code name. One thing about the team, they made up new code names for every mission. Once Joker and his armed men went inside, Terron and Carol started walking as if they going to the front of the line but they were going around to the back for Leyla to let them inside.

* * * * * * * * *

"Jennifer, you look amazing tonight. Girl, you look damn good!" Tisha shouted, excited to be out with Jennifer tonight. Laura, Tisha, Melissa, Jamey and Jennifer used to go out together all the time but ever since the accident Jennifer would not go out. This was the first time in a long time they'd all gone out together. Tisha was so pumped up that she backed right into Terron. The smell of his fragrance screamed Jimmy Choo's Man Intense and seemed to put Tisha into a trance. She turned around to see who the hell she'd bumped into and when she saw Terron, she was at a loss for words.

"Excuse you," Carol said to Tisha which made Jennifer turn around to see what was going on. She, too, was caught up by Terron's startling good looks.

"Excuse us. It's okay," Terron said to Tisha who just nodded her head, unable to speak.

By this time all the girls were looking at Terron. Then Jennifer did the most signature thing all girls do: she gave him a quick up and down scan and turned away. She was able to look into Terron's beautiful hazel eyes for at least five seconds and something started happening inside her body that she'd never experienced before. As she'd briefly looked him up and down she liked his build and she really liked his brown-skinned complexion. Jennifer had a thing for African-American men. He was around 225 pounds of sleek muscle and stood at 6'3" which was a little taller than Eric. She liked his bald head and chin strap. He looked no older than 25 years of age. She noticed Terron appeared to be checking her out just as much as she was checking him out. Then he smiled at her.

Tisha saw it and whispered, "Girl, he smiled at you. Damn! He looks good. Jennifer you better get him tonight."

"Girl, he was with his girl," Jennifer replied, acting like she wasn't looking at him but she was.

"I don't think so, not looking at you like that," Laura said.

On the rooftop using the scope on her rifle, Ashley had seen the look, too. "Carol, what's up with big brother? I saw that look on his face," Ashley asked, not taking her eyes off Terron and Carol until they got around to the back. Leyla was there to let them inside the club.

"What's up with that, big bro? I saw that look, too," Carol asked him. Leyla had a confused look on her face until Carol told her what was going on. Terron stayed silent with a smug look on his face.

The three of them started walking down a corridor, entered the kitchen where they cooked food for some of the guests and exited out to where the dance floor was beside the bar. The club had a full length balcony up top where the VIP area was. There were four bars altogether in the club. There were two large horseshoe-shaped bars on the ground floor and two long bars up top near the VIP area. Then there were two sets of spiral staircases that led to the VIP area as well. The DJ's booth was raised higher above the bars on the ground level. The speakers were embedded in the walls and ingrained in the flooring, pushing a massive sound throughout the club. There were also four cages with some of the most beautiful women covered in body paint. Black lights were trained on them, making their undulating bodies glow as they danced exotically. The first thing Terron did was look for all the emergency exits. He saw four of them and relayed that to his team. Leyla made sure she didn't walk with them as she headed toward one of the staircases that led to the VIP area where Joker was seated with his party of 10. "Okay, here I go," Leyla said to the team, working her stuff, making sure the Joker's eyes were on her the entire time as she made her way over to him. She kept her eyes on him, smiling, showing her perfect teeth.

Some of his men reached out to stop her, but Joker quickly said in a Russian accented voice, "What are you doing you idiot? Let her through." Joker rubbed the seat beside him, inviting Leyla to sit down.

She gingerly sat beside him. "Yes, what would you like to drink tonight?" Leyla asked him, smiling. Joker rubbed her hand then her thigh, but when he tried to push his hand upward she stopped him. "You just can't keep your hand still, can you?" Leyla teased him, showing her pearly white teeth, but in the back of her mind she was screaming, *"Creep!!"*

Joker couldn't take his eyes off of her. "I would like for you to get me a bottle of Ace of Spade and come join me please."

Leyla kept her eyes on him, smiling and still holding his hand. "Okay, give me five minutes and I'll be back with your order," Leyla told him standing up slowly. As she walked through his security team, she was able to surreptitiously place tracking devices on them. The device was so small it could fit on the tip of her index finger. She would smile and say, "Oh, excuse me," as she intentionally brushed against them, touching almost all of them. For the three she didn't touch, she told herself she would get them when she returned with the order. Once out of the VIP area Leyla told the team, "Transmitters are a go except for three of them. I'll get them when I go back to the table. But everybody else is a go." She walked down the corridor where Terron and Carol were waiting for her. Terron slipped her the poison to put into Joker's bottle of champagne. She took several bottles of champagne to the back of the bar and slipped the poison into one of them. She used a device that allowed her to slip it through the cork without the seal being broken. "Okay bitch, here I come," she whispered to herself, walking from behind the bar with the bottles of champagne in an ice bucket and glasses and ice on a tray. Once in the VIP area she tried to make it to the three men she missed to put a transmitter on them but she was unable to do so.

And it would've looked too obvious so she just walked over to Joker. She put her hand over her mouth, pretending she was coughing, but she was really talking to her team. "Three unmarked, sorry," she whispered. By the time she reached Joker she was smiling. "Here you go, sir."

"Please call me Joker. All of my friends do. Are you going to join me?"

Leyla smiled and grabbed the bottle of Ace of Spade, popped the cork and started pouring the champagne into glasses. She made sure not to pour the ones with poison into her glass.

"So, why is a beautiful girl like you working here? I'm pretty sure they pay you good money, but I see more for you."

Leyla started slightly, blushing but thinking to herself, *"He's got to be kidding me with that lame pickup line."* But what came out of her mouth was, "I did not know that you think of me like that. You probably say that to all of the girls, don't you?"

Joker zoomed in on Leyla with his eyes and sat a little closer to her, seductively placing a hand on her thigh. She placed her hand over his, making sure he didn't slide it under her dress.

On the ground floor, all the girls were on the dance floor getting their groove on. The club was dark except for the black lights stabbing the darkness. Tisha had two guys dancing with her and she was doing her thing. She was 17 years old and would be 18 next month, but she sure didn't look 17. She stood in the middle of two tall men and at 5'6" she fit right in. Plus, she had an added three inches from her Christian Louboutin red bottom shoes. Tisha rocked her body, swinging her long black hair around. Melissa was right beside her and started dancing with Tisha, kissing her on her full, pouty lips. Tisha smiled at her. One of the guys Tisha was dancing with tried to grab her by her small waist, trying to feel on her voluptuous body. Tisha was curvy in all the right spots. Her African-American honey-brown skin was lit up in perfume by Mon Paris Yves Saint Laurent. The young man just couldn't help himself.

Melissa pulled Tisha away from both dudes and started walking back to their table. "That was so intense, girl. Thanks. These fake I.D.'s really work," Tisha said, laughing with Melissa.

"I saw y'all two on the floor getting your freak on," Laura said. The three of them got up and started dancing with each other. Tisha and Laura put Melissa in between them and started dancing with her. Some of the guys started to look at them, cheering them on. The DJ put on some reggae dance music. Melissa was working her hips. She had both of her hands up in the air and she was crouched down with one leg up. She quickly put a hand down and grabbed the skirt of her dress, holding it so no one could see her "stuff." Melissa was a European American stallion. She was throwing her long, blonde hair around, making her 42 inch booty pop and twerk. Tisha had both her hands on Melissa's waist, holding tightly onto her waist band. Melissa was only 5'6" but her Gucci high heels made her look taller. Tisha looked into Melissa's ocean blue eyes and started kissing and telling her how much she loved her. Melissa smiled seductively, letting her curves show in a tight Dolce and Gabana red dress.

Upstairs in the VIP area, Leyla had already poured Joker a glass of champagne from the poisoned bottle, but he hadn't drunk it yet. Some of his men were about to drink it. Leyla knew she was going to have to do something to make him drink it, or her plan A would need to quickly become her Plan B. It was not a plan she wanted to implement, but she'd do whatever it took to stop the terror across the world. Plus, Joker was nice and besotted with her. He couldn't stop himself from feeling all over Leyla and telling her how much he wanted her.

By this time, she was sitting on his lap with her arms around his neck, kissing him on the cheek. She kept her eyes on the glass of poisoned champagne on the table. She was not leaving until she knew he'd drunk it. She also noticed that five of his men did not drink. But she was on the clock and time was running out. Joker finally got up and walked over to get his drink and Leyla gave a devilish smile as he picked it up. But one of his men bumped him, making him spill most of the drink on the floor. "Shit!" Leyla thought to herself because now she was going to have to shift to plan B. She was really hoping she wouldn't have to do what she was about to do, but she was a team player.

She took a deep breath and got up and walked over to Joker and put her arms around him and pressed her soft lips against his. She pulled him back over to the VIP seating where it was dark and sat him down and started rubbing on him. Then she pretended she needed to go to the bathroom and freshen up for him. He told her not to take too long. Leyla gave him a bewitching look as she left, biting her bottom lip. She walked away slowly making sure Joker saw all of her curves, looking over her shoulder and smiling at him like the devil in a red dress. Once she got to the spiral staircase, she whispered into her hand, saying, "I've had to go to plan B." The team knew what plan B was and did not like it, but it had to be done. Leyla walked past Terron at the bar and down some steps to her locker. Terron was at the bar drinking some Louis XIII. He glanced at Leyla as she walked past him. Terron turned around to take another sip of his drink but stopped, looking into Jennifer's engaging green eyes. He wanted to walk over to her, but instead he asked the bartender what she'd ordered. She told him so he paid for it. He was about to walk away so he could keep his focus on what was going on, but he started glowing, feeling something he had never felt before. "Blue Dragon, what does it look like up top?" Terron heard in his earpiece, bringing him back to the job at hand.

Leyla was in the lady's room slipping on a fake vagina. She pushed it up inside of her. It was filled with caffeine and a few drops of fentanyl, enough to stop his heart. She had to be very careful when placing it inside of her because he couldn't find out it wasn't the real thing. It fit like a glove would fit on her hand. "Okay, Little Mice is ready to go back and handle her business," she said to herself as she walked out and headed back to the spiral staircase and the VIP area. Once upstairs and as soon as she got within eye contact of Joker, she started strutting her stuff. She was working her art of seduction on him. He was sitting on the couch watching her every move.

Leyla sat on his lap, whispering in his ear in her sexiest voice, "Tell your men to leave, please."

Joker started smiling and told his men in Russian to go. Leyla knew exactly what he told them because it was her job to know all the languages on Earth as well as the language of the Watchers. But she played it off like she didn't know what had been said. After they left, Leyla slid her hand into Joker's pants, reaching for his manhood and started playing with it. She kept her eyes locked on Joker and he had his eyes locked on her, but for all the wrong reasons. His were filled with lust and hers was working the art of death. Once she felt his manhood at full erection, she pushed it deep inside of her. Well, he thought it was her. Joker grabbed her firm 34DD breasts and pulled one out, sucking on it while Leyla was working her hips and pushing herself downward onto his manhood.

One of his men came back upstairs to check on him, but when Joker saw that Leyla became frightened, he told his man in Russian to leave. But it was all an act by Leyla because she was working on the clock. It made the plan even better that one of his men walked in on them so that when it was time for her to exit, it wouldn't be so hard to do. Leyla looked into Joker's eyes and she could see her fiendish plan coming to fruition. A slightly evil smile crossed the African-American's beauty's face as she saw him slipping into darkness.

Terron and Carol were downstairs checking the club out, but he couldn't help looking at Jennifer. He noticed she was doing the same and then he heard Ashley in his earpiece say, "Little Mice, hurry the fuck up! Big brother is here! I repeat, big brother is here and he's walking inside the club doors now!" Terron and Carol were both ready for what might happen next.

"How many of them?" Terron asked.

"Ten at least and they're strapped to the hilt, too!"

Carol started walking toward them to try to give Leyla some time. But Leyla had gathered her stuff together and checked Joker's pulse one last time just to make sure her job was done, and it was. He was dead and Leyla closed his eyes, pushed him into a prone position on the couch and put his hat over his face. She kissed her fingers and touched his forehead and walked out of the shadows into the light. As she walked past one of Joker's men she told him in Russian that Joker said to leave him to rest. However, Emil was coming up the staircase as Leyla was going down. They both looked into each other's eyes and after they passed each other she faded into the crowd of people where Carol was waiting.

Terron was watching from the other side of the room. He had his eyes on Emil. He knew exactly when Emil found his brother dead because he started flipping out and all of their men went on alert, looking for Leyla because she was the last one seen with him when he was alive.

"Just get outside. We got you covered Little Mice and Bright Bird!" Ashley instructed. She and Todd got ready for the kill shot. Anything coming within range of Terron, Leyla and Carol were going to die. Some of Emil's men had earpieces and had gotten a description of what Leyla looked like. Then one of them saw Carol and Leyla trying to slide out one of the back doors. The man went straight after them with two other men. Terron was moving swiftly through the crowd, his hands on the triggers of his FN 57 fully automatic pistols with extended clips. They had to make sure that they got outside because of collateral damage. If they had sex inside the club, the death of Joker looks like a heart attack. But to start a gun fight inside would look bad for business.

Terron was walking toward the club doors with some of Emil's men in front of him. Then he saw Emil with a few of his men coming down the staircase and at the same time he walked into Jennifer, bumping her. What Terron and Jennifer had felt hadn't been forgotten by either one of them as their eyes locked with one another. But Terron had to quickly turn his attention back to Emil and his men. He had to beat them to that door!

Chapter Four

Leyla and Carol made it outside but were far from being in the clear. "Don't worry Little Mice. We got y'all," Ashley said in their ear and told Todd to switch to x-ray vision. The three men came out the back door behind the two women, raising their guns, but Carol quickly banged her birth daggers on the ground, disabling their enemy. They started to become delusional.

"Now Leyla!" Carol yelled and Leyla forcefully threw several birth daggers into the men chests, making them explode.

Terron shot out of the back door shouting, "Come on, we've got to go now!" pointing his two pistols with over 35 rounds of exploding ammunition that when voice activated, could switch to several different rounds of ammo by telling it to switch. Terron had his back to Carol and Leyla as he walked backward, counting down.

Inside the club, Jennifer was wondering why Terron ran out so fast. She was upset that she was not able to say anything. As she turned around, Emil and his men were walking towards her with their guns drawn. Jennifer just stood there looking then tried to move out of the way. Emil pushed her to the floor. Laura, Tisha, Melissa and Jamey ran toward her.

"Yeah, don't you touch my sister asshole!" Laura shouted out.

Emil was so mad that he turned around with his gun up like he was going to shoot Laura.

"Nooo!!" Jennifer yelled and ran toward her sister. But right before Emil was going to shoot, the back door blew off its hinges with a loud bang and Emil fell to the ground. Jennifer reached Laura and pulled her up and all five girls started running in the opposite direction toward an exit. Emil was knocked out and his men helped him get up.

Chaos was everywhere in the club. People were running everywhere trying to get out of the way of the men with the guns. Emil and two of his men stayed in the club as several of his men ran out after Terron, Carol and Leyla, but the three of them were walking quickly around a corner and out of sight. Now Ashley and Todd had a clear shot. "Keep coming, baby. We got y'all," Ashley said, keeping her eyes on her three team members. Todd kept his eyes on the alley, making sure no surprise came out at them. And sure enough, three gunmen ran out of the alley. Todd shot all three of them in the head.

Terron, Leyla and Carol got to their 2047 black hover Super Truck Extreme. Terron was behind the wheel and whipped out of their parking spot. Carol and Leyla grabbed AA12 assault shotguns, fully automatic that shoots 300 rounds in one minute. As they were pulling off some of Joker and Emil's men ran towards them yelling but were quickly taken out by Ashley and Todd. "Okay, it's time for us to go!" Ashley shouted. They didn't have to pack up anything because Semtex was laced in their weapons that they had a dime a dozen of.

Both of them ran to the edge of the roof and jumped just as the weapons they'd left behind blew up. They were coming down at a tremendous speed in a free-fall. Their black exoskeleton wing suits were fully equipped. It was made out of soft titanium; soft 24-carat gold; and Kevlar and magnets were embedded all over the suit to assist in stopping their fall before the wearer reached the ground. It was like a built-in parachute without the chute. They worked with Earth's maglev system. The suits were fully equipped with 100 rounds on the utility belt attached to the guns mounted on their shoulders; three-inch exploding rockets made out of Semtex and sulfuric acid; and Taser darts that produce 1500 watts of AC power. It was fireproof, bomb proof, bullet proof, crash proof and shock absorbent. The suits could accommodate two remote controlled, shoulder mounted machine guns that could fire 300 rounds of one-centimeter, razor-sharp titanium with magnesium ammunition inside the rockets. They could be activated with a simple movement of the eye. Its camouflage ability was phenomenal because of its chameleon feature that allowed the color/design of the suit to change to whatever a Hatchet Man or Woman leaned against or passed by. It provided scuba diving capabilities that allowed the wearer to stay underwater for up to two days if needed. There were grappling hooks connected to the utility belt that helped to pull them upward or drop them downward with rapid speed. And, there were jet packs with wings that could transport them from New York to California within an hour. These were the major capabilities of the suit.

Once Ashley and Todd reached the ground, the two of them moved swiftly to their black 2047 Super Truck Extreme. Terron, Carol and Leyla were on their way to meet up with them. And back at the club, Emil was out front looking for Leyla but saw no sign of her. He started to hear the sirens of the police coming and quickly left with his remaining men. But he still carried a mental vision of Leyla's face and he was not going to stop looking for her.

Jennifer, Laura, Tisha, Melissa and Jamey raced out of the club and got into their car just like the rest of the people in the club. There had been chaos in the club but they heard no shots fired, only that explosion. "Oh my God, Jennifer, I thought that asshole was going to shoot you!" Laura said in a voice that trembled, scared for her sister's life. She took a moment to hug Jennifer tightly as if she was never going to see her again. They pulled into their driveway safely. Laura was still a little shaken up at what had happened at the club. Jennifer could sense that and turned to her when they got out of the car and said, "We're good Laura. Take it easy and don't tell dad because he'll never let us go out again."

As both of them started walking toward the house Jennifer's mind kept replaying what she'd felt tonight when she'd seen Terron. Once inside the house Jennifer stopped Laura at the door and asked her, "Laura, did you feel anything funny tonight?"

"Other than that asshole that wanted to shoot us, no."

"Not that, Laura. I mean did you feel anything when you saw that guy?"

Laura stopped to think a moment about Terron then started smiling and said, "No."

"So why are you smiling, Laura?" Jennifer asked, waiting for an answer.

"Okay, he's cute as hell! Did you get his number?" Laura asked, smiling.

"No Laura, I did not, but I felt something that I've never felt before."

"Like what?"

"Like we're connected or something; it felt really weird like something running through my body."

"Jennifer, what do you mean?"

"It felt like, I don't know how to explain it Laura. It just felt weird."

Their father, Chris, was listening to them the entire time. He was in his bedroom with the door cracked so that he'd hear them when they returned from their night out at the club. He had a very concerned look on his face because of what he was hearing, but he was not going to say anything just yet. Laura and Jennifer headed for the kitchen to get something to eat. They stood around the island in the kitchen making turkey, Munster cheese, lettuce, tomato, onion and Hellman's mayonnaise sandwiches.

"You should've gotten his number, Jennifer," Laura said, grabbing two Pepsi's from the refrigerator.

Jennifer picked up her sandwich, took a bite and said, "I know, but if it is meant to be it will be."

Their father was still listening but now he was at the top of the stairs. He felt like saying something but he didn't. He just walked back to his room, closing his door quietly.

Chapter Five

The next morning Chris was about to go to work but decided to stop by Jennifer's room to see what happened at the club. "Jennifer, baby girl, could I talk to you for a moment?" he asked as he gave a short knock on her door and walked into the room.

Jennifer was still somewhat asleep, but she rolled over, pushing a swathe of long, inky-black hair out of her face, looking at her dad with sleepy eyes. "What's up, dad?"

"What happened last night at the club?"

Jennifer knew her father must have been listening to them after they got in because otherwise he wouldn't have known something had happened, so she would just tell him, hoping she would get some answers herself. She sat up in bed and reached over to her nightstand and grabbed a rubber band, putting her hair in a ponytail. She looked at him and said, "Everything started good and we're outside in line, waiting to get inside the club. Then this real attractive guy walked by me and accidentally bumped into Tisha. Dad, he looked really good…"

Before Jennifer could finish her sentence Laura walked into the room and sat on the edge of the bed. "Yeah dad, he was hot!" Laura shouted and Chris looked at her like she was crazy which made Laura calm down so Jennifer could finish talking.

"Anyway, for some reason he and I locked eyes and something happened…something like I never felt before…it was almost like magic. It felt like we were meant to be together. Have you ever felt like that, dad?" Jennifer asked, looking into her father's dark brown eyes, waiting on an answer.

Chris was smarter than that because he was not going to turn what happened into a story about him. "That's nice, but what happened? That's what I want to know about," Chris replied, looking at both of them.

They glanced at each other and Jennifer continued. "We get inside the club and we're dancing and having fun, you know just doing our thing, and then all hell broke loose in the club."

By this time Laura had turned on the TV in Jennifer's room to CNN and what had happened at the club was breaking news. "Oh my God, that's the club, dad!" Laura shouted and the three of them were quiet as they watched the news report.

Chris turned up the TV to hear better: "Last night at one of the many Jay-Z 4040 clubs, Joker Sevdeski was found dead from an apparent heart attack. He was a Russian crime boss in the notorious crime family known as The White Widow." They showed pictures of Joker and his brothers and Laura bellowed out, pointing at Emil's picture, "That's the guy that was about to shoot us at the club!"

When Chris heard Laura say that, he turned off the TV because that was enough for him to know what was going on. He surmised that somebody killed Joker and the media was covering it up. He turned to his daughters with a very serious look on his face and said, "Did he see y'all faces?" Jennifer and Laura looked at each other and Chris took that as a yes. "Look, I want y'all girls to be very careful because those guys are very dangerous people, and from what I know they're killers, too. Somebody killed one of them."

"But the news said that he had a heart attack, right?" Laura asked with a confused look on her face.

"The news media will say anything they're paid to say. Look, I'm going to work and I want y'all two to be very careful when you go outside, okay?" Chris instructed.

Jennifer got up off her bed and replied, "We will dad, but have you ever felt like I was telling you I felt before?"

Chris smiled and answered, "Yes, when I met your mother. I'll talk to y'all girls later. Be good."

"We will, dad," they said in unison as he walked away to go to work.

* * * * * * * * *

Chris didn't work too far from home. He worked at 10 Cherry Hill Road precinct in South Baltimore. "Yeah, Chris, how are you today?" Wendy asked, handing him a cup of coffee.

Chris worked with Wendy every day. She was like one of the guys, but very attractive. Both of them walked towards their desks, talking. "Wendy, I don't know how to raise girls. Man this shit is hard."

Wendy started laughing because she had no kids yet. She was 29, Latin-American and only 5'5" in height, but she was very tough and could do almost anything the guys could do. "Well, it's not easy raising two girls, Chris. I can't imagine how hard it is, but I'm a girl even though some might not think that I am."

"I think you're a girl and a good looking one, too," one of their coworkers said, looking over and checking Wendy out. She was built like a stallion with 36DD cups, 27" waist, 40" booty and thick thighs. She also had a cute face and pretty hazel eyes with long, black silky hair running down her back in a ponytail. Wendy just rolled her eyes and fanned her coworker away.

Chris just laughed but sobered quickly. "Wendy, something is going on. Did you look at the news today?"

"No, what's going on, Chris?"

"Well, you remember the Sevdeski brothers, right?"

"Yeah, the ones that got away with bombing the subway in New York, right?"

"Yes, that's them. Well, one of them was killed yesterday and the media is reporting that it was a heart attack at a club," Chris said, looking at something on his computer.

"Which one was it?"

"Joker."

"So, what's the sad face for, Chris?"

"His brother, Emil, tried to kill my little girls last night at that same club."

When Wendy heard that, it changed everything, making her pay closer attention to what he was about to say. "So what do you want to do, Chris?"

"Wendy, I don't know just yet; but something is going on and whatever it is, it is big. I just got to keep my little girls safe."

Wendy could hear the distress in Chris' voice and see his concern for his kids like any real father would have. "What do you need me to do?" she asked, looking at Chris as she waited for him to answer.

"Right now we need to check if Emil is still in the states, and if he is, where is he because he's not going to stop until he gets revenge for his brother's death."

"Don't worry about it, I'm on it," Wendy told him and started the process to run Emil's name, using their virtual computer, to see if it shows if he's staying anywhere in the United States. Chris' captain walked into their office space, asking them to go check out a homicide in Cherry Hill.

"Okay, we're on it," Chris told him and the captain left them.

"I can't find anything right now. You said the club that they went to was in New York, right?"

"Yes it was, why?"

"So the girls should be safe then, right?" Wendy asked, glancing at Chris, but quickly turning back to the virtual screen.

"If it was somebody else, maybe, but not the Sevdeski brothers. They have connections everywhere, Wendy."

Chris and Wendy left to go check out the homicide in Cherry Hill. It was a young teenage kid. He couldn't have been no older than 17. Chris and Wendy started doing their jobs like they always did by asking people in the neighborhood what happened. And just like always nobody saw anything. Even though he was doing his job, Wendy knew Chris had his kids on his mind.

"Hey Chris, are you okay?" Wendy asked.

"Yeah, I'm fine, Wendy. Are you ready?"

"I guess so because it doesn't seem like anybody is going to tell us anything. Let's go." As the two of them headed to their car, they could hear somebody yelling and it was coming from a house down the street. Both of them looked at each other.

"I guess you want to go check it out, right?" Chris asked Wendy and she nodded her head up and down in the affirmative.

They changed course and started walking down the street to where the yelling was coming from. When they reached the house they could tell it was a domestic situation.

"Get the hell out of here and don't bring your ass back here again!!" a dark-skinned, heavyset woman shouted, throwing some of her man's stuff out on the porch in a bag. One of the things which fell out of the bag was a gun. It fell out right in front of Chris and Wendy. The boyfriend looked at Chris and Wendy as if to say, "Please, not today."

"I hope you got a permit for..." Chris started to say but the guy took off running like a bat out of hell. "Seriously!! Dude, not today!!" Chris shouted, running to the car.

Wendy took off after the guy. "Stop!!" she yelled out, running after him with her gun drawn. She was pointing it at him but when she saw he wasn't going to stop she holstered it and ran behind him like a track star in the Olympic Games. He took her for a good run as he jumped several fences and Wendy did the same. She was in very good shape because she stayed in the gym lifting weights and doing intense cardio every day. She was built for this shit. The dude jumped into a yard with a pit bull. The dog almost got him but she was willing to take her chances with the dog. The dog was on a chain but it was long enough in length to cover the entire yard. Wendy had to think fast because she was about to leap over the fence right into the yard. Chris was in a black, 2049 armored Range Rover hover car with a supercharged BR6+ multi-shot, high-powered rifle defeat. It was a Santori black/jet-black, jet headliner with black piano wood in onyx with Alcantara trim and 42mm multi-shot glass and body. All police cars were heavily armed because of the constant cop killings in 2020. He was looking at the tracking screen to see where Wendy was located and swiftly rounded a corner to cut off the guy's escape. "Wendy, what is your position?" Chris asked her with his foot to the pedal.

But Wendy just leaped into the dog's yard and the dog started running towards her. She quickly grabbed her Taser, making sure it was on low voltage before she tased the dog. It gave the guy a jumpstart of two backyards on Wendy, but she was still on him, leaping the fences using two hands and one leap. The guy made it to the other side of another fence and turned around, laughing and giving the middle finger to Wendy. He turned around to take off again and turned right into Chris pointing his Taser at him.

"Get down on the…!" Chris started to order but the guy tried to take off running again, but he tasered his ass, making him drop onto his back.

Wendy leaped over the fence and cuffed the guy. "I had him!" Wendy said; breathing and sweating heavily as she dragged the guy up off the ground and marched him to the back of the Range Rover where she had him get into the back passenger seat, slamming the door.

Chris was laughing at her and said, "I know you had him, but I wanted to help."

Wendy turned to the guy in the back and said to him, "This isn't your lucky day, is it?" The guy didn't say a word. They drove down to Baltimore Central Booking to book him.

Later that day Chris' phone rang. It was Jennifer. She and Laura had just come back from food shopping. She called her father to see what he'd like to eat for dinner. "Dad, what's up?"

"Nothing much, just another day at work, why?"

"Well, I'm cooking tonight. What would you like for me to cook?

Chris thought about it as he was looking at Wendy working on the virtual board. She was trying to find some information on the murder from earlier today. Chris said, "How about some lasagna?"

"Let me guess, Wendy coming over tonight, right?"

Chris started laughing and told Jennifer, yes. He got off the phone and walked over to help Wendy with the case.

* * * * * * * * *

It was still early in the day after Jennifer made dinner, so she and Laura texted a few of their friends and told them to meet them at the mall in Towson for lunch. They took Jennifer's 2047 black hover Jeep Wrangler Unlimited. They met up with Tisha, Melissa and Jamey at the mall by Friday's restaurant. The entire time they were at the mall Jennifer couldn't help but think about Terron and the way he had looked at her, and the way she felt that night when she looked into his eyes and when she'd stood beside him.

Laura saw that Jennifer kept drifting off in thought and Laura had to bring her back. "Jennifer, where are you?"

"I'm right here silly. Why do you ask?" Jennifer asked, laughing slightly. However, she drifted right back to thinking about Terron again.

"See, that's what I'm talking about. You're drifting off again," Laura pointed out.

Jennifer started smiling and said to all of them, "Man, he is cute! That's what's on my mind."

All of the girls started laughing because they thought the same thing. "Yes girl, he is," Tisha agreed. "When I bumped into him I was at a loss for words," Tisha said, laughing as they walked into the Friday's restaurant together. A waiter took them to a table and the five of them sat down, grabbing the menus. "Jennifer, I can't believe you did not get his number. What's up with that?" Melissa asked, then told the waiter what she wanted to drink and eat.

"There wasn't enough time. However, he did pay for our drinks." All the girls started smiling and moaning then giggled. "I hope I see him again."

"Girl, we were in New York so what are the chances we'll see him again?" Tisha said. Jennifer had no response as everyone decided what they wanted to eat and started giving their orders to the waiter.

Chapter Six

After the girl's left Friday's they went their separate ways. On the way home Laura and Jennifer talked about what happened at the club. And Jennifer wanted to go out again. She was starting to come out of her shell and Laura liked that. She was down with it. By the time they got home their father was in the kitchen with Wendy, waiting for them. "Hi dad, hi Wendy," both girls greeted them together.

"Hi girls," Wendy said as she walked toward the dining room table, placing the last plate on the table. Wendy and Chris set the food out on the table which Jennifer had cooked earlier that day.

"We already ate at Friday's dad," Jennifer told him.

Wendy took a seat and Chris asked both his daughters to join them at the table because he wanted to talk to them. Jennifer and Laura glanced at one another and walked over to the table, taking a seat. "What's up, dad?" Jennifer asked with a puzzled look on her face.

Now that both girls were seated Chris started talking. "I did some research on the Sevdeski brothers and I want you girls to be very careful when you go out."

Jennifer and Laura were happy he didn't say not to go out, but just be careful when they did. They knew how their father could get when he was in his protective mode. Laura was curious to know what their father had found out so she asked, "They're not just any ordinary terrorists?"

"They're international and Emil is going to want some revenge for his brother's death."

"But they said on the news his brother died from a heart attack, right Jennifer?" Laura looked over at Jennifer who was nodding her head up and down.

Chris started smiling. He knew better than that because of what had happened inside the club. "Well, the news will say whatever it's told to say, but from what y'all told me it sounded like a different situation. It sounded like somebody wanted to kill somebody. Jennifer, that guy you saw in the club, was he with anybody else?"

"Yeah, he was with a girl but I don't think she was his girlfriend."

Chris looked at Wendy then turned his attention back to his daughters, saying, "If you see this guy again, don't think it's just a coincidence. Something else might be going on, okay? I want you both to play it safe."

Jennifer and Laura told their father they understood him and got up and went upstairs to bed. Laura went into Jennifer's room to talk with her for a while before going to bed. They closed the door just to make sure their father and Wendy wouldn't hear them. "So, what do you think about what dad said, Jennifer?" Laura asked, sitting down on Jennifer's bed.

"I don't know, but what are the chances that I'll run into him in Baltimore, Laura?"

Laura started smiling and said, "I don't know but if he was going to kill me I wouldn't mind him doing it."

Jennifer started laughing at her sister. "Laura, you're fucking crazy."

"I'm just saying if he's going to be the one to kill me…mmm right?"

Both girls started laughing again and before Laura left to go to bed she gave her sister a big hug and left the room. Jennifer began to undress and then got in the bed. She lay there for a while, thinking about what her father had said about Terron. A smile flickered across her lips and she turned off the light.

Downstairs, Wendy was about to walk out of the door to go home. "Chris, I'll see you tomorrow and try not to worry about the girls. I think they're going to be okay."

"I'll try not to but you know how I can get."

Wendy smiled and said, "Yeah, I do. But try not to get all worked up, okay?"

Chris walked Wendy to her car and watched her drive off. He walked into the house and locked up. Before he went to his room he checked on both his daughters and found them sound asleep. Then he walked into his room to do the same thing.

****

"Terron, I need to talk with you," Leyla called out, checking out Todd as she walked into the weight room where Terron and Todd were working out.

"What's up, Leyla?"

"I think the girl from the club saw me, and I just don't know…" she said, letting her voice trail off.

"You just don't know what, Leyla?"

"It was something about her that I can't put together right now. Did you get her number?"

Terron knew he hadn't gotten her number, but he had paid for the girl and her friend's drinks that night. "No, I didn't get a chance to but I did pay for their drinks." Leyla looked at him like he was crazy and by this time Carol had walked into the room.

"What's going on guys?" Carol asked because she saw how Leyla was looking at Terron.

"Nothing yet; just your brother trying to hook up with some chick from that club we were at."

Carol looked at Terron with a surprised look on her face because she knew he knew better than to do that. "Terron, is this true?"

"I didn't hook up with her. I just paid for their drinks. That's it!"

Carol walked up to him and said, "Terron, you know better than to do that more than any one of us. What were you thinking about?"

"I didn't do anything. I was just using her for cover, that's all."

Leyla and Carol looked at each other and Carol said, "Terron, you know you could have put her very life in great danger by interacting with her. Now we're going to have to make sure she's okay because one of our spies told us that some commotion happened inside of the club, and I think it was with the same girl."

Terron didn't like the sound of that because he didn't want to see anything happen to her because of him so he asked, "So, what can we do?"

"Our spy just so happened to be working behind the bar that night and one of the girls used a credit card so, we should be able to track them down from that," Carol explained.

Terron was so happy he could not only protect the girl but get a chance to see her again. "Okay, we're going to put a 72 hour watch on her and her friends just to be sure that Emil is not looking for them," Terron directed Todd, Carol, Leyla and Ashley.

"It sounds like to me somebody likes somebody," Todd said, laughing at Terron.

Terron was not laughing because he knew if the Elders were to ever find out he would be in serious trouble. "Todd it's not funny because if the Elders find out that could be the end of Dragon Team, so keep it on the low, all right? Let's go."

Todd nodded his head in understanding to his team leader and got up off the weight bench. Todd and Terron always went out together and always had each other's back. "Let me just change real quick," Todd said, running towards the men's locker room. Terron followed him so he could change his clothing. "Don't worry dude, I got your back. You know that, right?"

"Todd, I know you got my back. I just don't want you to put anybody's life on the line, you know?"

Todd smiled and whispered, "Yeah, I know, especially as you didn't get a chance to bang, bang, bang that ass yet!!"

Terron just looked at him, shaking his head. He couldn't do anything but laugh at Todd. But what they didn't know was that Leyla was watching their every move. She always peeked in on Todd to watch him change his clothing. Leyla had a thing for Todd; he just didn't know it yet. Her eyes were like x-ray vision trained on Todd's light-skinned, muscular body. She watched him take off his under-armor t-shirt and throwing it on the floor. Leyla loved looking at Todd's body and watching the breathing holes on his body take in air turned her on. He was 6' tall with brown eyes and most of all she loved looking at his tattoo of a dragon spitting fire on his back. She felt his breathing holes up and down his spine spoke to her. Todd and Terron laughed at something and she zoomed in, admiring his pearly white teeth. "My little Latin lover I'm going to get you," Leyla whispered to herself then she was startled by a tap on her shoulder.

"Bitch, what the hell are you doing?" Carol whispered.

"I'm not doing shit. What the hell are you doing, Carol?" Leyla whispered back, looking at Carol as if she was crazy or something.

"Leyla, I notice that every time Terron and Todd come to work out you're the first one to want to work out with them. And every time they go to the little boy's room you're nowhere to be found. What the fuck is up with that shit?"

"Leyla rolled her eyes and said, "So what bitch! You got me!"

"Do you have a thing for my brother?"

"No bitch, he's not the one."

Carol started smiling and turned to look at what Leyla was watching. Todd was just putting on his boxers. "Now I see why. He does have a nice ass, girl," Carol observed, slapping Leyla on the ass. The both of them walked back out to where Ashley was waiting for them.

"So let me guess, you caught Leyla looking at Todd, right?" Ashley asked Carol.

"You knew this all the time that I would go back and look at Todd?" Leyla asked with a surprised look on her face.

"Hell yeah, all the time. I don't know why you just don't let him know how you feel."

"Let who know how who feel? Todd asked, walking up to the three girls.

They all looked at one another and Carol quickly said, "One of the other teams think Leyla is a lesbian, that's all." Leyla looked at Carol as if she was out of her mind for throwing her under the bus like that.

Todd just looked at Leyla, smiling and said, "Well, I never see you with anybody. Are you?"

Ashley and Carol were doing their best not to laugh at Leyla, but Leyla did not find it funny. "Hell no, boy!! Let's go!" Leyla shouted, turning around and walking away.

As Terron walked out of the locker room Todd turned and looked at Carol and Ashley with a clueless look on his face and asked, "Did I say something wrong?"

"No, Todd you didn't. Let's go," Carol told him gently, grabbing his 22-inch arm and walking away with him.

"Did I miss something?" Terron asked Ashley and Todd.

"No, let's go see what the Elders want," Ashley said and all of them walked down the corridor together toward the board room.

* * * * * * * * *

Carol and Todd were the first ones to walk into the conference room. Grag was waiting for them along with Tara.

"What's going on?" Carol asked as she took a seat in one of the glass chairs around the table.

The conference room was all black except for the pictures on the walls. The table was made from good old oak wood, but the surface of the table was covered with tempered glass that would play missions on a virtual reality screen for any team that had meetings in the room. There was a hieroglyphic writing which read: *"Those that come before those in this room are Gatekeepers of Tripueler, and protectors of the Earth as Hatchet Men"* right above a picture of an American bold eagle with a dagger in its claws and blood dripping from the dagger. Right beside it was another picture of the all-seeing eye on the dollar bill.

"It took you long enough. Where is the rest of your team?" Grag asked as he stood at the right side at the head of the table. Tara was seated at the end of the table. At that moment Terron, Ashley, Leyla and Todd walked into the conference room and closed the door behind them. Tara nodded her head at Grag and he started talking.

"Dragon team, the reason we called this conference meeting is because after that successful night where you eliminated Joker Sevdeski, his brother, Emil Sevdeski, put out a world-wide hit on whoever had anything to do with his brother's murder."

"Excuse me, Master Chief, but after every job that we complete successfully, somebody always put out a world-wide hit on us. What makes this one any different from others put out there?" Todd asked.

Tara stood up and said, "What makes this one different is that Emil wants to kill some of the people that were in the club that night." That raised the eyebrows of all the team members because they were just talking about putting some surveillance on the girl and her friends. Tara pulled up the virtual reality screen showing them what Terron and his team already knew. "We believe that these people are in great danger from Emil. We intercepted some phone calls from Emil talking about this woman right here." She pulled up a picture of the girl.

From the look on Terron's face you could tell he was caught by surprise at what he saw and that he felt something. Carol saw the look on his face and kicked him in the shinbone so he could wipe the look off his face. He didn't and before Tara faced them he blurted out, "Why would he have some interest in her?" Terron asked Tara.

"We don't know. We were hoping one of you could tell us that, but our job is to protect the people and that is what we're going to do," she replied.

"Master Chief, do you have any information on the people?" Carol asked eager to get the information.

"Yes I do. This young lady's name is Jennifer Lin. She lives with her sister, Laura Lin, who was also at the club. Jennifer Lin is 23 years old and works at The World Trade Center in downtown Baltimore. I want a week of surveillance on her and her friends." She pulled up four more pictures and said, "This is Laura who's about to turn 18 in a few weeks. She attends Lake Clifton high school in Baltimore with two of the girls that were there that night. Their names are Tisha and Melissa, same age as Laura, and they also attend Lake Clifton high school," Tara said, pointing at each girl. "The three of them work at MacDonald's off of Richy Highway on Baltimore Court. And this one is Jamey. She's Jennifer's best friend, she's 24 and the two of them work at the same place. Oh, and one more thing. Jennifer and Laura's father work for the Baltimore Police Department. His name is Chris Lin."

Terron couldn't take his eyes off Jennifer's picture and Carol had to kick him again on his shinbone.

"We can't have anything happen to these girls and do not blow your cover under any circumstances. You may leave," Tara said and walked out with Grag.

Terron ran up to Tara to further talk with her and she stopped to hear what he had to say. Carol waited for him at the end of the hallway. "Tara, can I talk with you, please?"

"If this about the other day with the prisoner, I'd rather not."

"No, this is about what was just said."

With a frown on her face Tara said, "You know protocol, Terron."

"I know, but what was said by Emil?"

Tara and Grag found it strange that Terron would ask such a question outside of the conference room. "Terron, what's really on your mind?" Tara asked, walking closer to him. "He was just asking something I should've asked you. We'll go through proper channels." She could see Ashley coming to get him.

"Come on, Terron. Let's go. We have a lot of work to do," Ashley said as she walked up to them. Tara just looked at Terron, shaking her head as she walked away with Grag.

Once Tara and Grag were gone, Ashley shouted, "Terron, are you losing your freaking mind, bro'? You know once we leave out of the conference room nothing else is to be said about the mission!" What the hell were you thinking about?"

Terron had this foolish look on his face as he started walking toward Carol. Ashley shook her head as she walked behind him.

* * * * * * * * *

The sun was just coming up and sunlight was shining in Jennifer's face, waking her up. She rolled over and yawned. Her first thoughts were getting up and going to Montihello Park to do some artwork. She wanted to draw the beautiful landscape with her sister Laura. Jennifer got into the shower and yelled for Laura to get ready so they could ride to the park. Both of them loved to do art. It helped them find peace in a very un-peaceful world.

"I'm up!" Laura shouted from her room with her pillow over her head. Her alarm started ringing and Laura threw a pillow at it, trying to make it stop.

"Laura, get the hell up!" Jennifer yelled, running into Laura's room with a towel wrapped around her body and one around her head. She started tickling Laura, making her laugh.

"I'm up! I'm up!" she shouted. They calmed down and lay there, just looking up at the ceiling. "So you really want to go to the park today?" Laura asked.

"Yes, I think it would be real cool. Why? Do you have somewhere else to go today?"

"No, come on. I'm going to make us some breakfast so don't take forever."

Laura got up and went to take a shower and get dressed. She was just happy that her sister wanted to go somewhere instead of staying inside the house all day.

Jennifer walked down the stairs into the kitchen and went directly to the refrigerator to get the eggs, some turkey bacon, home fries, onion, green peppers and butter. She was feeling real good this morning.

Chapter Seven

In short order Terron and his team finalized their plans and headed out to implement their mission. Ashley was soon on the job. She was camped out in front of the Lin's home, watching for any sign of Emil or his men because from the latest report, they found out he likes to do his own work to make sure it's done right. Ashley loved doing this type of work. She didn't mind it at all. Her iPhone started to ring. She looked at the screen, smiled and answered, "What do you want Terron?"

"Any movement on our girl?" he asked from his New York penthouse in downtown Brooklyn.

Terron was living very well for himself. Most Hatchet Men did. His penthouse was fully loaded. It was 3,185 square feet, cathedral ceiling, three bedrooms, three bathrooms; a dining room, breakfast room, powder room and laundry room with both washer and dryer. It also had five-star concierge services and amenities: private gardens, mind/body spa, fitness center, children's playroom, rooftop club, porte cochere entrances and onsite parking. The price point was at $1.5 million dollars.

Terron had some of the most luxurious stuff in his penthouse. His walls were Indonesian bricks and he had a large, beveled window that resembled a cut diamond, creating a striking environment, especially at sunrise and sunset. He had sky-blue Lorraine France Saint-Louis lanterns, an Eagle Wolf Orca the Archipelago, and two stone and glass tables in his great room. There were two black Udine Italy Moroso biknit chaise lounges. And, there was a sub-zero, 36" wide French door model refrigerator in his kitchen with marble patterned quartz counters. These were just a few of the luxurious European designs in Terron's penthouse.

"No, no movement yet but I'm going to follow the Little Bird," Ashley answered as she kept her eye's on Jennifer's front door.

"Okay, good. Let me know if you see anything."

"Terron, you will be the first one to know Blue Dragon," Ashley responded and got off the phone. She turned her eyes back on the Lin's house and to her surprise Jennifer and Laura were coming out the door. They got into a black 2047 hover Jeep Wrangler unlimited Mercedes with Tectite gray Kevlar and took off. Ashley slowly pulled out behind them. She turned on her supersonic hearing device.

Inside the car Laura told Jennifer, "After we go to the park, I want to go to Subway to get something to eat."

"Okay, that's what's up. We're almost there."

Jennifer and Laura were doing something they loved to do and Laura just loved that her sister was getting back to her normal self. At times, Laura would see her sister stress-out about the death of her fiancé, Eric, but she seemed to be doing a lot better than a few months ago. Once they got to the park, Laura's watch started to beep and right afterwards Jennifer's watch did the same. "Shit, you know what time it is, right?" Jennifer asked Laura, reaching into her glove compartment and grabbing a medicine bottle with her name on it. "Laura, you got yours?"

"Yeah, I got it. I hate taking these damn pills."

"Me too, but we got to take them," Jennifer said, taking hers and making funny faces with the pill in her mouth, making Laura laugh.

"Jennifer, you always find some type of way to make a bad situation into something good," Laura told her as she took her pill. They reached their destination and both got out of the jeep and grabbed their art gear.

Ashley was just pulling into the park, driving very slowly toward Jennifer and Laura's jeep. She was making sure she wasn't noticed by them so she parked on the opposite of the jeep. She sat in her 2048 black hover Alfa Romeo 8c competizione pretending to fix her hair; but she was really watching Jennifer and Laura walk across the grass. Ashley hadn't been there for five seconds and Terron was calling her phone. "Terron, what the hell you want?" Ashley asked, irritated as she kept her eyes on Jennifer and Laura the entire time, getting out of the car.

"What is she doing?" Terron asked from his penthouse in Brooklyn.

"We just got to the park, Terron. Damn! Calm the hell down! From the look of things it seems she and her sister are going to do some art work."

Terron started smiling because he also liked to draw and he found that very interesting. "Wow that sounds like we have something in common. What else are they doing?"

Ashley looked at him through her phone screen like he was crazy. "Terron, are you losing your mind? Just take it easy. I'll keep you updated. I got to go," Ashley told him and hung up the phone so she could keep her eyes on Jennifer and Laura.

Terron just smiled to himself, feeling good that he and Jennifer had something in common. He was so pumped up that he went into the room where his easel and art materials were set up and started sketching Jennifer as he'd seen her that night at the club. Hatchet Men have photographic memory, so he was able to draw her exactly the way she'd looked.

Once into the park, Jennifer and Laura found a spot where they wanted to draw and set up shop. "Right here seems to be a good spot. What do you think?" Laura asked Jennifer.

"It seems fine to me. Let's do it," Jennifer replied jokingly and started setting up her gear, and once completed she started painting the landscape.

At first, Ashley couldn't tell what Jennifer was painting, but when it started coming together she was impressed with her work. She wanted to walk over to Jennifer and ask her a few questions about her work, but she knew that wouldn't be a good idea. So she kept her distance from the girls even though she'd already sat there for three hours. Then she began to feel like somebody was watching her watch them. She started to scan around the park to see if somebody was watching her but she saw no one. She felt a strong presence around her and started walking toward a tree where she thought she saw a shadow. When she got there whatever she saw was gone. Her phone started ringing and she saw it was Terron, probably calling to see what else was going on. She picked up.

"So Ashley, what does her art work look like?"

"Her art looked really good. I was surprised at her work," Ashley said as she continued to look around for someone, but saw nothing. She walked back over to where she had been observing Jennifer and Laura, still keeping her distance from them. She and Terron talked a few more minutes and ended the call. Terron was smiling as he brushed up his drawing of Jennifer from that night. However, she didn't have on the same outfit. He'd gotten creative and designed his own outfit for her.

Jennifer and Laura sat there for another hour, looking at the landscape of the pretty park and started talking about life. "Jennifer, do you think you'll ever get engaged again?" Laura asked, looking at her sister and hoping it wasn't a bad time to ask her that question.

Jennifer was caught off guard by Laura's question but she was still able to answer it. "Maybe one day, if I find the right guy." Laura started smiling and hugged her sister.

Ashley started smiling because she liked how Jennifer and Laura were very loving toward each other. Her thoughts were suddenly interrupted because she thought she felt somebody watching her again and just like before she went to check it out but saw nothing. Ashley did not like the feeling that someone was watching her and she couldn't find them. She saw Jennifer and Laura packing up and walking toward their jeep. Ashley walked slowly toward her car but was still on the alert for someone watching her. She still found nothing. So she just followed the girls again. But she made a mental note of what she'd felt today at the park.

* * * * * * * * *

Terron, Ashley, Leyla, Carol and Todd returned to the conference room to talk with Tara who was talking to Russian President Kurashsky about Emil Sevdeski. Terron had already told his team not to say too much about Jennifer, her family and her friends because he wanted to keep them safe himself. Terron and his team sat down and just listened to Tara talk with the Russian President. When she saw them walk in she started bringing the conversation to a close. Once the call was ended Tara turned to the team and asked, "What other information do you have on Jennifer and Laura Lin, Jamey Shea, Tisha Knight and Melissa Gray?"

Ashley wanted to say something about the feeling she'd gotten while she was watching Jennifer and Laura, but Terron had told her not to say anything about it yet. She was praying that nothing would happen because she would have to live with the bad decision she'd made in not telling. Terron promised her that he would make sure to keep a watch on them because of what she'd felt in the park. Terron wanted to do some more investigation into what Ashley told him.

"No, just that Jennifer is a very good artist," Ashley said, glancing at Terron but quickly turning her attention back to Tara.

Carol looked at Ashley and was glad she hadn't said anything about what she'd felt because if Tara found out about Ashley's intuition in the park, it would set off all types of alarms. And Terron probably wouldn't get the chance he was getting to be with Jennifer.

"Ashley, I want you to turn in a full report about what you saw, what you felt, what we should do next and should we put a team on them. Okay?" Tara said, looking Ashley directly in her eyes.

"Yes, I'll do that right away, Master Chief. But as of right now, I see no need for a team," Ashley said to Tara. At that moment Grag walked into the conference room to talk with Tara so she excused Terron and his team.

When they were outside the room, they headed to the virtual reality training room to train. Terron was up first and he liked to listen to music while he trained. One of his favorite songs was track 3 from Metallica's album "Death Magnetic."

Carol was in the control room by the control panel and ready to turn the music on for him. "Terron, are you ready?" she shouted and he nodded his head in a yes motion and she turned it on.

"I want it set to level 10," Terron told her and Ashley looked at Carol and Leyla as if Terron was crazy because at level 10 everything comes at you.

Todd walked over toward the balcony, yelling, "Dude how about a warm-up first? Are you sure about that level 10?"

Terron nodded in the affirmative. Some of the other Hatchet Men heard what Terron was about to do and came over to watch him fight. This training exercise was more advanced than the one Ashley had completed because not only was Terron going to fight Ghost-likes and Hatchet Men Ghosts, he was going to fight a simulation of the God Seth, something he'd never done before. Carol had a somewhat worried look on her face because the simulation was like fighting a real God and it can become life or death if he's not careful. At level 10 you feel the real deal and some Hatchet Men had been killed at this level of training exercise before. Word got out and dozens of Hatchet Men came in to watch Terron fight.

"Come on, I'm ready!" Terron shouted, taking deep breaths. His team didn't like what he was about to do but they couldn't stop him. Terron immediately started running when the music started playing. "Arrrrr!!" he roared. His technique was not to be quiet. He was trying to heat up so his breathing holes would take in more oxygen so he would become stronger in battle. He could've used his team's powers by having them to transfer theirs to him. However, if they were in battle it would make them powerless but make him super-strong and they would only have the strength of regular humans. He wouldn't do that. He was on his own.

The time was set for 10 minutes in the virtual reality room. The doors were locked and he had to survive to get out. Terron grabbed both of his Tabar axes from behind his back, leaping into the air and simultaneously twirling around like a tornado, killing two Ghost-likes. Before he hit the ground he threw one of his axes at a Hatchet Man Ghost hologram, killing it. Terron hit the ground in a crouch then took off running toward his axe, sliding across the ground like he was sliding to first base. He quickly grabbed his axes, leaping 20' right back into the air, doing a front flip several times; defying gravity by running upward on the side of a wall to the top of the roof of a simulated building.

Two simulated Hatchet Men Ghosts leaped out, thrusting with their swords at Terron. He quickly kicked one in the chest, sending it flying into the air but it bounced back onto its feet and advanced toward Terron, trying to kill him with the help of the second Hatchet Man Ghost. Terron used one of his daggers to stab one of the Hatchet Men several times in the chest and the hologram disappeared. Terron took off running, leaping across to another roof top. The building was about twenty stories tall so he had to be very careful, although he knew he had gravity in his favor.

Carol stood up in the balcony, feeling intense because she knew how stubborn Terron could be. "Come on, Terron. You got six more minutes," Carol whispered to herself.

Leyla and Ashley saw the worried look on Carol's face and both of them went to the balcony and stood on each side of her, holding her hand. "He'll be fine," Ashley told her with a slight smile.

Suddenly, two dozen Ghost-likes blazed down from the sky at once. "Oh shit, here he comes!" one of the Hatchet Men watching shouted, pointing at the hologram of Seth coming from afar.

Carol gripped onto the rail of the balcony and whispered to Ashley and Leyla, "I wish he would have taken our powers just in case."

Leyla turned to her with a smile. She whispered, "Now you know that wouldn't be Terron. He'll be fine." Todd stood on the side, watching as he cheered Terron on.

Terron heard loud thunder coming from behind him and the sky turned completely black. He got goose bumps all over his body because this was the first time that a hologram of the God Seth had appeared in his training and something felt different. Seth was about a quarter of a mile away from Terron but once the hologram saw him it started running toward him with his steel rod that could shoot lightning. Every time Seth hit another God or Hatchet Man with his weapon, it would send an electric pulse, paralyzing them and then he would kill them.

Terron took off, running in the opposite direction, leaping from one building to another. He opened a hatch on a roof and saw stairs. He started running down the steps. By the time he was down four levels of stairs he heard the hatch's door ripped open and he knew Seth was there. Terron glanced upward but kept on moving. This was the first time he was going up against Seth. He had heard about other Hatchet Men going up against him but they had not been successful.

* * * * * * * * *

Tara and Grag were just coming out of the conference room and as they walked down the hallway they saw and heard all the commotion coming from the training area. "What the hell is going on there?" Grag asked Tara as the both of them walked toward that area.

"There's only one way to find out," she replied. When some of the Hatchet Men saw two Elders coming their way some of them dispersed quickly. "What the hell is going on here and where is Terron?" Tara asked Ashley, Carol, Leyla and Todd once they reached the balcony.

"He's in the training room on level 10," Carol replied.

When Tara and Grag heard that, Ashley noticed strange looks on both their faces. Grag's seemed to say, "You go Terron!" Tara's look was worry. "What the hell is he thinking about? He's not ready for a level 10. How long has he been inside?" Tara asked, walking over to the simulation control board.

Carol looked at her and said, "What are you about to do?"

Tara looked at the board and asked, "Which God is he about to fight?"

"Seth and it's his first time."

"Who the hell authorized this shit?" Tara asked, mad as hell. She pulled out her top secret security clearance card so that the computer could scan her eyes. Nobody said a word just like she thought they wouldn't.

Chapter Eight

Terron was in the building, hiding behind some cubicles with both of his Tabar axes in his hands, ready. He heard when Seth entered the room. He could feel his energy and it was so dark he felt a little frightened; and for a quick second he closed his eyes. But then he remembered when his mother used to train him and Carol and she would always say, "A little fear is good but just don't let it consume you." Terron quickly opened his eyes, staying focused on what was going on right now. He took over 20 deep breaths, trying to make a lot of oxygen circulate within his body so he could have the maximum strength he would need. Once he felt he was ready, he slowly started to make his way toward Seth. He looked up, trying to get a good look at Seth. And what he saw he was not ready for it. Seth's face was skull and bones on fire with worms crawling in and out of his face.

Terron swiftly dropped down, whispering, "Shit!" That was all it took and Seth was on him. He started running through the cubicles trying to find Terron. But Terron was able to leap over two cubicles and take off running. Seth was right behind him. He clipped Terron's foot with his rod, making Terron fall to the ground, but the shock from Seth's rod didn't knock him out but it dazed him. He was stumbling as he tried to get away. However, Seth leaped into the air, coming down hard on Terron with his rod. But Terron used both his axes to block the blow and quickly gained his balance, moving faster than a speeding bullet.

Tara, Grag and Terron's team were looking down from the balcony, watching as Terron was fighting for his very life. "Aunt Tara, what the hell is going on in there!" Carol cried out loud.

"He's been fucking lucky, that's what! He shouldn't be in there!" Tara shouted. Even though she had top security clearance, it was still going to take the computer some time to stop the simulation.

"Come on Terron, you can do it," Todd whispered and Leyla grabbed his hand. They stood there together, watching their team leader, trying to survive from the hologram of Seth.

Terron was running down some spiral steps. Then Seth started leaping down the steps so Terron did the same and eventually bolted out of a door to the outside where the landscape changed and the images were different. The setting was that of Tripueler. Carol asked Tara where was Terron because she didn't know the setting. Terron kept running and he heard a voice that whispered in his mind, "Don't run. You are one. Stand and fight as the one that fights before you!" Terron thought he was hearing things because of the blow to his head.

Terron ran out of space and he stopped and turned around and Seth was right there. As soon as he faced him Seth punched Terron in the chest, sending him flying across the sky and right onto the ground. His body bounced several times before hitting the ground and almost leaving him unconscious. In the training area you could hear Tara, Ashley, Leyla, Todd and Ashley shouting for Terron to get up. Seth leaped into the air then started coming down with his rod lit up like a Christmas tree full of lightning about to finish Terron off.

"Terron, call your birth sword, Royal Ron, now!" Terron heard that same voice tell him.

He quickly shouted, "Royal Ron, come to me!!"

Unknowingly, he unconsciously held out his hand and everything started happening in slow motion. None of the other Hatchet Men knew what the hell was going on because this had never happened before during training. Lightning struck several times and by the time Seth landed over Terron, his birth sword, the Zweihander, was in his hand. Seth banged his pole on the Zweihander several times and by the eighth time a bright light took over the room, making it hard for anybody to see what was about to happen next. Terron's birth sword released an exploding electric pulse which sent Seth flying across the sky, and right after that the training room doors opened. And standing there was Tara, pissed off at Terron.

He was still dazed and on the ground but he was able to see the Zweihander sword, hovering in front of him. It was the most beautiful sight to his eyes. He was able to analyze it and record it with his eyes before it disappeared. It was chrome and very shiny, about ten feet in length; six inches in width at the very bottom; and seven feet from the bottom the sword widened to a foot in width. There was a hieroglyphic writing from the tip to the hilt of the sword which read: *Only the birth handler can handle me because I am one with whom I belong to and there is nothing I can not kill by right. I can slip between stars, moons, planets and can live within the sun. I can take life or let life live. I am a weapon of mass destruction.*

The handle was made out of solid gold and titanium from Tripueler with gems like amber, citrine, moldavite and amethyst. There were also black gems embedded at the tip and base of the sword of jet and schorl. Terron was able to record all of this before the sword disappeared before his eyes.

"Terron, who the hell authorized this training?" Tara shouted. She was very angry.

Terron glanced at Carol who stood behind Tara and was able to read her lips without her saying a word. He looked at his Aunt who was standing in front of him and said, "Mom gave me authorization, so take it up with her. And why did you shut down the program? I was doing fine."

Tara walked right up to Terron, looking him straight in the eyes and said, "You were what?"

"I had it under control. Why did you stop the program?"

"You had nothing under control Terron, and you could've been killed."

"I've done this program over a thousand times and defeated it every time. And where did that sword come from?"

Tara started smiling and then chuckled. "Terron, that's how I knew you were about to die because that sword is a Hatchet Man's last line of defense in the program when you're up against a God. Boy, you were dead and didn't even know it. I don't want you doing that ever again, Terron. Do I make myself clear?" Tara warned, standing no less than a foot from him.

"Yes, I understand," Terron replied angrily and stalked away.

"Terron, hold the hell up!" Carol shouted, running up to her brother.

"Carol, right now I don't want to hear it."

Carol jumped in front of him, softly placing her hand up against his chest, stopping him. "Hold on bro' I'm with you. Just chill out for a second." Terron huffed and puffed, turning his face away from Carol, but she gently turned it back to her and asked, "What the hell happened in there? Something was very different this time. What was it?"

"Something different definitely did happen. I've never seen that God before. And that sword, where did it come from?"

"You heard auntie, she said it was the last line of defense."

By this time the rest of their team was standing with them as Terron said, "Yeah, I know, but it didn't feel like it. It felt like it belonged to me and somebody told me to call on it for help. When I did that, it came to me."

Ashley walked up to Terron and said, "So what are you saying, Terron?

Terron looked at each of them and said, "Something else is going on. I can feel it. It all started when they brought that prisoner onto the base that day that I've been feeling like this.

All of them looked at one another and started to walk away because some more Hatchet Men were coming down the corridor toward them. Once they reached their quarters where they knew it would be safe to talk, they continued their conversation. "Terron, do you want me to look into this for you?" Ashley asked him.

"You do know the type of danger you could be putting yourself in by doing this, right?"

Ashley shrugged her shoulders. "It's not anything I didn't sign up for as a Hatchet Woman, so I'm in. I'll check on the computer when I can and I'm going to start with that simulation of that God Seth. That was his name, right?" Carol nodded her head indicating that was the name.

"Terron, so what do you think is going on?" Leyla asked, looking a little confused about everything that was going on.

Terron just smiled slightly and said, "I really don't know but we're going to find out. Todd, when is the next time you go to work at the prison?"

"I told Master Chief I'll volunteer next month so I guess then, why?"

Terron walked up to Todd and looked directly into his eyes and said, "I want you to find out everything you can about that prisoner they brought in that day we were on top of the base."

"I'm going to get on it ASAP!"

Terron was not about to ignore how he'd been feeling and he felt Jennifer had a lot to do with it as well. He didn't know how she fit into it all but he knew she was a part of what was going on with him. He could never forget how she'd made him feel that night at the club.

* * * * * * * * *

Tara reached her quarters and immediately called Terron and Carol's mother who was on another Hatchet Man's base in California, underwater off Catalina Island. Most of the Watchers stayed there and would come to this base. It was very top secret.

"Long time no hear from, Tara. What brings you to call me?" Zenny asked, looking at some papers in front of her.

"I'm calling because your son claimed that you gave him authorization to use the Watcher simulation program. I'm calling to see if that is true because if not, he is going to the hole for a year. Did you give him authorization?"

Zenny did not even lift her head and responded, "Yes I did, for him and his team. Why?"

Tara was shocked that she would approve him and his team for such a high level program, knowing that he could be killed. "You know what could happen during that program, don't you?" Tara asked.

Again, Zenny didn't lift her head as she continued to look at some papers, replying, "Yes Tara, I know. But I'm very busy right now, saving the world. So I'll see you soon. And on that note…"

Tara did not like how Zenny had brushed her off, but she was Tara's Commanding Chief and rank was a real big thing in the Hatchet Men world. So she just replied, "Okay, I'll see you when you can get here."

Once Tara signed off the screen, Zenny lifted her head in disbelief at what Terron was doing. Even though she'd told Tara she had approved the authorization, she really hadn't. "What the hell are you doing, Terron and Carol?" Zenny whispered to herself, hoping the two of them were not up to no good.

Chapter Nine

The team was on their way out of their quarters when Ashley grabbed Terron and pulled him to the side, asking, "Why did you want me to lie like that? Please don't tell me it's because you see something in this girl, Terron?" Carol was talking to Todd, standing about 10 feet away from where Ashley was talking to Terron. Leyla was keeping her ear tuned in to Terron and Ashley's conversation because she was waiting to hear what Terron was going to say next.

Terron started smiling and said, "Something tells me you don't approve of what I'm doing."

"Terron, you do know what could happen to me behind this, right?" Ashley had the most serious look on her face, waiting on his answer.

"I know and I'm very thankful for all everybody is doing for me. But it's something about that girl when I saw her. I felt something powerful when she was around me. Right now there's so much going on around here that I feel this girl might have some answers for us all."

"I hope she's worth all of this, Terron because if what we're doing ever gets out, we're in big shit dude. I got your back," Ashley said and pushed out her fist for Terron to bump it with his.

"So you're going to do what needs to be done, right?"

Ashley scrunched up her face and replied, "Don't I always and I always have your back." Terron nodded his head and hugged Ashley in thanks.

The five of them walked down the corridor toward the elevators. Ashley was going to hang around to see what she could find out while Terron, Carol, Todd and Leyla returned to New York. They would travel in an Agusta Westland Aw 101 Merlin aw109Luh helicopter to their cars in Manhattan. It was time for them to get back to their day-to-day jobs. Terron and Carol had some real estate to sell in the Upper East Side on 56th Street in Manhattan. Leyla was going with Todd to help him take some pictures at his studio in Brooklyn.

Ashley had gotten clearance that could get her into the prison to find out anything on anybody being held at the prison. She walked down the corridor with her team to the elevators. She would get on one and they would get on another. When they arrived she entered and turned around and said, "I'll see y'all soon," then threw up a peace sign as the doors were closing. The other elevator came and the rest of the team got on it and headed up to the top of the base. The semisubmersible where Terron and his team attended school was fully equipped. It wasn't like a regular semisubmersible because it belonged to HUWP and had the latest technology and equipment that the world has ever seen. As the elevator sped to the top, the semisubmersible was emerging out of the ocean. Not only was it made out of the strongest metals known to man, the corridors have high-tech cameras everywhere and mini machine guns beneath every camera that can shoot exploding bullets, moving simultaneously with one another. The corridors are also lined with fluorescent blue lights which light up as you walk past them as well as stationary lighting. The floors were concrete but the corridor walls were solid steel. The semisubmersible would emerge out of the Pacific Ocean about 20' above sea level only when there were incoming or outgoing aircraft to and from the semisubmersible. Otherwise, it would stay underwater deep into the Pacific Ocean.

The prison held the world's most dangerous criminals alive and some would never leave and die at the prison. There were terrorists, religious cult leaders, racist leaders and the most notorious of them all — Hatchet Men Ghosts. The prison was housed at the very bottom of a building that was built underneath the submersible underground at the bottom of the ocean. The school was five levels up and the Hatchet Men Shadow's living quarters were two levels above the prison. The training area for the Hatchet Men was three levels above that. Terron and his team didn't live on their base but they did have rooms that they used. Only the real young Hatchet Men Shadows stayed on the base until they successfully completed enough missions and got reassigned to a penthouse or mansion.

When Terron and the team got to the top of the base, their helicopter was less than 50' away and about to land. "I hope you know what you're doing because if she got…" But before Carol could finish, Terron stopped her.

"Ashley is going to be good. Now let's go."

The four of them got on the helicopter and headed to New York. The ride wasn't that long and in short order they were there and getting into their cars. Carol and Terron got into Terron's midnight blue Range Rover with white leather interior. It was bullet-proof and bomb-proof and loaded with the world's best technology and high-tech guns that Hatchet Men used. It also had aggressive high-speed driving for chasing cars. "Are you ready to do this?" Terron asked Carol as he turned on his hover car.

"Yeah, I guess," she replied.

Todd and Leyla got into his 2049 midnight blue Aegean Bentley GT coupe. His car was just as equipped as Terron's Range Rover. The only difference is that Todd's car had turbo boosters, picking up speeds over 300 miles per hour and from zone to 60 in 0.5 seconds. Leyla looked over at Todd and he asked her, "What's up?"

Leyla wanted to tell him so badly how she felt but she wasn't ready yet. So she just said, "Look, don't be driving like a madman, Todd. A bitch is not trying to die," she said laughingly.

Todd looked over at Leyla laughing as he turned on some rap music from the late 19th Century. It was Drake's album "Thank Drake Me Later," track 4 and said, "Come on baby, you don't trust the kid? I got this."

Leyla started blushing as she put on her seatbelt, shaking her head as Todd quickly took off, head bobbing to his music. He took off straight into the air, weaving in and out of traffic as he performed rollovers and zigzagged in the air. If the truth were told, Leyla liked it. She was getting a little bit excited from the ride.

Terron and Carol had reached the property they were going to sell. Carol was on her tablet, checking over everything about the property so that when the potential buyer arrived she could quickly run through everything with them. The longer a potential buyer takes to say they're buying, the more they're likely not going to buy. "Terron, you're ready to do this?" Carol asked, looking over at him as he was parking.

Terron glanced at her, smiling and as he got out of the car said, "Hell yes. Let's get this money."

The both of them walked into the penthouse and they started role-playing; Carol acting as a potential buyer and it was Terron's job to sell the property to her.

"Let me go over a few things with you," Carol said.

"Okay, go ahead."

"How many square feet?" she asked.

"It's a luxurious buy at 3,184 square feet."

"Well, I have two kids. How many bedrooms are in this penthouse?"

"It's just what you need with three bedrooms. Come let me show you, right this way," Terron invited her. "The first bedroom is right through the foyer to the right. It's 13.5' in width and 14.5' in length and has a full bath. As we walk right down here, this is the second bedroom with a full bathroom just like the first, although this bedroom is a little bit smaller."

Carol stopped him and said, "I have two boys and if they don't have the same size rooms it's going to be a problem with them."

Terron smiled and nodded his head as if Carol was a real potential buyer, and took control of the situation. In real estate, when dealing with the one percent, you must show control, but in the most respectful manner. Terron smiled and said, "It's only smaller by a few feet but because of this problem, come, let me show you. Please come." Terron gently took Carol's hand and led her to the master-suite, opening the door as if he was her knight in shining armor. Terron started talking to her in a very excited way saying things like, "Is this what you like? The master-suite is 25.5' in length and 15' in width with a very large master bathroom and a view to die for. Just take a look," Terron said with a smooth smile.

Carol was grinning as she walked over to the bedroom's floor to ceiling window where the view looked out over New York, hugging her brother. "Without a doubt you sold it to me."

"Who do we have coming first?" Terron asked at the same time the doorbell rang.

They left the bedroom and made their way to the front door, opening it. It was an African-American woman about five feet tall and dressed in the latest black-on-black, full style Dolce and Gabana dress. She had on red, six-inch red bottom heels with a red leather Ralph Lauren purse and red Louis Vuitton sunshades. Terron walked over to her, complimenting her on how beautiful she looked and went to work.

* * * * * * * * *

Ashley was still at headquarters on the semisubmersible as she worked down below in the prison. She was in the central control room doing her job. There were a few other Hatchet Men working with her. Ashley was just waiting for the right time and right opportunity to perform Terron's request and it finally came.

"Ashley, we're going to grab something to eat. Do you want anything?" one of her co-workers asked her.

Ashley glanced over her shoulder and smiled slightly. "Yes, I'm starving. Get me two cheeseburgers, a large fry, one vanilla milkshake and…what is that hotdog that it takes forever to make?" Ashley asked but she was really buying time.

"Oh, my Hatchet dog. You want one?"

"Yes, please get me one."

"I got you," he said as she was reaching into her purse to get some money.

Ashley started smiling and turned back to her fake assignment. Once they left she went straight to work. The control room they were in had no cameras because it was the room which controlled all the cameras. She grabbed from her purse the flash drive she used to decode anything from anywhere without being detected by anyone. She was fully focused on what she was doing because she knew she only had about 30 minutes to get whatever she needed to get. "Come on, boot up," Ashley whispered to her computer. Once she was in she started to smile and said, "Yes!" She typed in the date when the prisoner came to HUWP and as the screen pulled up the information the only thing that she was able to see was a name and she whispered, "Cynthia, ancient one Hatchet Men Ghost." She quickly started to download what she could.

Somebody really didn't want her to see anything because as she was trying to copy everything to her flash drive the computer started to kick her out. "What the fuck?" she almost shouted and looked at her watch because she knew her co-workers were on their way back. She was listening out for them using her supersonic ears and heard them coming from three corridors away. She kept listening as she tried to get more information but the computer would not let her back in, and now her co-workers were less than 20 feet away from the control room. However, by the time they got to the door she was done. She acted as if she was starving, grabbing the food and smiling. She sat there for a few minutes, eating some of the food then told her co-workers she was going to take the remainder with her. Ashley was thinking she couldn't believe she hadn't been able to get clearance on the prisoner. She found that very strange.

Chapter Ten

Todd and Leyla went to his studio to do a photo shoot of an up and coming rock group and their manager was pissed because Todd was 15 minutes late. "You know we pay you by the hour, right? And not by the photo and we do have other things to do, right?" the manager said sarcastically, giving them a rude look. "And who is this? It doesn't matter. Let's get to work!" she shouted, snapping her neck and fingers while walking away from Todd and Leyla.

"Oh no this bitch didn't just do that!" Leyla whispered angrily under her breath, ready to set her straight.

Todd heard Leyla and stopped her with a soft touch to her hand and holding it. "Chill, I got this. Just follow my lead."

Leyla liked the fact that Todd was holding her hand. For a moment she was in a daze by his words and the gentle way he'd touch her. But she was brought back to Earth by the ignorant manager talking to the rock group.

"Okay, where would you like to take the first photo?" Todd asked as he started setting up his equipment. Leyla was giving him a helping hand, still glazing over him when she was abruptly interrupted by the manager.

"I need you to hold these, thanks," the manager said, shoving some papers at Leyla.

It took everything in Leyla not to snap on the manager. Leyla said to herself so she wouldn't say the words aloud: *Bitch, I will cut you down!* But the words that came out of her mouth were, "Ma'am, I can't hold these for you because I have other stuff to deal with." Then Leyla smiled and put the papers down on a table beside her.

The manager looked at Leyla as if she'd lost her mind for not holding the papers. As she walked away she said, "What type of help are you? If it was up to me your job would be over."

Leyla was about to let her have it but Todd gently touched her again and whispered, "Don't worry, I got this. I got you."

His words seemed to calm Leyla down some. He was going to get the manager back in his own way. "Okay, I need the group to stand over there," Todd directed them. Once there he said, "Now I need you to back up some for me, please, because the flash might hurt your eyes," he said to them and the manager.

"Exactly where do you need me?" the manager said sarcastically as she walked backward.

"Back up just a little bit more. The light isn't good for your eyes. Trust me on this." Leyla saw where Todd was going with this and she was trying not to laugh out loud.

"What about us dude? Will the light affect us?"

"No, no you'll be fine."

"Just back up a little bit more!" Todd shouted as he started snapping pictures of the rock group.

The manager had stopped about a foot away from a couple of duffel bags behind her. She took another step backward. "Woooo!" she yelled, falling backward right on her ass. All of them started laughing at her. She was the only one who didn't find it funny. She was so mad she grabbed her phone and called her boss to find out who was Todd's boss.

"Okay, now we can get to work," Todd said, looking at Leyla, giving her a small smile. She felt good that he had taken up for her.

The photo shoot went well and when it was all over their manager walked over to Todd and asked, "Where is your supervisor?"

"You're looking at him now and you can go. You needed to learn a good lesson on how to deal with people because your attitude stinks. Now, goodbye."

Leyla looked at her, laughing as the manager walked out highly upset at what had happened during the shoot. "Thanks Todd," Leyla said, kissing him lightly on the cheek and a spark sizzled between them.

Todd glanced at her. He actually liked the kiss she'd given him. He turned back to what he was doing, but Leyla saw his glance and what it said.

* * * * * * * * *

Terron and Carol sealed the deal with the lady who came to buy the penthouse. "Boy, you were great Terron. You did that with style. I need to incorporate those tactics into the sales approach I'm taking," Carol said, laughing and then smacked Terron on the back of his head.

"You better find your own client! That one's mine!" Terron said in a joking manner, chasing Carol throughout the penthouse. When he caught her he started tickling her, making her laugh out of control. His iPhone started ringing and when he saw it was Ashley calling on a secure line he stopped and answered it. "Talk to me."

Ashley was just getting into her black Alfa Romeo and it was just as equipped as Terron's and Todd's. Ashley didn't say a word until she took off into the air. "You're not going to believe this." Terron put Ashley on the speakerphone so Carol could hear what she had to say. "Well, I looked up the prisoner you told me about and guess what?"

"What did you find out?" Carol asked, walking over to Terron, waiting to hear what Ashley had to say next.

"The only thing that I was able to get on her was a name…just a name."

Terron and Carol looked at each other because that was weird. Ashley had the highest clearance there was among the Hatchet Men and Women at the HUWP prison. Both of them found this very odd. "Something's not right about this. But what did you find out about her?" Carol asked.

"The only thing I could find out is that her name is Cynthia and beside her name was written 'ancient one Hatchet Man Ghost' then the system very abruptly kicked me out. I've never seen anything like that before, ever," Ashley told them as she was checking her rearview mirror to see if anyone was behind her.

"Okay, we know we've got some investigation to do. Are you on your way here?"

"Yeah, I'll be there in less than twenty," she replied and got off the phone.

Terron and Carol found it strange that Ashley was not able to get information on the prisoner that came in that day. "So, what are we going to do?" Carol asked Terron as he walked over to a window, looking out of it. She walked up behind him.

"Well, we can't ask Mommy so we're going to have to figure it out on our own."

"But Terron, shouldn't you at least know about her because you're an ancient one, right?"

"Yes, that is why it's bothering me so much because I should have known her." Terron turned to Carol with a serious look on his face and said, "This is why I got to get down to the bottom of all this. I told you, the day she came to HUWP I felt something; and I got the same feeling that night at the club when I saw Jennifer."

"Oh, now you're on a first name basis with Jennifer?" Carol teased him, laughing.

Terron turned around and started chasing her around the penthouse again. One thing about Terron and his team, they loved one another and would ride and die for each other.

Chapter Eleven

Jennifer and Laura were almost home from the park. They stopped at a 7-Eleven in South Baltimore to get something to drink. Laura made two slurps: one for Jennifer and one for herself. Jennifer grabbed a big bag of cool ranch Doritos but as she walked toward the counter, she felt someone watching her. It made her stop and turnaround as she put her items on the checkout counter.

"Miss, is this it?" the woman behind the counter asked, bringing Jennifer back from her search of who could be looking at her.

Laura walked up and put the two slurps on the counter. "Add these to that, please," Laura said, smiling slightly at the lady as she paid her. Then she saw the look on Jennifer's face and tapped her sister on the shoulder, asking her if she was okay.

"Yeah, I'm fine. Let's go," Jennifer replied and both of them walked out and got into her Jeep.

Jennifer started looking in the rearview mirror, looking for anybody that she thought was watching them.

"Jennifer, are you okay?" Laura asked with some concern.

"Yeah, I'm fine. It just feels like somebody is watching us."

Laura started looking around as Jennifer backed out of the parking slot to head for home. "Well, I don't see anybody. I guess we're good, right?" Laura asked Jennifer, making her smile. "What's so funny?"

"You said that as if we've done something wrong, that's all."

Laura stuck her tongue out at Jennifer, making her laugh again as she turned up the volume to Spliff Star. They started singing in unison. It didn't take long for them to reach their house. They got out of the truck and went inside, hugging each other.

* * * * * * * * *

The Sevdeski family was mourning the loss of Joker Sevdeski. His mother took it harder than anyone else in the family. The viewing was at the family mansion in Moscow in Russia. It sat on 100 acres atop a hill with a one mile curving driveway up to the door. The only other way to get to the mansion was by helicopter. Over three dozen armed guards protected the perimeter around the mansion. The landscape was beautifully maintained by a dozen workers. The viewing of Joker was attended by mostly family and a few of Joker's friends. He left behind two young boys and his wife was pregnant with their third child. Some of Joker's girlfriends were there as well but knew to keep quiet.

Tony Sevdeski felt his wife's touch on his arm as his son, Emil, stood beside him. They walked her to the master bedroom as she cried all the way. Before they entered the double oak wood doors, she stopped and grabbed her husband with both hands, bringing him closer to her.

"I want you to bring the son-of-a-bitch to their knees! I want their wife to cry just like I am. I want you to promise me that Tony!" Mrs. Sevdeski told him in Russian-accented English. Tony nodded his head at her. She turned to Emil, grabbing him a little gentler and said, "I want to see the son-of-a-bitch who killed your brother before you kill him, Emil. Can you do that for your mother?" Emil nodded his head in a yes manner and she turned and walked slowly inside to her bed, sitting on its edge quietly. Her husband told one of their daughters to stay with her.

Tony and Emil walked outside to talk about what needed to be done. "Emil, what we need to do is call some backup and find out what government agency was behind this because we have no quarrel with anybody else. Everything with the Jamaicans is over, right?"

"Yes dad, and whoever was behind this were professionals on another level and it wasn't about drug turf. I feel it was about the weapon that we're working on getting."

Tony squinted his eyes at his son and said, "I do feel that, too, and that is why I'm calling some of our friends to have a meeting at a club in Ukraine. We're going to get the fuckers who took your brother, my son from us. Blood for blood. Now go get the helicopter ready to go to Ukraine." Emil nodded his head and walked off, getting on a satellite phone to call his team.

His father walked off across the grounds and pulled out his satellite phone and called in some help from someone he would have to pay a great deal of money to. But money was no problem at all for the Sevdeski family. Tony stood at 5'7" and weighed 175 pounds with brown eyes, black short, straight hair and a set of stained teeth. He was formerly KGB and when that organization was disbanded he became a part of the FSB (Federal Security Service) of the Russian Federation. And he still had a lot of friends in very high places.

* * * * * * * * *

"I want this done today! Not tomorrow, today!" Yolanda shouted as she walked into the control room at HUGP (Hatchet Man University Ghost Project). Their operations were in the cold Antarctic deep underneath the ice in the ocean. It was a large ice mass that was 100 feet in length and width, and seven feet in thickness with three feet of steel in between. The large sheet of ice ran on a hydraulic press that could lift the ice about 10 feet into the air with doors that could slide apart, revealing a hidden semisubmersible which could emerge from underneath the ice for incoming and outgoing aircraft without their being detected by any ships, other planes and submarines passing through that were not a part of HUGP. Deep down in the ocean, ice surrounded the base.

As Yolanda stood in the control room one of her Ghost-in-training walked in and said, "Ghost Leader, you have a call on Earth's landline. It's Mother Russia calling."

Yolanda's entire demeanor changed from angry to devilish. She left her second in command Ghost Leader in charge and walked down the corridor toward a padded room. Inside the room were several phones that were linked to seven contacts, representing each continent on Earth. Only one person from each continent calls on one of the seven phones. As Yolanda entered the room she closed the large steel doors behind her. She picked up the phone and asked, "Where and when?"

Tony was on the other end of the phone, looking out over the grounds of his property saying, "I just finished viewing the body of my oldest son. Now it's time to see what's in the shadows." That was code for Yolanda to start looking at some of the Shadow teams in New York. One thing about Ghost teams, they knew everything that was going on because Hatchet Men Ghosts and Shadows had a signature killing style, smell and when they were around each other they could feel each other's presence. But Hatchet Men Shadows hadn't seen a Ghost in over a century. They thought the Ghosts had died off, but that was far from the case. The Ghosts had been growing secretly underground.

"I'll call you in a few days with some information. What's your number?" Yolanda asked as she twirled a medicine ball in her left hand.

"Three a head."

That brought a smile to Yolanda's face because she was going to get paid three million a head for the job. She was going to take the job on her own, but she also didn't want to underestimate the Shadow team even though she was an Elder Ghost and could stand on the battlefield; could hold her own in the virtual reality training room; and she was very active, engaging in small battles, running back and forth to Tripueler to see Kali.

Yolanda needed a little background information on whether the Hatchet Men Shadows were involved in any way. Back in her control room she had her second in command to turn on the monitors. At HUGP they had the ability to see anything, anywhere in the world real time or they could go back in time. She had the Ghost to dial back to the night Joker was killed at the club and specifically focus in on Joker as well as any Hatchet Men Shadows in the vicinity. The monitor scrambled for a minute and then it cleared and she saw a voluptuous African-American woman playing with Joker's manhood. Her name popped up on the screen as "Leyla." Yolanda continued to watch them for a minute and whispered in an exasperated voice, "For God's sake, give the man some head, will you? I don't believe there's a class on killing with sex; she's an amateur."

On another monitor, a man was sitting at the bar gazing intently at a woman across the room. The name popped up as Terron. "Hmmm. What's the story behind you two?" she wondered as she watched them. She had her Ghost to identify the woman and others at her table. The names Jennifer, Laura, Tisha, Melissa and Jamey displayed over the heads of the women, identifying each. Yolanda nodded in satisfaction. The monitor also picked up another woman named Carol. When Yolanda turned back to the first monitor she saw Leyla walking quickly away from Joker.

Yolanda watched the monitors from all angles four times: first through Leyla's eyes, then from Terron, Carol, and Jennifer's eyes. Again, she saw how Terron and Jennifer looked at one another. "What the hell is up with y'all two?" Yolanda mused, watching them and then seeing Emil come into the club and find his brother dead and start flipping out. She watched everything and when the shooting started outside at the back of the club, she shouted, "Stop!" She told the young Ghost to turn the angle around to where the shots came from. Once he did, she started searching for the shooters.

And Yolanda found them, which brought a big smile to her face. She was able to see two shadows from a quarter mile away on the top of a skyscraper. To the human eyes they couldn't be seen but to the eyes of an Elder Ghost it was not hard to spot them although she couldn't see their faces clearly. Then the names Ashley and Todd popped up and she said, "Bingo." Now she knew there had probably been a Hatchet Man Shadow team involved in the killing. "Well, somebody knew how to cover themselves well. I can't wait to kill all of you," she said to herself. Yolanda continued to watch everything play out and by the time she was done, she had enough information to study Terron, his team, Jennifer and her group of friends. One thing was for sure, Yolanda was going to get down to the bottom of everything that very night.

Chapter Twelve

"As soon as I have some more information I'll get back with you. Where do I need to go first?" Yolanda asked the person on the other end of the phone line. She was leaning against a desk, twirling the miniature medicine balls in her hand. "The New York night club 4040? I'm on it. I'll call you when I got something," she said and ended the call. Now that she had identified the Hatchet Man Shadow team she went back to her control room to review everything again but in detail. If there was a camera in the room or on the street nobody was safe from HUGP. Sometimes Yolanda would catch a Shadow slipping and she would watch them.

"I need a visual of the 4040 Club in New York again," she told her second in charge. She leaned over his shoulder to look at the different ways she would perform the hit. She was on point with all the angles that showed how the Shadow team was able to set up the killing that night. "Okay, now give me a visual inside the club right before the shooting." The young Ghost typed in the data and when the inside of the club appeared on the monitor at the start of the night, Yolanda immediately started to put the puzzle together. Once she saw Leyla working as a waiter, she knew something was up. "Hold up, stop, now go back," she directed the young Ghost. "Stop there and enlarge her face for me." Yolanda started visualizing herself in the club, trying to insert herself as a member of the Shadow team. She looked over at the VIP area and knew that's where Joker and his friends would sit, but they hadn't arrived yet. "Okay, stop it right there until I get inside the virtual room. Then play it for me." She quickly strutted to the virtual reality room and once inside, told her young Ghost to start the simulation from the start of the night of the killing inside the club.

Yolanda started to scan the club as people were walking around. She saw the full length balcony on the upper level where the VIP area was located. She also saw four bars and two were shaped like horseshoes on the ground level. The other two were up top. She started walking around, looking for anything out of order. She saw the two spiral staircases that led to the VIP area and the DJ booth which sat higher than bar level. Then she looked at the four cages that had ladies dancing inside of them. As she moved on she thought she saw a face she knew. Yes, it was Terron casually checking out the exits in the room. She was watching his every move. It was as if she was there herself. But what really caught her attention was Leyla walking toward Joker and strutting her stuff for his men, making sure Joker's eyes were on her the entire time. Yolanda started smiling because she knew what Leyla was up to. "I see you jumping out of the shadows" she was thinking and continued to watch Leyla as she was walking through Joker's men, placing tracking devices on them. "Oh she good, real good," Yolanda whispered to herself as she watched Leyla make her way through the crowd of men to Joker. Even though the tracking devices were very small, Yolanda knew from centuries of training how to spot a

Shadow at work. She continued to watch the hologram of Leyla come down the stairs and walk down a corridor to meet Terron and Carol. "Come on, y'all can do better than that. You're such amateurs. I see you and you're supposed to be living in the shadows." She watched Terron pass what she bet was poison to Leyla and watched Leyla walk into the kitchen and slip the poison into a bottle of champagne. To the human eye, everything looked normal. But to an Elder Ghost it was not hard to spot. Yolanda yelled to her young Ghost to fast forward the simulation until she told him to stop. He did so until Yolanda shouted, "Stop!" She took a good look at the hologram of Terron talking to the bartender as he looked at Jennifer from the bar. But what she saw next really caught her attention. As Terron walked away from the bar he started glowing. "What the fuck?" she whispered to herself, taking a closer look. Yolanda looked at Jennifer to see if there had been a connection but she really couldn't tell. So she turned her attention back to Leyla who was with Joker again in the VIP section again, having sex. "That's the oldest trick in the book. Men are always thinking with their dicks and that's what caused his death." Yolanda could tell what caused Joker's death before it happened.

Once she finished reviewing all the details and had gotten all of the information she needed from that night, she had her young Ghost to stop the simulation and she walked out of the room and down the corridor to make some calls to her sister and brother to see if they'd heard anything. More than likely Tony had already put out a worldwide alert for the people responsible for his son's death. A group of young Ghosts walked past her and some of the young males couldn't help but check Yolanda out, but at the same time making sure she didn't notice them. Well, at least they thought she hadn't noticed them. Yolanda was a very beautiful Latin American woman. She was 5'6" in height with calm, brown eyes which could turn red with wickedness in a second. She was petite with long, black hair which had white and pink streaks. She had two tattoos on her body. One was a female warrior stepping on a dragon's neck, cutting the head off. The second tattoo was a hieroglyphic which read: *Born a Ghost die a Ghost. Daughter of Kali.* "I can see you watching me. Watch out before you catch a reckless eyeball charge," she called out to the group that passed her. The young Ghosts quickly turned forward and took off. With a smirk on her face Yolanda continued down the corridor to call her sister Maryse, to see if she'd heard anything.

* * * * * * * * *

Maryse was on it because she already had eyes on Jennifer and Laura in Baltimore. She was already working over a young Shadow, pounding her fist into his face. The 225 pound young Hatchet Man Shadow was tied to a chair in an abandoned warehouse in South Baltimore. She was questioning him, trying to get some information. Maryse was about to work him over some more but her iPhone started ringing. "It's your lucky second to breathe, but not hard," she told him. She walked over to where her phone lay and answered it. "Yolanda, what's going on, sister? I didn't get anything out of this young one yet, but it's far from over with him," Maryse said with a ghoulish look on her face as she looked at the young Hatchet Man Shadow tied to the chair.

"Well, see what you can get out of him, but I found something you might want to see. I'll send it to you." When they finished their call Yolanda sent Maryse everything that she'd seen in the virtual reality room."

Maryse took time to watch the video her sister sent her from the beginning to the very end on fast forward. Hatchet Men and Women have the ability to look at things and comprehend them faster than the normal human. When she was done she looked over at the young Hatchet Man Shadow with a devilish look and then a sinister smile. She casually walked over to him, crouched down and ripped the tape off of his mouth and said sarcastically, "I have all the information I need right here in my hands and head, so technically I don't need you anymore. But this is what I'm going to do for you. I'm going to give you a chance to save yourself."

Maryse stood up and walked over to a table about 50" from the young Hatchet Man and lay her phone on it. She turned to him and said, "This is what I'm going to do for you. If you can get this iPhone on this table within ten minutes, I will not kill you. Does that sound fair to you?"

The young Hatchet Man started laughing and shouted, "Just let me loose and I'm going to kill you!"

Maryse started smiling and walked toward him with a pair of wire cutters she pulled from her pocket and started to set him free

Chapter Thirteen

The moment Maryse cut the young Shadow free, he sprang into action. He leaped at Maryse, trying to grab her by her shirt. She leaped back, doing a backflip, kicking the young Shadow in the face, causing his mouth to bleed and him to stumble a few feet backward. He threw up his fists and his eyes blackened and he said, "Is that the best you got, bitch? Fuck that phone! I'm going to kill you!" He leaped into the air and Maryse did the same, pushing the palm of her hand into his chest, making him fly backwards through the air; but he was able to land on his feet. Maryse looked at the watch on her wrist. "You wasted two minutes," she said. The young Shadow glanced at his two titanium razor-sharp daggers beside the table. "Go ahead, grab them," Maryse taunted him. "From the looks of things you're going to need them, bitch!"

The young Shadow ran over to the table and quickly grabbed his two daggers. Maryse stood there smiling, waiting for him to come to her.

"Arrrrr!" the young Shadow yelled out, running toward Maryse, giving it everything he had as he tried to stab her.

But Maryse was too fast for him. She was moving her body in all types of ways, using her hands to block his daggers. She started backing up as the young Shadow kept advancing toward her. She quickly turned around, running toward a wall and the young Shadow ran behind her. Maryse ran up the wall, executing a backflip in midair. She was very good when it came to battle. She was an Elder and was not about to let a young Shadow take her down. She was 5'4" tall and weighed only 120 pounds with a petite, feminine look that could throw an opponent off until they went toe-to-toe with her. She came down out of the air, wrapping her legs around his neck so fast that the young Shadow couldn't believe it. Maryse smiled as she punched him in the face several times. He quickly started hitting her with his elbow two times before she was able to lock her legs around his arm.

The young Hatchet Man Shadow was twice her size and built like a world champion bodybuilder and stood 6' in height. He was not able to escape this 5'4" African American. She was a hazel-eyed beauty with shoulder length blonde hair and a pretty white set of teeth. But what separated Maryse about her from him, her hieroglyphic said: *I am the beginning of your end.* And there was a tattoo of a Watcher killing other Watchers. Fighting her in battle was like fighting five grizzly bears at once. He slammed her two more times before she broke his arm and immediately pushed him halfway across the room where he landed on his back.

Maryse flipped to her feet with her fists up to her face, taking deep breaths through the breathing holes all over her body to make herself stronger. This young Shadow just didn't know how old Maryse really was because from just looking at her you would think she was 23 years old because she stopped aging after her 23rd birthday. She was well over 500 years old and was one of the best of the best from the Ghost teams.

The young Shadow thought he had a window of opportunity because he had his two Southwestern Bowies. Maryse saw him glance at her, trying to scan her body for a weak point. This was something Hatchet Men did in battle with one another. She started smiling. "What's wrong little soldier? You want to stab me with your little knives…hmmm?" Maryse asked him sarcastically, making him become furious and breathing hard.

"Arrrr!" the young Shadow yelled as he charged toward her from across the warehouse.

Maryse just stood there, ready for him. She looked at her watch. "Your ten minutes are up now! It's time to die!" she shouted at him.

The young Shadow leaped into the air with both Bowies in his hands, twirling them around and then he tried to stab Maryse, but she was too quick for him. He flipped several times in the air still trying to stab Maryse, but she leaped above him, locked both her legs around his neck and made a clean break, killing him. As his lifeless body hit the floor, she leaped off of him, rolling twice before getting to her feet. She grabbed her iPhone and called Yolanda.

"Were you able to get anything out of him before you killed him?"

Maryse chuckled and said, "No, he was a tough one, but I think his iPhone will give me what we need. Just give me a few hours."

"Good, I'll see you soon then, right?"

"Sooner than you know," Maryse said to herself as she got off the phone, glancing at the dead young Shadow, saying out loud, "You never had a chance, boy." She started scanning his iPhone and then she ran across something she felt would help her and started smiling. "Well, well, well, what do we have here? It looked like a Shadow team was up and biding its time to go to work. Maryse grabbed her things and before she boarded her submarine she made sure to tell one of her young Ghosts to dispose of the body. Then she was on her way back to HUGP to join Yolanda.

* * * * * * * * *

Jennifer was downstairs in the kitchen making breakfast for herself and Laura. "Good morning, princess, and thank you," Chris greeted her as he picked up the coffee Jennifer had made for him. He lifted the cup to his nose, sniffing it and with a big smile started drinking it. "Damn, this is some good coffee, baby!" Jennifer smiled as she continued cooking breakfast. Wendy pulled up in the driveway and started blowing the horn. "That's Wendy," Chris said. He walked over to Jennifer and gave her a slight hug and kiss and said, "You two have a good day today. If you need anything, please call me, okay?"

"Got you dad and don't forget your lunch!" Chris had almost forgotten the lunch Jennifer had packed for him before she started cooking breakfast. He was headed for the door but stopped, letting Wendy inside. Laura had come downstairs dressed and grabbed a piece of toast, munching on it.

"Good morning Jennifer, good morning Laura," Wendy said as she walked into the house, closing the door behind her.

"Good morning Wendy. I made you a lunch bag," Jennifer said as she handed the bag to her.

Wendy started smiling and took the bag, saying, "Jennifer, you didn't have to. Thank you."

"I know Wendy, but y'all always working so hard so I took the honor to make you and dad something to eat."

Chris walked over and gave both his daughters a kiss on the cheek before he walked out with Wendy and they drove off.

"Laura take a seat and eat. We have some time," Jennifer told her as she ran up the stairs to get dressed.

"Uhhmoof!" Laura shouted with a mouth filled with food, letting Jennifer know she was eating.

Outside and a few houses from the Lins, Terron patiently sat in his car, waiting for Jennifer and Laura to start their day. When they finally walked out of their home, his iPhone started ringing. He transferred the call to his car's speakerphone so that he could keep his eyes on Jennifer.

"Peeping Tom," Carol teased, but Terron didn't find her funny.

"You're not very funny, Carol. Don't be mad because I found somebody good for me." By this time Jennifer and Laura had gotten into Jennifer's black Jeep Wrangler, pulled out their driveway and drove off down the street just like she always did. Terron had been watching her for a few weeks so he knew exactly where they were going to go next. He had her schedule down to a science for everyday of the week.

"I can't believe you're going to give her some diamond earrings, Terron, and you don't even know her. What's up with that?" Carol asked while she and Leyla got dressed for training.

"Yes, I'm giving her diamond earrings but you're forgetting what they're for, Carol."

"Yeah, whatever Terron. I know there's a tracking device in them but such a very expensive one. Why is that, ummm?" Carol questioned him, smiling slightly and giggling with Leyla as they continued to get dressed.

Terron didn't find it very funny at all because he did have his feelings tied into it; and knew if somebody at HUWP found out he would be put up on charges. "Carol, are we really going through this again? I thought I told you why already. Is Todd in place because I'm pulling up behind her at the coffee shop she stops by every day?"

"Yes, he's in position. Didn't you go over this with him about 100 times already?"

"Yeah Terron, you got my baby doing your dirty work," Leyla shouted in the background behind Carol.

"I would do it for you so what's the problem?"

"Nothing, big brother. You know we got your back," Leyla called out to him, smiling.

"Okay, because she and her sister are getting out their car to walk inside now," and he transferred the call to their earpieces so that they all could individually hear what would be going on with Todd. Carol took out her earpiece and motioned for Leyla to take out hers.

"Leyla, when are you going to tell Todd how you feel?" Carol asked, looking at Leyla with a straight face.

"I don't know Carol. I'm just not ready yet, you know?"

"No, I don't know because if it was me I would have told him how the hell I felt, flat out. So, next time you better tell him or I will."

Leyla turned her head and looked at Carol as if she'd lost her mind for about five seconds before she said, "You better not tell him because I would never do that to you." There was a pause and then both girls burst out laughing. They put their earpieces back in and started listening to what was happening with Todd at the coffee shop.

* * * * * * * * *

Todd was already on point, playing his part as a janitor working in the shop as he watched Jennifer and Laura walk inside the shop like they always do. He had been working undercover for two weeks and had built a good relationship with Laura, making Leyla jealous. But she knew it was part of the job. Todd went straight into action.

"Good morning Jennifer and Laura. How've you been?"

Laura started laughing before she answered. "I'm doing just fine now."

Todd gave a little laugh which made Leyla get slightly mad and she sucked her teeth and rolled her eyes. Carol tapped her with her elbow and Leyla gave her a crazy look. Todd knew something was going on between Carol and Leyla but he kept his cool while talking to Laura and Jennifer.

"Jennifer, you will never believe this but sometime yesterday a guy stopped by, giving this to me to give to you," he told her, reaching into his pocket and pulling out a small case that had the diamond earrings inside.

Terron was listening from outside in his car in front of the coffee shop, hoping that his plan would work. He started biting his fingers. Whenever Terron got nervous he would do that.

"Boy, I know you better not be biting on your fingers," Carol yelled into his earpiece.

"Carol, shut the hell up!" Terron told her, making Carol and Leyla laugh. Todd wanted to laugh but he kept a serious look on his face as he gave Jennifer the small box.

Jennifer and Laura looked very surprised. "What is it?" Laura asked with a little bit of nervousness in her voice as she slowly took the box from Todd's hand. However, her eyes almost popped out of their sockets when she slowly opened the box. She slammed the top closed and quickly tried to give the box back to Todd, saying, "I can't take these! You have to give this back to whoever gave it to you."

"I can't because I don't know the guy. He just told me to give it to you and that when the time comes you would know who gave it to you. I guess he knows you or something."

Terron heard Todd and started smiling, but listening and hoping that Jennifer would buy it, and she did.

"Let me see!" Laura asked, grabbing the box from Jennifer, looking inside and was just as amazed. "Yo', if you don't want these can I have them?" Laura asked a little sarcastically as she smiled.

Jennifer snatched the box from her sister, smiling once she had her hands on it again then her smile turned to a frown. "No, you can't have them!" Jennifer said, opening the box again and looking at the earrings, wondering who sent them to her.

"So, you're going to keep them, right?"

"Yeah, I guess. Thank you for giving them to me," Jennifer said. She sat the open box on the table and just looked at the earrings as Todd walked away.

"Okay playboy, are you happy now because we got some training to do today and we're running late." Carol said, hoping that Terron was ready to go train. "If we keep coming in late Tara is going to kill us so let's go now!"

Terron looked intensely at Jennifer's lovely, smiling face one more time and drove away from the coffee shop. He started thinking to himself that now he's got to figure out how to approach Jennifer later in the week.

"Now you and Todd need to get your asses here before Tara starts looking for the two of you. Let's go!" Carol shouted again and Terron started laughing and drove back to HUWP. Todd would meet Terron there.

Jennifer and Laura stayed at the coffee shop, drinking coffee and listening to music. Jennifer couldn't take her eyes off of the diamond earrings in the box.

"You know if you don't want them I will gladly take them off of your hands, you know," Laura replied, smiling as she took the box from Jennifer's hand. She took one of the earrings out of the box, trying it on. How do I look?"

Jennifer laughed and replied, "No, I'm going to keep them, so stop asking me and put that back in the box."

Laura rolled her eyes and sucked her teeth as she took the earring out of her pierced ear and put it back into the box. "Boy, you are lucky."

"Why do you say that?" Jennifer asked Laura while checking her Facebook and Instagram pages for any new posts.

"Because it's like the beginning of a perfect fairytale story: you get the right guy and he gets the right girl."

That made Jennifer smile because Laura felt she was perfect for somebody. "Why thank you, Laura for feeling that way about me. And since you feel so highly about me, you can wear the earrings first." Jennifer gave Laura a wink, hugging her tightly. "But just for today, Laura."

"Thanks, Jennifer, and you best to believe I'm going to rock them good!" Both of them started laughing and continued to drink their coffee.

Chapter Fourteen

"It's about time you girls got here. Come on before Tara starts wondering why we're not training," Carol said in an irritated voice to Terron and Todd. The both of them were quickly getting dressed.

"You ready, bro'?" Terron asked Todd as he zipped up the outfit he trained in. Their outfits were black and gray and made out of a strong, flexible rubber infused with Kevlar and 24-carat gold. There were small lines of silver throughout the suit, light sheets of magnesium and titanium. And, small lines of magnets and copper wire are integrated within the suit to help whoever is wearing the suit feel as if though the virtual reality simulations from the training room are real. It was almost like their exoskeleton wing suit. If the training is on a level 10 or higher, they could go into cardiac arrest if they're given a deadly blow in the virtual reality room. This mostly happens when a Hatchet Man Shadow goes up against a God. The suits also had a special tap-out button to quickly take them out of the training if they feel it has gotten too rough.

Terron and Todd both started smiling as they walked out of the dressing room together and headed for the training room. Carol, Ashley and Leyla were waiting for them. And this time, Terron had Carol to turn the level up to 15. At this level they would be training again with the hologram of Seth but, the Gods Eurus and Zeus would also join them in the training.

"You better know what you're doing big brother because if this comes back to bite us…ooohhh!" Carol said, pounding her balled fist into her other hand.

"Man I got this. We're good so chill. What we need to focus on now is this training we're about to face because last time it was no joke. I hope you're ready?" Terron asked, looking at all of them before they stepped into the training room. Everyone nodded their heads, looking at each other. Then the five of them walked into the room together and the doors closed behind them.

Everybody knew what was going on except the Elders. They were the only ones who didn't know yet. This was a forbidden thing for them to do. If they got caught they could be put in the hole and held up on charges because any young Hatchet Man Shadow has to get authorization from their Elder, and that was not going to happen. There were dozens of young Hatchet Men and Women Shadow teams above them in the balcony, cheering Terron and his team on as the lights went out and the virtual training began. "Okay Shadows, it's time to play. I hope you're up to it?" Terron challenged them as he pulled his two, twin gold and silver fully automatic Fn 57 pistols that shoot explosive rounds with two forty-shot extended clips.

The virtual reality room was set for the year 2025 in the old New York City in East Side Manhattan. This was a few years after the world went up in smoke. There were no flying cars, trucks, bikes or any type of hover vehicle. There were no maglev cities. Everything was on the ground. Carol, Todd, Leyla and Ashley walked over and stood beside Terron. Each of them had the same model guns as Terron and his team were ready to use them.

"So what's the plan?" Todd asked, scanning the area around them, making sure nothing surprised them. The hologram of Manhattan was at its worse. The city was in ruins with buildings barely standing.

"Terron, why in the hell did you pick this place to come to?" Carol inquired as she quickly pointed her guns at a movement which turned out to be a dog running towards her.

Terron started laughing, holstering his guns and responded, "Because stuff like that dog keeps us on point. We must be able to identify the good, the bad and the very ugly..." Terron's voice trailed off when suddenly they heard a rumbling from the sky as the ground started to somewhat tremble. At the same time all of them drew their weapons, ready to go. "Everybody look alive," Terron whispered, scanning the ground when about two hundred yards away he saw some Ghost-likes marching toward them.

"Do you see that?" Ashley whispered.

Terron signaled for them to split up into two groups. Terron and Carol went to the right of the street and Todd, Ashley and Leyla to the left. Both teams pressed their backs up against the ruined walls of a building.

"Terron, what's next?" Todd asked.

Terron looked all around, trying to see the best place to take down the army of Ghost-likes. Once he saw a location, he whispered through his earpiece, "Todd, I want you to get on the rooftop of that store. Ashley I need you right where you're at. And Leyla, are you up to being the bait, sis?"

"Oh, why the hell I got to be the bait?"

"Because, the bait has to be pretty enough for the Ghost-likes to want, come for her, and that's not me."

Leyla started blushing and responded, "Well, since you said it that way, sure I'm up for it."

"Carol, get to the top of the building and when I say 'go,' I need you to come from the sky, blasting their asses back to hell." Carol nodded her head and took off running to the building, running up a wall, scaled it quickly and got into position. The Ghost-likes were almost upon them. When they got within 50 feet of them, Terron whispered, "Leyla, now run your ass off toward Carol."

Leyla took off from behind the wall, shouting as she ran, and the Ghost-likes took the bait. A dozen of them started shooting at Leyla, causing her to quickly leap behind a wall and start shooting back because no one from the team had started shooting yet. Carol grabbed her Fn 57 fully automatic pistols and Terron kept his eyes on the creatures and whispered to Carol, "Not yet, they're almost within the drop point. Not yet. Come on…now Carol now!!" Carol shot her grappling hook into the building and took a running leap off the side of the building; shooting at the Ghost-likes with her pistols, killing them.

"Terron, are we going to help?" Todd asked, ready to get to work on the Ghost-likes, but Terron told him not yet.

Terron readied his pistols for what was to come next. Once Carol and Leyla had dispatched all the Ghost-likes on the ground, several dozen more came falling from the sky. It started to thunder and then rain started to fall very hard, making it almost impossible for them to see through their human eyes, but not through the eyes of a Hatchet Man. Their vision quickly adjusted to the weather. "Now!!" Terron yelled, running from behind the wall, shooting the Ghost-likes down. It was so easy for Terron and his team. Five Ghost-likes started charging toward Terron, making him leap into the air, executing several front flips with both of his pistols at his side, shooting three out of the five Ghost-likes in the head. He leaped onto the shoulders of one of the two left, wrapping his legs around its neck and shooting it in the head. He swiftly leaped off that one and onto the other one, twisting his body and snapping the Ghost-like's neck like a twig.

Todd was surrounded by seven Ghost-likes with flaming swords. He grabbed his Belduque and started destroying them one by one until they were all gone. The more Terron and his team excelled, the more the young Hatchet Men and Women Shadows came to watch them. Terron and his team were the best of the best. Carol, Ashley and Leyla stood back to back, reloading clip after clip until they were all gone. Ghost-likes kept dropping from the sky, but as fast they dropped they were liquidated.

"This was easier than I thought," Carol said as she scanned the skies for more Ghost-likes.

"Yeah, just a little bit too easy if you ask me. Keep an eye out," Terron said as he reloaded and started walking through the ruined city. "Come on, let's go this way." Terron took the lead and the rest of the team was right behind him. They started to walk over what was left of the Brooklyn Bridge.

Chapter Fifteen

"Terron, did you hear that?" Carol whispered, scanning the Brooklyn Bridge as they were slowly walking across it. The bridge was barely standing with cars flipped and overturned all along the entire length of the bridge. The bridge's sidewalk was destroyed so they had to walk around wrecked cars and trucks.

"Come on, we're almost on the other side," Terron told them as he crouched down with one of his pistols in his hand.

They came upon a wide crack in the bridge and had to jump across it to the other side. And from the look of things the area looked like a recently fought war zone. The more they walked the more spoils of war they saw. Several fighter jets screamed over their heads, making them look up. "What the fuck?" Todd snarled, pointing his weapon to the sky.

"Terron, I see something straight ahead," Leyla said and she took off running and left the bridge as she ran towards smoke and flames. The others ran behind her.

"Please, help me, please," a soft-speaking voice said from underneath some rubble on the ground. A building had collapsed on some people.

"Leyla, good job," Terron said. "Ashley and Carol set up a perimeter around the area."

"Miss, if you can hear me we're going to get you out. Just hold on, okay?" Leyla shouted. Then everyone heard booms going off a few blocks from them. They were on the other side of the bridge in Brooklyn.

"We're going to check it out!" Carol yelled and she took off with Ashley and Leyla, running in a crouched position toward where it sounded like an active war was going on.

Terron and Todd started digging, using their superhuman strength to lift big boulders out of the way until they reached the woman beneath the rubble. Once they pulled her out she disappeared back into the training area where all of the young Hatchet Men and Women were looking at the score board. They saw that Terron and his team got 50 points for saving the woman.

Back in the virtual reality room, Carol, Ashley and Leyla ran right into a war zone. Several dozen Ghost-likes were trying to overrun a small army of soldiers. "Ashley, take the right and Leyla get on the rooftop, now! I'm going to help them out on the ground. Go!" Carol, Ashley and Leyla moved like bolts of lightning. Carol zigzagged her way around the Ghost-like's fireballs until she got to the ditch where the soldiers were hunkered down. One of the hologram soldiers thanked Carol for her help. Lela and Ashley got in position and started shooting at the Ghost-likes, plucking them off one by one. Once the battle was over, the holograms of the soldiers disappeared back into the control area. The team received 100 points for assisting the soldiers.

Ashley and Leyla ran back to Carol. "Okay, where to next?" Ashley asked. No sooner had she asked the question, then the gunfire quieted down and the sky turned red. Rain continued to fall hard and right before the women's eyes large bolts of lightning from the sky began to hit the ground.

"Terron, are you and Todd seeing this? What the hell is going on?" Carol asked through her headset as they ran toward another ruined building for cover.

Terron and Todd were still helping people when they started to see the same red sky and lightning that the women were seeing. "I don't know, but where are you?" Terron shouted as he and Todd found cover after moving all the people into an adjacent building because the rain was coming down real hard and the wind had picked up speed. "We're about 100 kilometers away from you and Todd."

"Can the three of you make it back to us?"

"I don't know but we can try." Just as she said that, the front of the building Todd and Terron were in collapsed down on them. "Shit! It's going to take us some time, but we can get to you, Terron," Carol said.

"Well, it's going to take us some time," Terron said, looking at all the rubble they had to dig out of. "Watch your backs out there."

Carol had a look on her face she didn't want Ashley and Leyla to see. Leyla walked up behind her and her expression quickly changed as she turned around to face the two women. "We're going to make our way back to Todd and Terron. Keep your eyes open," Carol told them as she took point. The three of them started to fight their way through the storm.

"Carol, look!" Leyla shouted, pointing toward the right of them.

Carol and Ashley looked and couldn't believe what they saw. Three bolts of lightning hit the ground, making the ground rumble all throughout the virtual training center where the young Hatchet Men and Women were watching. "Carol we've got to move fast!" Ashley shouted, but right before their very eyes Seth, Eurus and Zeus appeared and started running toward the women.

"Carol, what do we do?" Ashley asked in an urgent voice.

Carol turned to Ashley and Leyla and her eyes became slits, making them turn reddish-yellow. "We fight in the name of the Shadows!" she yelled and all three women took off running towards Seth, Eurus and Zeus. They slammed their hands together, hard, making their birth weapons appear in their hands then they leaped into the air.

Ashley pulled out her steel webbing which was razor-sharp, throwing it around Zeus and making him stumble backwards; Leyla had her Southwestern Bowies in her hand as she charged toward Eurus; and Carol had her Katar in her hands as she was descending from the air onto Seth. Then Eurus, Zeus and Seth attacked the women at the same time. Seth grabbed Carol's Katar with two fingers and twisted her and her birth sword and threw them into a building. Carol hit the building so hard that an imprint of her body was left as she slowly slid to the ground. Her birth sword had ripped through the brick wall right beside her head, and barely missed her face.

Eurus shot Leyla in her chest with two lightning bolts, making her fly across the sky where the force embedded her into a ruined rooftop, knocking her out cold. Zeus grabbed Ashley's steel web net from her, balling it up into his hand and threw it at her with such power that it pushed her through three cars, causing her to flip several times where she landed on the ground. She was left disoriented and spitting up blood as she struggled to get back on her feet.

All of the young Hatchet Men and Women watching them on the scoreboard saw the impact the women's bodies were taking from the three hologram Gods and knew Carol, Ashley and Leyla should be taken out immediately. However, the system was set on a timer and only an Elder could stop the simulation. Ashley, under Terron's order, had set the timer for 20 minutes. In the past, most Hatchet Men Shadows wouldn't survive past five minutes when going up against one God, not to mention three of them.

"This don't look good for them," one of the young Hatchet Men Shadows said to a comrade.

Chapter Sixteen

Terron and Todd had finally dug their way out of the ruined building. "Carol, Ashley, Leyla do you copy?" Terron asked through his earpiece but got nothing. He and Todd started scanning the terrain with their long-range vision. What they saw made them take off running toward Carol, Ashley and Leyla with great speed. The women were fighting for their very lives against Seth, Eurus and Zeus. Terron and Todd's eyes turned reddish-yellow. "Todd, you go high and I'll go low!"

"Got it!" Todd took off, leaping onto the side of a building, moving posthaste up the wall. Terron glanced at Todd to see exactly where he was so that he could time his attack just right. Todd leaped into the air, banging his hands together, calling his Spanish Belduque birth sword and it appeared in his hands. He was able to leap down and stop Zeus before he gave a deadly blow to Ashley who was still down on the ground. "Ashley, get up! I need you!" Todd roared. He was barely able to stop Zeus. He was overpowering Todd slowly but surely. Todd had a grimace on his face as Zeus was getting the upper hand with his mighty sword pounding on Todd's Belduque.

Terron ran as fast as he could and slid underneath Seth as if though he was sliding for home plate at a baseball game. He reached Seth just as he held Carol over his head about to break her back. Terron kicked Seth in the leg, bringing him down onto one knee, making the young Hatchet Men and Women Shadows that were watching cheer him on. Seth tossed Carol into the air but she was able to land on her feet, sliding a few yards leaving an imprint of her feet in the ground. She was about to say something but Terron told her to go. So she took off to help Leyla fight Eurus.

Terron was able to scan Seth's body as the two of them slowly circled each other. Terron slammed his hands together and his two twin Tabar axes appeared in his hands. He couldn't believe how built Seth was. He stood at 12 feet and Terron was barely half his size and build. Terron noticed Seth's grayish-blue skin and that his eyes were bloodshot just like fire; and on Seth's spinal cord he had several breathing holes that made it very easy for him to break anything that came his way. On his deltoids, biceps, forearms and triceps were very huge muscles. Terron took a deep breath, cracked his neck and back, preparing himself to fight with Seth.

"Arrrr!" he shouted, leaping into the air, dicing and slicing his twin axes at Seth, but was not able to connect any blows because Seth was too fast for him. Terron hit the ground quickly sweeping his feet which caused Seth to fall on his back. Terron leaped into the air very quickly and was descending down over Seth, about to give him a deadly blow. But Seth extended his hand, making a lightning bolt shoot from his hand into Terron, sending him flying through the sky. Terron landed on his feet but before he was able to stop his feet dug up ground and buried him to his knees. Seth started charging toward him. Not too far away Todd and Ashley were fighting with Zeus. Zeus grabbed one of Todd's ankles as he was trying to kick him in the face and threw Todd into Ashley, causing them both to tumble into several cars like a bowling ball into pins. Zeus shot into the air and his shadow covered the sky above Todd and Ashley. Todd quickly grabbed Ashley, leaping out of the way just in time before Zeus stepped on them as if they were bugs. He made everything shake as his feet hit the ground. He stood at 13 feet tall and was strong enough to rip a skyscraper from out of the ground. He picked up a car as if it was a football and threw it with great force at Ashley and Todd. His 600 pounds of muscle made it very easy for him to do so. They dodged it, rolling several times over the ground.

"I'm tired of this shit!" Todd shouted, leaping to his feet. "H and H!" he called out. Todd's AA 12-assault shotgun, fully automatic, appeared in his hands. It could shoot 300 exploding rounds a minute. "Eat this! Arrrr!" Todd shouted again, shooting Zeus, causing him to stumble backward under the assault of the explosive rounds.

"H and H!" Ashley shouted, doing the same thing as Todd and from the look of things the double assault seemed to be working. Then Zeus raised both his arms and two shields appeared in his hands, blocking the exploding rounds from Ashley and Todd. Then he extended one of his hands and a lightning whip appeared. He whipped it out and wrapped Todd and Ashley within it and flung them into the air. Todd glanced back as they began to fall back down and saw that they were going to hit a bus, but he was able to grab Ashley to help her absorb the impact.

Further down the street, Carol and Leyla were in some trouble of their own. Eurus was throwing them back and forth around in the air as if they were rag dolls. "What the hell are these guys made of?" Leyla shouted to Carol, giving her a glance as she was flipping to her feet. Carol was breathing heavily as she scanned Eurus, trying to find a weak spot.

"The same thing we're made out of, just three times our size and a hundred times our strength. I'm trying to find a weak spot on him. Are you ready?" Carol asked.

Leyla nodded her head and both of them took off running toward the giant called Eurus, leaping into the air at the same time. Carol landed on Leyla's shoulders, leaping off just before Eurus created a sonic boom from his fist which hit Leyla, making her fly backward over the bridge into the water.

"Leyla!" Carol screamed as she saw her friend hit the water like a shooting star. Carol rapidly threw two flash bangs onto the ground, temporarily blinding Eurus. Then she dove into the water after Leyla, diving down to her and bringing her up to the surface, swimming with her as fast as she could toward land. She immediately started CPR on Leyla, giving her mouth-to-mouth. "Come on, Leyla! Breathe girl, breathe!" Carol glanced back to see what Eurus was doing and to her surprise, he vaulted into the water just as Leyla started spitting up water from her mouth and nose. "Are you okay?" Carol asked, rubbing her across the back several times in comfort.

"Yeah, I'll be fine. What about Eurus?"

Carol started helping Leyla to her feet. "Come on, we've got to move now!"

The two of them ran toward some ruined buildings to hide. Leyla was still a little shaken up from that hit from Eurus.

Chapter Seventeen

Terron was hidden from Seth in what was left of downtown Brooklyn. He ran into the subway but Seth started pounding the ground with his fist, ripping it apart as if it was paper. "You just don't stop, do you?" Terron silently asked Seth. Terron flipped over debris on the ground as he continued to run toward a dark train tunnel. He was able to make it back above ground and less than 50 yards away stood Seth, watching him. "How the hell is he able to find me so easy?" Terron asked himself. Terron knew there was only one thing to do: fight!

Terron grabbed his two battle axes and started charging straight towards Seth as Seth did the same toward Terron. Both leaped into the air together and the clash of their weapons sounded like an Earthquake and both flew into the air away from each other, hitting the ground hard. Terron flipped to his feet and so did Seth. They charged one another again but this time Seth ducked the swing of his two axes and punched him, sending Terron flying across the sky and through the wall of a building. He stumbled to his feet but Seth pounded down on top of him. He threw Terron across the ground and through several walls of a building where he was finally embedded into a truck. Terron was disoriented by this time and the scoreboard reflected that he'd taken a lot of beating and it was looking as if he would experience cardiac arrest pretty soon. Blood was gushing out of his mouth and nose plus, he was starting to get double vision which made it hard for him to see. Seth leaped into the air, extending his sword behind his head, about to cut Terron in half.

Carol and Leyla landed right in front of Terron just in time to block Seth's blow with their birth weapons. "Terron, get up now!!" Carol screamed just as Seth threw a bus at Carol and Leyla, sending them flying into a wall.

"No!!" Terron shouted, stretching out his arm to Carol and Leyla who were crying. All the young Hatchet Men and Women were just looking on in shock, not knowing what to do. Terron did his best to get to his feet but wasn't able to do so. By this time Zeus and Eurus were there standing with Seth. The three of them stood side-by-side. Terron struggled to get up again, but he'd taken too many hits from Seth. Eurus leaped into the air about to strike Terron with his fist but was blinded by a flash bang being thrown by Ashley and Todd. They quickly helped Terron to his feet.

"Don't worry brother, I got you," Todd assured Terron.

"What about Carol and Leyla?" Terron asked with concern.

"Ashley got them. Come on, we've got to go now!"

But suddenly, Todd was stabbed in the back by Seth and lifted into the air on Seth's sword. By the look on the Young Hatchet Shadows' faces and the scoreboard, Todd's body was about to enter into cardiac arrest.

"Nooo!" Terron yelled, leaping up into the air and twirling both of his battle axes in his hands, zooming in on Seth's right calf. Seth moved just like Terron thought he would, giving Ashley a clear shot at his right calf. "Ashley, aim low, now!!" Terron shouted and Ashley let loose her 300 rounds into Seth's calf, making him drop Todd right into Leyla's arms.

"I got you baby! Terron, what now?" Leyla cried out.

"Go! Get him out of here, now!" Terron urgently shouted just as Zeus punched him two stories into the air where he landed in what used to be the Supreme Court in downtown Brooklyn but was now just a pile of rubble.

* * * * * * * * *

Tara and Timtim were just landing on top of the semisubmersible and Tara was wondering why Terron and Carol were not there to meet her. "It seems your nephew and niece are at it again," Timtim said, knowing that Terron and Carol were up to no good. Two dozen Shadow soldiers met Tara and Timtim and the rest of the Elders that were with them, escorting the Elders to their quarters. Tara was not about to go there right now. She was upset.

"I told those two to stay out of the training room and stay off of mix level." Timtim started smiling and Tara glanced at him wondering what he was finding so funny. "What the hell are you finding so funny, Timtim?"

Timtim's smile faded and he stopped in his tracks, looking Tara directly in her eyes. "You know, just as I do, you can't stop a star from shooting, burning and most of all, feeling alive. I think it's time you tell them."

Tara was not ready to hear what Timtim was saying to her. All she had on her mind was finding Terron, Carol, Ashley, Leyla and Todd. And it did not take her long to find them because all she had to do was follow the young Hatchet Men and Women Shadows to the training room Terron's team were in and the rest was easy.

* * * * * * * * * *

By this time Terron had to separate himself from his team so they could get out of there. He told them to use their emergency "quit" button to leave the simulation, but they didn't. Terron left them and was staggering around the ruined city of Brooklyn when Seth, Eurus and Zeus landed in front of him and started surrounding him. Terron stopped and took several deep breaths, trying to prepare himself for what was next then Eurus punched him into Zeus and Zeus kicked him into Seth's hands that slammed Terron so hard into the ground it left an imprint of his body.

Ashley and Carol tried one more time to help Terron while Leyla stayed with Todd who was still unconscious, but it had no effect on Seth. Zeus saw them and threw them both into the ground. Seth stood over Terron, looking at him then leaped into the air, and was descending over Terron to finish him off with his sword when something amazing happened. A bright, white light shone blindingly over Terron's body and when he looked up he saw the same sword that helped him before — the Zweihander. Terron quickly grabbed it and instantly felt a power that was unbelievable running through his body, causing him to feel stronger than ever before. Seth's sword hit the Zweihander and Seth was sent flying over the Brooklyn Bridge and back to Manhattan.

Terron got up fast but everything was moving in slow motion. He turned to Eurus and Zeus and to his surprise they appeared afraid because they started backing up, trying to still stand tall, but he and the young Hatchet Shadows could see that they were acting differently and not the same as before. Terron took a good look at the Zweihander in his hand. "What are you, and where do you come from?" he whispered to himself. Then a power overtook Terron's body and his eyes turned into blue flames. He started grunting and at the same time charging towards Eurus and Zeus. Terron leaped into the air about several stories high and as he was about to come down onto them the two holograms disappeared as the simulation was stopped. Terron and his team were surrounded by three teams of Shadow soldiers along with his Aunt Tara and Uncle Timtim.

"Terron, you need to calm down, now!" Tara shouted, reaching out to him but Terron was too hot, just like a shooting star.

"Aunt," Terron muttered, and rapidly cooled himself down. Terron dropped to a knee and Tara told the soldiers to take him and his team to a holding cell until later and Todd to the jail's hospital. As the soldiers were taking them all away Tara stood there, watching Terron look at her like the little boy she always knew and loved.

Timtim walked up beside her and whispered, "You have to let him find himself because if you don't, one day somebody else might do it for you, and then what?"

Tara turned and looked into Timtim's eyes, crying a little but quickly wiping away any tears before anyone else could see them, and walked away.

At the jail, when Todd regained consciousness he saw that he was in the jail's hospital and knew they were more than likely in big trouble with the Elders. Todd sat up and rubbed his head as a nurse walked into the room.

"It's good to see you're back with us," the nurse said, smiling at Todd as she checked his vital signs. "Well, everything seems okay with you."

"What the hell happened?" Todd asked the nurse.

"You went into cardiac arrest but you pulled through, and I must say that's a first."

Todd had a confused look on his face. "What do you mean, that's a first?"

"Because every time somebody tries to go against the Gods at the level your team was at, they never make it."

"Hold up, you mean to tell me that nobody ever made it at that level before?" Todd asked. But by this time Tara and Timtim were walking into the room.

"That is right, Todd," Tara replied, looking at the nurse who knew to leave and she did so with haste.

"Where's the rest of my team?" Todd asked, trying to get out of the bed and stand on his feet. Several soldiers walked into his room, pointing their Fn 57 pistols at Todd's head.

Todd took a deep breath and slowly put his hands up stating, "So I guess we messed up this time, right?" Tara told the soldiers to take Todd to the Judgment Room and walked out.

But before the soldiers took Todd, Timtim told them to step out of the room so that he could talk with Todd. Once the soldiers were gone Timtim said, "Before you go up for judgment make sure you talk with Terron and the rest of your team. You're going to have two choices."Todd knew that one of the choices was death, killed on the spot. "I'm listening."Timtim started smiling and said, "Good. Well you know one is death and your second choice is a very dangerous mission in the mid-East to finish the job you started at that club by taking out the remaining Russian mobsters."Todd was a little bit confused because Timtim was telling him instead of Terron. But Timtim knew that so as he was walking out of the room he stopped at the door and said, "Todd, you must tell Terron not to buck this job and for him not to argue with any of the judges because he will get your team killed for not listening to rules! Rules have been in place in our society for eons. Without rules our very structures would fall overnight. So I tell you so you can tell your comrades while you're in the holding pen together." Timtim turned around and fully faced Todd and continued, "Terron has a greatness inside of him that has a need to come out. All of you do, but he is very different than others and I'm very sure you know that." Timtim turned back around and walked out, leaving Todd thinking hard.

Tara didn't want Todd to see her so she was waiting around a corner for Timtim and asked, "Did you tell him what I wanted and expected of them?"

"Yes, I did. Now the rest is up to them." Tara had a worried look on her face because she knew that she and Timtim would not be judging them alone.

Once Todd was taken to the holding cell where the others were, one of the soldiers started taking the glove-like manacles off. They were made of titanium, rubber and had gold stripes, metal nets and magnets. They fit a prisoner's hands perfectly and tightly. After the prisoner's hands were inside the gloves, the soldier turned on the magnets with a remote control causing the prisoner's hands to ball up into fists and the magnetic pull would bring his hands together, making it impossible for him to separate them.

"Terron, Ashley, Carol, where is Leyla?" Todd asked once the manacles were off and the soldier had left.

"She's being held in another holding cell. Wait, they're bringing her back now," Ashley said as she was looking out the laser bars, being sure not to touch them.

Two soldiers brought Leyla inside the cell. As soon as her manacles were off she ran to Todd, giving him a big hug. "Whoa, I'm happy to see you, too," he responded, hugging her in return. Leyla went even farther, giving Todd a passionate kiss. "Whoa, I didn't see that coming," Todd said in surprise.

Carol walked over to them and said with sarcasm, "I wanted to tell you that Leyla had a thing for you, but I was never able to tell you. I guess you know now."

Todd was at a loss for words. But he knew that he had to tell Terron what was told to him by Timtim. Nevertheless, he grabbed Leyla by her shoulders and whispered into her ear, "We'll continue this conversation about us, but right now I have to tell Terron and the rest of you what was said to me by one of the Elders." Leyla was somewhat in a trance by Todd's words but she was able to give him a head nod meaning she understood.

Chapter Eighteen

The Elders sat inside of the judgment chamber having a discussion about Terron and his team and what needed to be done. The judgment chamber was almost like a federal courtroom but more upscale. Five Elders would sit on the bench, judging Terron and his team. Tara, Timtim, Barrin, Backgril and Zenny would be the judges today. All five of them put on their traditional black and midnight blue robes with gold stripes. They sat in soft leather chairs positioned at a higher level than where Terron and his team would be standing. There was a bannister above their heads that had big, bold words inscribed that read: *"In Isis, Osiris, Lugh, Sorey, Ra, Hera, Lu Tung, Ares, Poseidon and Ho-sien Ku, We Trust."* The walls were thick, oak wood with ancient hieroglyphic writings and Egyptian symbols trimmed in gold. There were different galaxies on the walls in full color. The rug on the floor was gray, very thick and soft. In this court process the defendants stand and to the Elder's surprise, Isis was watching on the screen.

"Isis, this is unusual. What brings you to judgment today?" Zenny asked with a little worried look on her face.

Isis looked at her smiling, showing her lovely pearly, white teeth. "No, I decided to sit in on this one. I'm just here, but I will give no ruling."

Zenny whispered, "Thanks." Then she told the soldiers to bring Terron, Todd, Ashley, Carol and Leyla into the judgment chamber for judgment and sentencing.

Once summoned, it took about five minutes for the guards to return with Terron and his team because there were so many young Hatchet Men and Women Shadows in the corridor, cheering the team on.

"Why is everybody cheering and chanting our names," Leyla asked Todd.

"Because nobody ever made it as far as we did in the simulation room and lived."

When the team heard that, it made them feel very strong. Young Hatchet Shadows were running up to them, wanting to just touch them. The soldiers had to form a circle around the team to keep them from being touched. This was the first time they'd had to be judged before. As the judgment chamber doors opened and Terron, Carol, Ashley, Leyla and Todd walked inside, all the judges, even Isis, were looking, trying to see what the commotion was all about. One of the soldiers told the judges, "All of the young Hatchet Men and Women Shadows were trying to touch them. We had to put up a wall to stop them, Lady Tara. I'm going to have my team disburse them."

However, once the doors closed you hardly heard any noise. Tara was about to say something but Isis wanted Terron and his team to know she was there watching and said, "No, leave the young spirits alone. This is the first time in ages anyone got as far as they did," Terron turned to Isis, slightly smiling, but she was not done speaking yet, "even though they broke all the rules and the rules are there for a reason." Her smile went away and was replaced by a stern look at the entire team. Terron's smile went away, too.

Tara and the Elders didn't know what to say and just looked at one another because Isis had said she was not going to butt in. Isis turned to Zenny, nodding her head for Zenny to take over; and she did quickly because Terron was her son. "Terron Elenius, Leyla Jones, Ashley Carne, Carol Caine and Todd Green you are brought here today on charges of disobeying direct order 151 from the Elders. How do you plead?"

Terron was the leader so he was the one who would make a statement; nobody else unless he told them to. Terron was going to do all the talking today. He looked at every one of his teammates and smiled, whispering, "Trust me, I got this." Todd immediately dropped his head because he knew Terron was going to do what he wanted to do, not what he was told to do, and this could be their death sentence if the judges didn't see eye-to-eye with them. And to make matters worse was something that didn't happen a lot: Isis was watching.

"We plead guilty with reason!"

Zenny and Tara's hearts dropped into their laps. Timtim, Barrin and Backgril supported their chins with their hands. And even Isis stopped what she was doing to listen attentively to what Terron was about to say next. Plus, everybody at HUWP were watching on multiple TV screens throughout their base. You could hear a pin drop on the ground.

Terron took a deep breath and said very firmly, "I know what I told my team to do was very reckless, dangerous and suicidal, but for the sake of Tripueler, Earth and our very survival as Shadows something has to be done. From my recollection nobody for centuries, no Hatchet Man or Woman Shadow, have been able to go up against a God and get us as far as we did. Not to mention it was three Gods and we survived. I swore an oath to withhold and I'm going to live by it. We have to be ready to fight whenever and whoever. I mean no disrespect to any of the Elders or Gods that I swore an oath to. I just want to be able to do my part as a Hatchet Man Shadow, that's all. And if that's too much then I'm sorry and ask that all punishment be placed on me."

Terron turned his attention to Isis and continued. "I don't know what it is inside of me, but I have an urge inside of me telling me what I need to do so that our will on Earth can be done. I have a fire inside of me wanting to come out that I can't explain. I just feel it!" Terron stopped and dropped to one knee, but Isis told him to stand.

"Terron, you have broken rules but in this case I see good and reasonable cause why you did what you did. But your crimes can't go unpunished because of the high risk for copycats. You already know what you have to do. Now, the question is, do you accept?" Zenny and Tara were hoping he accepted the mission that Todd told him about earlier.

"Yes, and with honor we accept."

All of his comrades cheered him all throughout the HUWP base. Terron looked at his team and smiled. Zenny quickly dismissed them from the judgment chamber. When Terron and his team walked out of the double doors it was as if they were stars walking down a city street, but instead they were on a semisubmersible deep out in the ocean.

"Terron, man we're stars! Look!" Todd shouted, looking at all of the young Hatchet Men and Women trying to touch them. The soldiers escorted the team to their quarters. "Man, this is starting to get real crazy, dude," Todd said, looking at Terron, waiting on his response.

Terron cracked their door a little and saw dozens of young Hatchet Men and Women Shadows outside. "Damn, we really did it!" Terron said, closing the door and leaning against it, thinking to himself.

Ashley and Carol walked over to Terron, smiling, and Carol said, "So what do we do now, big brother?"

Terron glanced at all of them and said, "We're going to do this mission and then I'm going to get my girl."

Carol punched Terron in the arm, making him laugh. "So, she's your girl now, right? You better not get us caught up with this girl, Terron, for real!" Carol told him, pointing her finger in his face.

"Man, I got this, sis, just chill. Todd, start putting together what we're going to need for the mission."

"Got you."

"Ashley, I need you to come up with a real good entry and exit plan. Can you do that?"

"Can a cat lick its balls? I got this," she replied.

"Carol, I need you to check out what and who we're going up against and Leyla, you need to get whatever contacts we have there on the ground and what we'll travel in.

I got you, baby," Leyla responded and went straight to work.

"Todd."

"Yeah bro'."

"Make sure you pack me something very big, okay?" Terron said.

A devilish grin appeared on Todd's face as he replied, "I got you. Trust me." All of them went to work, preparing themselves for the mission.

Chapter Nineteen

Terron, Carol, Todd, Ashley and Leyla walked toward the Sikorsky CH-53E super-stallion cargo helicopter as it landed on the semisubmersible. On the roof of the semisubmersible, young Hatchet Men and Women Shadows were cheering for Terron and his team. "This is unbelievable," Carol said as she was looking at everybody cheering them on.

"What's so unbelievable?" Terron asked Carol, glancing at her.

"The way they're all cheering our names. Okay, enough of the star treatment. Let's get focused on what we're about to deal with," Carol told all of them as they boarded the helicopter. She yelled out each area as she started doing the system checks: exoskeleton suits, shock absorbers, rocket launchers, taser darts, heavy weaponry, Kevlar body armor, shoulder armor, and camouflage systems, scuba diver systems, grappling hooks and jet fuel systems. Everybody checked off and Carol yelled, "All systems a go!"

"Whooray!" the team cheered together. Carol gave a thumbs-up to the pilot and she took off.

"Okay, listen up. When we get there who do we have on the ground for escort?" Terron asked.

Leyla went straight to work, pulling up a virtual touchscreen of the ISI (International Service Intelligence) they had on the ground. "His name is Sim and he goes back 10 generations of good service to the HUWP." The team took a good look at Sim because this was the guy they would have to trust with their lives once they were on the ground. "What's up with our weapons?"Todd started smiling as he responded, "I thought you would never ask, Terron. We have Fn 57 pistols and AA12 assault shotguns, fully automatic that shoots 300 rounds a minute. And for you, Ashley, I got this." Todd gave a wicked wink at her before he showed her the ADS assault rifle that shoots over 700 explosive rounds underwater at a range of 25 meters. Then for Carol, Todd pulled up on the virtual screen a camouflage SA sports Empire Beast that has the speed of 1000 feet reverse cam efficiency and mechanical aluminum parts with illuminated scope and the quiver set up like a backpack carrying over 300 rounds of explosive carbon arrows.

"You're going to make a girl kiss a boy," Carol said gleefully as she downloaded the virtual model into her exoskeleton suit. "I'm going to love this shit here!" Carol was like a kid in a candy store.

"Okay, we'll be there in two hours," Terron said. "I want everybody to stay sharp once we hit the ground because it's going to get ugly. But we're Shadows and we always get through. Ashley, show us what we're walking into."

Ashley pulled up the area where they were going to hit, looking for the Russian gangsters. Ashley began explaining the layout of the base they would be attacking. It was a mini-fortified fortress high up in the middle of some mountains. This was not going to be an easy mission for them because they had to get the Russians at their base before they transferred the nuclear warheads to North Korea. At the bottom of the mountain were several dozen soldiers with assault weapons and heavily armed vehicles with K9 advance units from Hatchet Men Ghost teams. The dogs can detect anything once they were on the ground. "Okay, for some reason these dogs were left behind with them by some Ghost that used to work with them back in World War II," Ashley pointed out.

"I wonder if there are any Ghost teams left on Earth." Leyla said with a quizzical look on her face.

Ashley looked at her and said, "We'll find out in due time." Then she continued telling them about the layout of the mountains. "Ghost teams helped them build this place and we're going to help destroy it. Now in the middle of this mountain is a MS6 rocket repel missile station. Right above that are XKM tracer missiles that can take down a mountain, and right above that are four remote controlled 175 caliber machine guns, one on each side of the four corners of the mountain. And, at the very top is a small runway for a plane and a helicopter pad with an EMP that goes off every 10 minutes. There is also a watchtower with sonar that can pick up anything in the sky within 10 miles of the mountain."

The team knew they would have to rely on their exoskeleton suits once they were within 10 miles of their jump point. They would also have to rely on their jet packs to get them as close as possible without being detected. "So is everybody ready for this?" Terron asked, looking at his teammates one by one.

"Fuck yeah!" Carol shouted as she made a fist and raised it up and the rest of the team did the same.

The pilot told them they would be over the area where they were jumping in less than two. The five of them put on their helmets as the back of the cargo doors opened. "This is it! Wooo!" Terron shouted as he jumped and the rest of the team followed. The night would give them a little bit of cover but their advanced camouflage suit made it look as if they were a part of the sky.

"Jet packs, now!" Carol shouted through their earpieces.

All of the team activated their packs and took off, moving quickly. They were 4,000 feet into the air and dropping quickly even though they were using their wing suits to help them slow down. They had to get within the area of the mountain before they ran out of jet fuel as well as turn off their jet packs before getting detected by the gangsters. Timing was everything on this mission.

Chapter Twenty

Ashley was looking at her watch so that she could tell everyone else when to turn off their jet packs. "60 seconds to shut down!" came through their earpieces. Terron was in the middle of their formation and Carol was to the right of him. Ashley was to the left of Terron, Leyla was to Ashley's left and Todd was beside Carol. All of them had their jets on full throttle.

Carol looked at Terron and said through the earpiece, "When we turn off these jets we're all going to have a word with you about your little friend from the coffee shop." Terron couldn't say anything because if anybody was to find out what he was doing, he could be stripped of his rank and thrown into jail.

"Twenty seconds and counting!" Ashley shouted, glancing at her watch to make sure they turned off their jet packs in time. She started her countdown at ten and when she got to one she shouted, "Now!" One by one they quickly turned off their jet packs, cooling them with nitrogen gas.

Leyla glanced at Todd and saw that he was having trouble with his suit. "Todd's in trouble!" Leyla shouted because his nitrogen gas was not working. They only had about three seconds once they got in range of the Russian base and radar could pick them up. Todd couldn't get his nitrogen gas to work so he just disengaged the jet pack so they wouldn't be detected by Russian radar.

"Well, we know we're not leaving by using our jet packs," Terron said as they were free-falling toward the only blind spot on the mountain. The team was in a circle, free-falling fast. Carol asked Ashley how long it would be before they hit the ground.

"We've got three minutes before the EMP goes off again," Ashley told Carol who then turned her attention to Terron. "Now, you and this chick; what is really going on, bro'?" Carol was about to give Terron a lecture on Jennifer.

Terron knew he had to keep it real because they were all putting their lives into this mission. "Look, I'm going to keep it real with you. I really like this girl and I want to see her again. I don't know what it is about her but I felt something the first time I saw her."

"Was it in your pants, Terron?" Carol teased, making everybody laugh except him.

"No Carol, not in my pants. It's something I can't explain. It's something like I feel when I'm with y'all but very different." All of them looked at each other before Terron said anything else.

"Terron, she's not one of us, bro' but I'll back you on it," Todd said, giving Terron two middle fingers up before pushing off from the pack.

Terron turned to Carol and she did the same as Todd. So did Ashley, but Leyla gives him the middle finger as they all pushed off from him. Terron started smiling at that and pushed downward.

As they got closer to the ground, the magnetic maglev system that was built on Earth slowed them down just in time because the EMP went off. Once they were on the ground with weapons up and all systems on go, Terron took the lead with Carol behind him, Ashley behind Carol with Leyla behind Ashley with Todd bringing up the rear. It was completely dark on the mountain but their eyes instantly adjusted to the darkness.

"How much time do we have with the dog repellant before them damn dogs find out we're here?" Carol asked Ashley.

"Ten minutes and then they're on to us," Ashley told her, looking at the two guards ahead of them. She nodded to Terron, letting him know she was going to take them out.

Terron nodded his head and at the same time saw three other guards that he was going to put down. Both of them started making their way to the guards. Ashley was crouched down with both of her Knight Templar razor-sharp daggers, one in each hand. She circled around and came up behind them, directly in the middle. There were sandbags on each side of each guard which kept them from seeing her. She took a deep breath and as she exhaled she vaulted over the sandbags, bringing her hands in quickly with both daggers in her hands then pushing them out and throwing both of the Knight Templar daggers at the two guards, hitting them in their heads and taking them out. Ashley's feet touched the ground before the guard's bodies did.

Not too far away, Terron crept up on the three guards that were equipped with Beretta AR-70s, talking and drinking when they should have been looking out. Terron had already planned in his head what he was going to do to them. He crouched down and started creeping slowly towards the box of supplies that were stacked up like a small wall. He lightly clapped his hands together, making his birth axes appear in his hands. Terron's facial expression changed to that of a predator in the jungle about to kill his prey as he started to take a few deep breaths. On his last breath he leaped over the boxes of supplies, throwing both axes and killing two of the guards. The third one turned right into Terron's fist. Terron stood over him and kept pounding him in the face until he was dead.

"I'm up," Todd whispered, crawling toward five guards and Leyla flanked his left side.

"Whenever you're ready," Leyla whispered back, taking deep breaths as she watched the five men.

Todd banged his hands softly together, making his birth Spanish Belduque appear in his hands. Leyla did the same, making her Southwestern Bowies appear in her hands. When Leyla heard Todd say, "Now!" she sprang into action, throwing both Bowies into two of the five guard's chests, killing them. Todd leaped into the air, landing on two of the guards with his Belduque slicing and dicing the other three before they could pull their Beretta model 72s.

"We're in," Leyla reported.

Carol was already going into action with her Katar in her hand, crouched down low and moving in fast on the three guards sitting in a tent laughing and drinking. Carol stabbed the first one through the tent, making an entrance through the hole she'd made. A second guard tried to grab his Glock model 30 45mm from his holster but Carol quickly cut off his hand and stabbed him in the heart. Blood spurted into the third guard's face and within the blink of an eye Carol stabbed him in the forehead, killing him.

Terron walked into the tent and looked at the carnage Carol had wrought. "Damn, couldn't you have done it a little…bit less mess…hmm?"

Carol looked at Terron and said, "I got the job done right. Now let's go." She wiped the blood off her onto a dead guard's body and walked out of the tent.

Terron just started smiling and shaking his head as he said, "It's going to be a long night." He took the lead and the others followed him as they continued on their way up to the top of the mountain.

* * * * * * * * *

Tony Sevdeski and Emil Sevdeski were both on top of the mountain with over five dozen men and women, fully armed with Marks carbine choice Anderson AR-15s, drinking some Louis XIII, having an early celebration. The North Koreans were coming to get their nuclear weapons and they were almost there. "This is going to be good for us but let us not forget about my son! To Joker!" Tony said, looking at his son, Emil, and all the soldiers making the toast with him.

Emil called on his satellite phone to see how far away the North Koreans were. He ended the call and started smiling and said, "Our allies are here. We should be seeing them soon. Turn off the EMP!" Emil walked over to his father who had a sad look on his face.

"Emil, we must not forget about Joker and those damn Hatchet Men. I want their bodies in front of your mother, alive, so she can decide what to do with them."

Emil saw the look in his father's eyes and could see that he was very hurt. He gave his father a big hug and kissed him. "I won't let you down, dad. I'm going to kill them damn Hatchet Men for Joker," Emil promised, walking away toward the helicopter landing pad. Tony kept on drinking.

Chapter Twenty-one

Terron and his team continued to kill as they made their way up toward the top of the mountain. "How much time do we have before the dogs can smell us?" Carol asked Ashley.

"About one minute," she replied.

Terron had his eyes on some of Tony's men that had SLR 106ur caliber 5.56 with a capacity of 30 and barrel length of 8.5, ready to kill; but their downfall was that they were drunk. However, they had dogs that were very fast because they were former Ghost team dogs and Terron knew it. "Those dogs have been around for centuries. It's going to be a shame to kill them," he said

Ashley crouched down beside Terron and said, "I know, right? Such a damn waste."

"Maybe not, Ashley," Carol whispered. "We can use our taser darts, but we got to be quick about it. So what do you think?"

Terron and Ashley both agreed to do it. "Let's get to work," Terron said and they went into action. Carol and Leyla used their taser darts to take out the dogs. Terron, Todd and Ashley killed the guards with their birth weapons.

* * * * * * * * * *

Emil and Tony were outside, watching the North Korean's five helicopters fly toward them. "This is going to be a good day my son. And after this we're going to get them damn Hatchet Men one by one." No sooner had Tony uttered those words when they heard missiles launched from their mountain, shooting down each of the five helicopters from the sky.

"What the hell is going on?" Tony screamed in disbelief. Emil started yelling to his men to go and check it out. The dogs started going crazy when Tony shouted, "Let the damn dogs go, now!" The guards released the hounds and they took off running toward the lower level of the mountain. "Emil, they're here! I can feel them!" Tony yelled, grabbing a Colt AR-15 Az government model that shoots explosive rounds; and each bullet was hand-packed with Semtex made to kill Hatchet Men. Tony started running behind the dogs.

"Dad!" Emil shouted, running to grab a Heckler and Koch model USC carbine caliber 45 Acp, and took off right behind his father.

"I'm going to kill them!" Tony kept shouting as several guards ran alongside him.

Emil looked up to see the debris falling from the last helicopter blown out the sky. "Fuck!" Emil called out as he ran down the porch steps.

* * * * * * * * *

Terron and his team were slowly creeping their way down a brick corridor in the mountain. "We've got company and they're coming in hot!" Ashley suddenly shouted.

Terron zoomed in with his eyes and saw about a dozen dogs out front. "We got dogs! Taser now!" Terron ordered. But these dogs were able to quickly maneuver out of the way of the taser darts.

"Fuck! We're going to have to..." Before Ashley could finish her sentence she was attacked by one of the dogs. It slammed her up against the wall and started shaking her arm which was gripped between the dog's sharp teeth. These dogs were not your ordinary German shepherds. They had the jaw pressure of a lion, the claws of a tiger, the speed of a cheetah and the strength of a gorilla. Their genetic makeup extended as far back as five centuries in the making. "I need some help over here!" Ashley yelled, fighting with the German shepherd, trying to snatch her arm away from its grip. Terron had to focus on the other two dogs that were charging toward him as well as more guards who had started shooting. He banged his hands together and his birth axes appeared in his hands. Terron smacked both dogs with his axes, sending them flying off the side of the mountain. Ashley couldn't get a good shot on the dog with her other hand because she had to stop the dog from taking her arm off with her free hand.

But Leyla ran through the gunfire, flipping and rolling, maneuvering through the dogs as well as the guards advancing on them. "I got you, sis!" Leyla shouted, leaping into the air, taking aim and shooting the dog three times, killing it. Once Ashley got her arm free she looked at it. If she was a regular human she would have lost her arm and more than likely her very life. "That damn dog was really trying to take my arm off."

"Damn, he got you good. Wrap that shit up. We got to keep it moving," Leyla told her brusquely, masking her concern. Leyla covered Ashley while she tended to her arm then both women started running, shooting at the guards shooting at them.

Carol was running through the heavy gunfire, leaping over sandbags, flipping over the ground and when she landed on her feet she had her SA Sport Empire Beast in her hands, letting loose explosive rounds, killing anything in their way; and with her Semtex, C4 and fire arrows. Then she shouted through her earpiece, "I got Tony and Emil in my sight!" She aimed and whispered, "I got you now," then suddenly, there was an explosion!

* * * * * * * * *

Tony and Emil continued on, running toward the gunfight. "I want all of them dead! None of them are to get away!" Tony shouted as he started shooting at Todd, running toward him.

Then suddenly, an explosion went off, separating Emil from his father. He was stumbling, trying to stand up. His vision was blurry and his ears were ringing. "Dad, where are you?" Emil called out, stumbling his way through the fire as he looked for his father. He saw some of his men on fire, screaming for help as they ran past him. Emil continued to look for his dad but couldn't find him. Then he saw Leyla killing some of his men with arrows of fire. As he took aim to kill her, Todd leaped into the air, throwing several knives, stabbing him in the back. Then he ran his Spanish Belduque across his throat so that he could bleed out slowly. Emil fell to his knees, gurgling and holding his throat as blood ran down his fingers and hand. Emil looked at Todd, trying to grab his leg. Todd pushed his hand away.

Tony was on the ground, bleeding profusely from the blast that had separated him from his son. Terron walked over to him and started smiling as Tony was struggling for air. "It's over Sevdeski. It's all over," Terron told him, looking into a dying man's eyes.

"This…is far…from…over…" Tony gasped out, taking his last breath as his soul passed on.

Carol ran to Terron and said, "We got the nuclear weapons. Everything's a success! It's time to go."

Everyone back at HUWP were cheering Terron and his team on, even Tara and Timtim. "Our ride is here and our contact, Sim. It's time to go," Leyla told everyone. Sim was from Iran. He was six feet tall and 210 pounds of muscle. He had brown eyes, white teeth, a full beard with long black hair and he dressed very well. As Sim walked toward the group, Leyla called out, "Sim, it's good to see you."

"No, it's good to see you. I see you're still working out, yes?"

Leyla started blushing and quickly glanced over at Todd to see his reaction, but Todd didn't show any.

Ashley walked over to Todd for some help and to get his attention off of Leyla and Sim. "Hey Todd, can you help me out?"

"Yeah, what's up?"

"Take a look at this. Damn, this shit hurts," Ashley grimaced as she showed him the dog bite on her arm.

"Yeah, that does look bad. Let me get something for it." Todd walked over to his pack to get something for Ashley's wound.

Leyla quickly walked back over to Ashley and whispered, "Was he jealous?"

Ashley smiled and said, "Yes, but here he comes." Leyla walked away as Todd came back with some medicinal items to clean Ashley's wound so that she could heal quickly. Afterwards, he bandaged her arm. "This should do it until you can get into the healing incubator."

Terron and his team were able to stop Tony and his son Emil from selling nuclear weapons to the North Koreans and successfully got the nuclear weapons back to their base with no further interruptions. "HUWP, we're on our way back with the package and all threats are dead. I repeat, all threats are dead," Terron said over the radio.

"We hear you loud and clear, Shadow team, we hear you," one of the young Hatchet Men replied and everybody back at the base started cheering them on.

Terron, so I guess you're going to want to start working right away on your little pet project, right?" Carol asked and Terron started to smile, already pulling up his virtual reality screen so he could locate Jennifer. "You know bro', you're kind of creepy," Carol said, laughing at him.

Chapter Twenty-two

Jennifer had just started her workout at the gym with some of her girlfriends. "Jennifer, how many sets do we have to do?" Jamey asked as she was doing planks. "Man, this shit hurts, girl!" Jamey shouted to Jennifer, screwing up her pretty face.

"Okay Jamey, you can stand up now," Jennifer said.

Jamey quickly got up, shaking her body loose. "Thank God! Two minutes a plank can become stressful girl. You like to work hard!"

"Well Jamey, I don't see it any other way. Now come on, we've got some weights to lift," Jennifer told Jamey and they walked over to a bench and picked up some light weights and started doing some shoulder presses.

"So Jennifer, did you find out who the guy was that got you the earrings?" Jamey asked.

"No, not yet. He hasn't stepped out of the shadows yet," she said, gently touching the beautiful diamond stud in her ear.

"Girl, you're damn lucky. Why can't it be me?"

Jennifer smiled and said, "But what if he's ugly, then what?" Jennifer replied.

Jamey gave a laugh and started rubbing Jennifer's shoulders. She leaned over one shoulder and said, "Well, if his money is long, fuck it."

Jennifer shook her head at Jamey saying, "Is everything with you always about money?"

Jamey wasted no time and immediately nodded yes. Jennifer playfully mushed Jamey in the face then they walked over to the pull-up bars.

But over in a corner of the gym by a weight bench two men were watching Jennifer and Jamey work out. One man couldn't help himself. He had his eyes on Jamey the entire time. Jamey stood at 5'7" in height with bright, white teeth, a pretty face with caramel colored skin and black, curly shoulder-length hair. Her body was very curvy with an apple bottom and flat stomach. Even though she hated working out she did it because she knew it worked for her. But if Jamey or Jennifer could see how the two men were watching them, they would leave the gym.

"That's it girl! Go! You can do it!" Jennifer shouted to Jamey as she was doing her pull-ups.

"Man, you…got me…fucked…up!" Jamey shouted breathlessly, pumping herself up to keep doing the workout.

"That's right, pull that ass up! Yeah! I like it!" Jennifer cheered Jamey on.

"Okay, what else do you want me to do?" Jamey gasped as she finished her pull-ups. Jennifer started smiling and gave her a devilish look.

"Why are you looking at me like that? I hope you're not trying…" but before Jamey could finish her sentence Jennifer ran over to the treadmill. "What the fuck Jennifer?"

She walked back over to Jamey. "Well, we can talk about the party. Come on, I don't want to hear it. Let's go." Jennifer grabbed her iPod so she could listen to music while she worked out and Jamey did the same. Jennifer set her treadmill for 20 minutes and so did Jamey. After about five minutes into their session Jamey's phone started to vibrate. She looked at it and there was a message from her mother letting her know she needed Jamey to pick her up today. Jamey tapped Jennifer on the shoulder to get her attention.

"What's up?" Jennifer asked, taking one of her ear buds out of her ear as she continued running on the treadmill.

"My mom just messaged me, telling me she needs me. Are you going to be good because I've got to go."

"Yeah, I'll be fine. I'll call you when I get home," Jennifer told her. Jamey left the gym with a guy she and Jennifer knew.

The two strange men turned their attention to Jennifer because Jamey was leaving the gym with someone else. "Well, one is better than none at all, I guess," one of the men said to the other. Both of them pretended to work out but kept their eyes on Jennifer the entire time.

Jennifer continued to run on the treadmill for about 30 more minutes. Once done, her watch alarm pinged letting her know it was time to take her pill. Instead of taking it then, she went into the locker room to take a shower. When she was about to undress she got a text message from Laura reminding her not to forget to pick her up in 20 minutes. "Shit! I almost forgot about that. Damn!" She hurriedly grabbed her stuff because she didn't have enough time to take a shower.

Jennifer walked outside about to get into her Jeep when her watch pinged again letting her know it was time to take her medication. "Damn!" Standing outside her car she started digging in her purse for her pills and when she located them she saw a shadow coming up behind her. She quickly turned around and saw two big men walking up on her. One was white and the other was Spanish and one of them tried to grab her by the arm. "Get the hell off of me!" Jennifer shouted, punching the man in the face and then kicking him in his balls.

"You bitch!" the man shouted, holding his nuts. But the other man was able to get behind her with a chloroform soaked rag, pressing it over Jennifer's nose and knocking her out. "Man, throw that bitch in the van!" ordered the man she had kicked in the balls. Her wrists were zip-tied and she was thrown into the back of a van containing several other women that appeared to have been kidnapped as well, and taken away.

* * * * * * * * *

"What the hell!" We got to turn around now!" Terron shouted and by the look on his face Carol knew something was very wrong.

"Terron, what's going on?" Carol asked as she saw him hurry over to the pilot to let him know where to take them. When he returned Terron started playing the live video from Jennifer's earrings and everyone couldn't believe their eyes as Terron fast-forwarded to when Jennifer left the gym.

"What the fuck is going on, bro'? She's been kidnapped!" shouted Todd. All of them were watching to see what would happen next.

Terron looked at his team and what he was about to ask them to do could get them in more trouble, but Tara had already told him to keep a watch over Jennifer. "I've got to help her and if you don't want to come I truly understand." All of them said they would go with Terron to help Jennifer.

Carol pulled him to the side just to make sure Terron's head was on straight because if he messed this up it could put Jennifer in great danger with her attackers. "Terron, are you sure you're up for this?"

"Yes, I'm good. We just got to get there fast because nothing has happened to her yet from what the video is showing."

Carol saw the look on Terron's face and knew he was not himself. She gently took his hand and said, "You know from the look of things the type of people who have her, right? And what they're going to do to her if we don't make it there before they get to their destination, right?"

Terron looked at her and replied, "I know and no matter what happens to her I'm going to love her, the same as I do now."

Carol hadn't known that Terron felt that way about Jennifer because he'd never acted like this with any other woman before. She nodded her head with a slight smile, happy for him. "Don't worry, bro'. We're going to get her back in one piece," Carol assured him. The other team members continued to watch the activity on the virtual reality screen.

* * * * * * * * *

They had transferred the women into the back of a truck and one of the men in the truck told the driver to pull over so he could go into the back with the girls. The driver argued with him but he pulled over anyway. Another truck following the first truck had four men in it and that truck pulled over as well. The guy got out of the first truck and took a piss before he got in the back with the girls. He was a very big man. He was 6'5" tall Caucasian, weighing 250 pounds. He was a cigarette smoker and heavy drinker; and he was drunk.

Although Jennifer was still unconscious, the man wanted her. He walked over to her and pushed up her exercise top and bra, grabbing her breast. But one of the girls started yelling at him to stop. The other girls were too terrified and traumatized to say anything. So he turned from Jennifer and went over to her. He had wanted her before they even found Jennifer. "Bitch, you should've just shut the fuck up! Now, I'm going to have you first," he said in a slurred voice. He hit on the wall of the truck so the driver could start driving again.

He pulled a small pint bottle from his pants pocket and drank the last of his whiskey quickly, throwing the empty bottle up against the wall of the truck right beside Jennifer; the noise making her start to move in and out of consciousness. Her vision was very blurry but she kept getting glimpses of a man raping a girl on the floor right beside her.

"Bitch, I told you to be quiet but I guess you wanted some, so you got it!" the oversized man said to the girl with a drunken smile. He was on top of her, grunting and sweating as he violated her very precious prize, as if her life meant nothing. She tried to kick him off but he was too large over her, holding her bound wrists over her head. Plus, her wriggling around seemed to excite him so she became still. He was paying no attention to Jennifer.

Jennifer started to feel something take over her body when she saw the girl give up. It was like nothing she had ever felt before. She started throwing up as if she was being possessed by a demon. By the time she was done Jennifer didn't feel like herself at all. Then all of her senses became super acute. Her hearing became supersonic and she was able to hear a young child crying in Baltimore. Her touch became super sensitive and she could feel every material the cold steel of the truck was made of. Her smell was enhanced and was sharper than that of a super blood hound. And her sight was like nothing she had ever experienced. She was able to see through the walls of the truck at long range and she now had precise target vision. Suddenly, she felt a powerful strength surge through her body. But it didn't frighten her. What was happening to her?

But the sight of the girl being raped drove her, with her newfound strength, to quickly pull her wrists apart and break the zip-ties binding her. She shrugged out of her backpack from the gym and pulled out her knife she always carried. Then she leaped to her feet and jumped on the man's back, slicing his throat, clean and quick. Blood spurted out of the man's neck into the girl's face, making her scream. Jennifer stabbed him several times in the chest to make sure he was very dead. She grabbed the man's Beretta model 72 stuck in the waistband of his pants, scanning it quickly and with her x-ray vision was able to shoot through the wall of the truck, hitting the driver in the back of the head, killing him. His foot hit the gas pedal and the truck picked up speed, going off the road and hitting a tree, smashing the entire front end of the truck into an accordion shape. The other vehicle behind them screeched to a stop a distance away in the event the truck exploded.

"What the fuck happened? Shit!" one of the men shouted, grabbing his M&P 15 T 5.56mm, looking around for any other vehicle coming their way and waiting to see if anyone survived the crash.

Chapter twenty-three

Jennifer stumbled to her feet and made sure everyone was okay and started cutting the other girls free from their zip-ties. She quickly pulled a towel from her backpack and wiped the blood from the face of the girl that had stood up for her, helping her to her feet and cutting the zip-ties from her wrists. "Come on! We've got to run now!" Jennifer shouted to the girls, kicking the truck's back door open because she could smell the strong stench of gas and knew the truck was about to catch fire. She looked around and for some reason she knew they were way out in Sykesville, Maryland, around farmland. Then Jennifer saw four men running toward them with guns as they were getting out of the truck. One of the gunmen raised his Colt AR-15 Az government model, taking aim at one of the girls who was about to run away, shooting her in the head, killing her. Her lifeless body fell in front of Jennifer. "You son-of-a-bitch!" she screamed.

Jennifer felt a coldness engulf her entire body, making her laser focused on the man who shot the girl. In the blink of an eye she pointed her Beretta at the man's head and pulled the trigger, killing him. The other men started emptying out of their vehicle and Jennifer started shooting at them as they returned fire, somehow able to flip and leap and dodge their bullets.

"Come on!" one of the girls cried out for Jennifer to run with them. She turned and started running with the girls through some wheat fields while still shooting at the gunmen, trying to hold them off. Some of the girls were tired and out of breath, but Jennifer made them run.

"We've got to keep moving. They're right behind us and there's no time to stop. Let's move!"

One young girl turned to Jennifer and asked, "Were you in the military or something?"

Jennifer glanced at her as they both ran and said, "No, why?"

"Because the way you handled that man in the truck was cool."

Jennifer thought about what she'd said and somehow was able to rewind the entire episode in her mind and replay it in seconds.

"Are you okay?" the young girl asked her because Jennifer's eyes had glazed over.

She blinked and smiled as she responded, "Yes, I'm fine." Jennifer saw what seemed like a farm across the field and told the girl to keep running behind her and the other girls followed. She was able to zoom in on the men behind her to actually see how far behind them they were. They didn't have a lot of time to get to that farm.

* * * * * * * * * *

Terron and his team were watching the virtual reality screen and Terron felt a very strong connection between him and Jennifer. "Did you see that?" Carol asked Terron in disbelief as Jennifer calmly killed the gunmen with a perfect shot and flipped and leaped to dodge the other gunmen bullets.

"Hell yeah, I saw that shit!" Leyla shouted and Terron started smiling. "I knew you were one with us," he whispered to Jennifer through the screen but Carol heard him.

"Okay, so what is the plan, flyboy?" Carol asked Terron as she performed her system check of all her weapons, making sure everything was ready to go. The rest of the team started doing the same.

"We're going to drop down over them and we're coming down hot! Are we ready?" Terron asked, glancing at each of his team members. They all nodded their heads, ready to fight.

Carol walked over to Terron and asked, "Why didn't we know about her?"

"She's probably just overly athletic, or she's just really nice," Terron replied, thinking about what they'd seen her do, but trying to shrug off what was before their very eyes.

"No, brother, she is one of us. We just don't know what side yet," Todd said.

Terron responded quickly, "That's why we're going to keep this to ourselves until we find out more about her, okay?" All of them agreed to keep it a secret for him.

* * * * * * * * *

"Come on this way, follow me," Jennifer instructed the young girl with her. The other girls were not too far behind them. She saw the farm and pointed toward it. "You see that farm, we've got to make it there for help, okay?" The young girl nodded her head at Jennifer as she tried to catch her breath from running. "Come on, follow me," Jennifer said softly and they started to run toward the house. "Let's go around the back," Jennifer whispered and they ran around to the back. They started looking around and heard some pigs and chickens in a beaten down wooden barn. There was a very rank odor coming from the barn.

"Maybe it's these dirty-ass clothes hanging on these clotheslines smelling like that," the young girl said, looking around very unsettled. So was Jennifer. She still had the Beretta in her hand. As the young girl pushed some of the hanging clothing apart, something startled her.

"Oh my God! There's shit on these clothes!" the young girl shouted, shaking her hand to get it off because she had touched shit.

Jennifer and the young girl could hear music coming from inside the house. She wanted to take a look in the barn but instead she started banging on the door of the house. The other girls came around the corner of the barn yelling, "They're right behind us!" Just as Jennifer turned away from the door, it was flung open and a man immediately grabbed Jennifer and tased her until she fell unconscious. The young girl started screaming, trying to get the man off of Jennifer, but another man came out and grabbed her and pushed a cloth soaked with chloroform into her face, knocking her out cold.

The other girls were screaming, too, and by this time the gunmen were there to help round up the rest of them. "Okay, the rest of you bitches get the fuck in the house, now!" one of the men shouted, pointing his Colt model 1911 at the girls. One of the girls tried to run and a pit bull was called from inside the house by the man who had Jennifer over his shoulder. "Get that bitch, boy!" he hollered and the dog took off after the girl running into the wheat field, calling for help. But they were deep in Sykesville, Maryland with no help anywhere.

"I'm going to take these two bitches into the barn," said the man who had Jennifer over his shoulder to the men escorting the rest of the girls into the house as he looked down at the knocked out girl on the ground.

"We didn't get a chance to have fun with them yet," another man complained.

"Too late for that," he said. These bitches are trouble. I'm going to lock them away with the rest of them trouble-making bitches."

* * * * * * * * *

Terron and his team had already jumped from the plane. Terron pulled up his virtual touchscreen where he saw a man carry Jennifer and a young girl across his shoulders into a barn. Both appeared unconscious. His face became enraged and his eyes were turning red.

"Terron, don't do it!" Carol shouted as if she knew what he was about to do, and she was right.

Terron turned off the wing magnets in his exoskeleton suit so he could free-fall faster by reversing the gravitational pull, making him shoot downward as fast as a cannonball being shot out of a cannon. Then he set the magnets to turn back on within ten seconds before he touched the ground.

"So what do we do now?" Leyla shouted, looking at Ashley, Carol and Todd.

"We go with the flow. Fuck!" Carol shouted and made the same adjustments to her suit as Terron except she set her suit for seven seconds. She made her virtual grappling hook belt become reality and shot downward like a bullet, just as Terron had done. Ashley, Leyla and Todd did the same.

In the barn, Jennifer and the young girl had regained consciousness. The man bound both girl's wrist with zip-ties and attached them to hooks as if though they were two slabs of beef. "You fucking pig! Leave her the fuck alone! She's just a young girl!" Jennifer shouted, making the man laugh as he glanced at her while sharpening his knife. That cold feeling Jennifer had experienced in the truck was engulfing her body again. She felt powerful and not afraid of him at all.

"Okay bitch, you can get it first then." The man started walking over to Jennifer to gut her like a pig, and suddenly someone was shooting through the roof of the barn and killed him. Jennifer was breathing very hard and her heart was in her throat out of shock at what had just happened. Then she looked upward as something came crashing through the roof of the barn. Now she was beyond shocked! It was the man from the club!

Chapter twenty-four

Terron had pulled out his Fn 57 pistol and used his x-ray vision to shoot the man endangering Jennifer, killing him. His suit reversed the magnets, but it wasn't enough. He had to release his grappling hook, making it shoot back up to Carol. She caught it and hooked it to her belt as she slowed down. Carol sent her grappling hook to Ashley and Ashley sent hers to Todd and he did the same to Leyla so that they all were helping to slow Terron down before he hit the ground.

As Terron came crashing through the roof of the barn he was happy to see that Jennifer was okay. He slowly hit the ground, got up and walked over to her. She was looking at him in shock! Then she seemed to shake it off as he was about to cut her down and said, "No! Help her first. I'll be fine." They could barely tear their eyes away from each other but Terron turned to help the young girl. Jennifer yanked both her wrists apart, and the zip-ties fell off. Then the rest of the team dropped through the roof, ready and armed with AA12 assault shotguns that were fully automatic and could shoot 300 rounds in a minute. Carol was the only one armed with her SA Sport Empire Beast with 300 rounds of explosive arrows to shoot. She walked over to Jennifer and asked, "Are you okay?" Jennifer nodded her head and ran over to the young girl, giving her a big hug and scanning her to make sure she was alright. She glanced over at Terron in amazement. She wondered how he had known she was here.

Carol introduced the team to Jennifer. His name was Terron, Jennifer was thinking to herself. She liked that. Terron seemed to be stuck in a trance as he looked at Jennifer so Carol walked over to him, clearing her throat saying, "Team leader, what now?"

Carol's words brought him back to reality. He quickly pulled up a Browning high-powered 9mm with rounds that exploded on impact and could also be switched to disintegrating rounds or taser rounds. Terron walked over to Jennifer and gave her a rundown on the weapon, telling her the rounds were explosive, disintegrating or taser and it was up to her which type she used.

Without hesitation Jennifer grabbed the gun, handling it like a professional and said, "I'm going to disintegrate these assholes." Terron tried to tell her to stay in the barn with the young girl but his suggestion just went into one of her ears and out the other.

Carol grabbed Terron as Jennifer walked beside Leyla across the barn to look through a crack in the barn door at the house. "She's going with us and please take a good look at her. She is different, Terron."

Terron knew what Carol was talking about. She hadn't hesitated in taking the Browning 9mm and he bet she could use it as well as they could. He took the lead, scanning the house as the team and Jennifer advanced toward it. They had hidden the young girl in the barn. They stealthily made their way to one of the windows and Carol peeped in. She could hear a man yell, "Shut your mouth, bitch!" The man was zipping up his pants and grabbed his bottle of beer. There was a woman tied to the bed with no clothing on and bleeding from the mouth with blood covering her chest. But, Jennifer had told her there were also several other men in the house they couldn't see and each of them had a girl in a room having their way with them. Five other women were being held captive in chains in the basement. And there was loud music playing which is why they probably hadn't heard the gunshots through the roof in the barn. The man was taking a beer break and he walked toward the window to look out. As he lifted the window, Carol shot him with one of her disintegrating arrows. The woman on the bed looked as if she couldn't decide whether to scream or faint as the man disintegrated. Carol pushed the window higher and put a finger to her lips, silencing the woman. None of them were prepared for the smell of urine and fecal matter coming from inside the house. "What the fuck?" Carol whispered as she leaped through the window first. Then one by one the team leaped through the window, rolling across the floor as they assumed a crouched position with their weapons ready.

    Since Carol was the first one inside, she crouched down and started walking toward the room's door, pointing her SA sport with disintegrating arrows, ready to shoot anything walking through the door. Ashley was behind her then Leyla then Todd. Again, Terron tried to get Jennifer to stay back but she ignored him and leaped through the window as if she was one of them. Terron couldn't believe his eyes but he leaped into the room right behind her. Once they were all inside Leyla cut the girl free as the rest of them started to make their way throughout the house. Carol used her x-ray vision to shoot one of the men through a door in the head, killing him with a disintegrating arrow. "Room one clear," she whispered through her earpiece. She went in and helped the girl up off the grimy mattress that was saturated with urine and fecal matter.

Ashley was up and she was about to clear room two that had two men inside having their way with the two women inside. Ashley had two Fn 57 pistols with built-in silencers in each hand. She took several deep breaths and quickly opened the door. Before the door was fully open both men were dead from shots to the head. "Room two clear," Ashley reported. Todd and Leyla crept downstairs to free the women in the basement.

Terron and Jennifer were at the last room about to breach the door. "You ready?" he whispered, looking into her beautiful green eyes. He was so close to her they could have kissed. She nodded her head firmly and both of them crashed into the room, taking care of business, killing and disintegrating the last three men in the house. "We're clear," Terron reported to the team as Jennifer freed the two girls in the room. But one of them was badly hurt and needed medical assistance.

"We've got to help her," Jennifer said, helping the woman up and taking her outside for some fresh air.

Carol quickly called 911 to get the police and a paramedic to come and told Terron they had five minutes to get out of there. Terron walked outside and over to Jennifer and said, "Look, we have five…" But before he could finish his sentence Jennifer reached up and passionately kissed him on the lips. She looked into his eyes and said, "I know who you are now. Go, I'll be fine. Just keep in touch." Her soft hand was gently cupping his jaw. He turned his head slightly and left his kiss in her palm, smiling.

Carol shook her head at her besotted brother as she grabbed him and took the gun from Jennifer. Ashley and Leyla went back inside, sprinkling a special powder over the entire house. Todd ran to the barn and brought out the young girl they had hidden there then Ashley and Carol sprinkled the powder in the barn, too. Once they were all clear of the buildings, Ashley pushed a button on her exoskeleton suit and the house and barn burst into flames. Carol could hear sirens coming closer. "Terron, we've got to go, now!"

Terron leaned forward to give Jennifer another kiss, but she reluctantly pushed him away and said, "Go, I got this." Then Jennifer turned to Carol, Leyla, Ashley and Todd telling them, "Thank you all so very much! What a pleasure it has been to meet all of you!" Carol nodded her head briskly and Ashley, Leyla and Todd smiled and nodded as well. Then Terron and his team took off into the wheat field's shadows right before the police and paramedics arrived. Leyla stayed for a while, camouflaged in the wheat fields, watching Jennifer and the girls until the police and paramedics arrived; and to listen to what was being said to the police. Once she was satisfied everyone was in good hands and their team wasn't being implicated in any way, Leyla took off to join her team on the plane.

* * * * * * * * *

Jennifer was talking to one of the policemen when her father and his partner, Wendy, pulled up. Chris ran toward Jennifer in disbelief that it was her. He couldn't believe it until he actually looked into her green eyes, seeing that it was his baby girl. Wendy was right beside him.

"Jennifer, what the hell happened?" Chris asked in alarm. "Are you okay? How did you end up here?"

Jennifer started explaining to her dad what had happened to her from the time she left the gym until she was kidnapped. She told her dad about waking up in a truck and seeing a man raping a young girl. She went on to tell her father, Wendy and an officer about everything that happened after that up until now, except about the part with Terron and his team. She explained that the buildings must have been rigged to kill the women after the men had their way with them and left because everything suddenly started burning, but they all got out in time. As the girls huddled together, they let Jennifer do all the talking because they were so grateful she had kept them from getting killed. And, because they had been so terrorized, drugged and traumatized they felt they had only imagined the other people who had shown up to help them.

Chris couldn't believe this had happened to his baby. Once Jennifer was done giving her statement, her father took her home. Laura was at the window watching when her father's car pulled up in front of the house. Wendy followed, driving Jennifer's Jeep with Jennifer's purse she'd found lying underneath the car, and pulled it into the driveway.

"Jennifer!" Laura shouted, running out to her big sister and giving her a huge hug as she walked into the house. Jennifer was so happy to see her sister and to be back in her home and her room. "Oh my God! I can't believe that you went through all of that, Jennifer. I knew something was wrong when you didn't show up to get me. I felt it in my bones that something was wrong. I'm just happy that you're home with me now," Laura told her, causing Jennifer to hug her and kiss her on the forehead.

They sat on Jennifer's bed and turned on the TV. The news was on. Jennifer stood up, listening to what was being said about the men that had kidnapped her and the other girls. Her father walked into her room and told her to turn the news off, thinking it would upset her. But Jennifer wanted to hear what the news had to say about the men.

"Today in Sykesville, Maryland, a sex trafficking ring was single-handedly taken down by an unknown woman who had also been kidnapped. The girls were being taken to a farmhouse located on a large parcel of land on the other side of the wheat fields. The girls were being trafficked into, as well as out of, various states. Their kidnappers have not been captured," the news correspondent reported.

"Okay girls, enough of that," Chris said, turning off the TV. Wendy had brought up Jennifer's purse and was standing in the doorway, listening at Chris talk with his girls. "I think you should go to bed and get some rest," Chris suggested to his daughters. He kissed them both on the forehead before he walked out, shutting the door behind him.

"Is everything okay, Chris?" Wendy asked as the two of them walked down the stairs together. He was her partner and she felt his concern.

"Yes, it's good. I'm just happy nothing bad came out of that situation today," he replied. But he still had a worried look on his face.

Wendy gave Chris a comforting rub on the back as they walked into the kitchen. She sat down at the table while he made some tea for the both of them.

Up in Jennifer's bedroom, Laura plopped down on Jennifer's bed and asked, "Jennifer, what the hell happened out there? I know you were scared, right?" She wanted to know more about what had happened with Jennifer.

"Laura, I want to be real with you so you can't tell dad or anybody else. You have to promise me that you're going to keep what I tell you a secret."

Laura nodded her head quickly, indicating she would because she was anxious to hear what Jennifer had to say.

Jennifer told her about leaving the gym and forgetting to take her pills right before she was kidnapped.

"So wait a minute, you're telling me you didn't take your pills yet? How is that so?" Laura asked with a curious look on her face because she remembered what her dad always told them about taking the pills.

"I don't know but what I do know is that's one of the reasons I'm alive right now." She continued to tell Laura about what she'd seen, what she'd felt and how she'd reacted when she was kidnapped by the men, especially when one man started raping a young girl. Laura's eyes got big and she couldn't believe what she was hearing from Jennifer and she wanted to know more. Jennifer got up and went to her purse, grabbed her pills and marched into her bathroom. Laura followed her. Jennifer opened the pill bottle and flushed all the pills down the toilet.

"Jennifer! What the hell are you doing? Have you lost your mind?" Laura whispered loudly.

She looked at Laura and said, "No, I'm freeing my mind and I think you should, too, Laura."

Laura was confused as she walked behind Jennifer out of the bathroom and asked, "Why?"

"I've never felt like I did today ever in my life, and I like it."

Laura stood there, thinking about what her sister had told her, but she wasn't ready to stop taking her pills just yet. "I don't know Jennifer. I'm going to still take mine for now."

Jennifer smiled and sat down on the bed, listening to whatever she wanted to. In her very house she could sit and listen to people talking in their homes down the street as if they were right beside her.

Laura stood there watching her sister for a moment and had to ask. "Did they drug you, Jennifer?"

Jennifer started laughing and said, "No, silly. They used a little chloroform to get me in the truck and that didn't last long. I'm good and you're going to see one day what the hell I'm talking about, Laura." Jennifer gave her little sister a big hug then Laura walked out of the room and headed to her room to get ready for bed.

Epilogue

"Terron, you know we're going to have to tell the Elders eventually about what we saw with Jennifer, right?" Carol said to him, looking at him with a serious and concerned face. Terron was crouched down, barely listening to Carol as he watched Jennifer's house. Just the mention of her name made him want to glow. The connection was that strong. Now that he had met her, fought beside her, there was no turning back his feelings for her. Carol walked up to him, slapping him on the back of his head.

"Ow! What the hell was that for?" he whispered with a scowl as he rubbed the back of his head.

"Because, Terron, I'm talking to you and you're not listening! This is serious shit! So act like you know it, dude!"

Terron slowly nodded his head at Carol. He knew she was right. So, he stood up and both of them vanished into the darkness from which they'd come.

* * * * * * * * *

"Chris, what are you going to do?" Wendy asked with a great look of concern on her face.

"I don't know. I might see if she would get some counseling. I just hope this doesn't make her afraid to go out and do things she want to do."

"No, she should be fine, Chris. She is a big girl and she's proven she can definitely take care of herself; that we do know. I've got to go. Thanks for the tea. I'll pick you up in the morning," Wendy said, picking up her keys from the kitchen table and walking towards the door.

Chris walked her to her car and then walked back inside his house. He went to Laura's room, peeking in on her then closing her door. He walked down the hallway to Jennifer's room, doing the same thing, but looking at Jennifer a little bit longer. He'd sensed something different about her today. It was as if the entire kidnapping situation hadn't fazed her at all. She had seemed so composed and in control. Chris closed her door and went to his room, undressed and sat on the side of the bed. He opened his bedside drawer and took out a bottle of pills. He took a deep breath then he took one. He put the bottle back, turned out his light and went to bed.

But Jennifer was not asleep yet. Her back had been to her father and she was still smiling as she listened to everything.

Hatchet Men

* * * * * * * * *

Everything is good and right with Jennifer for now, but the war between the Shadows and the Ghosts has yet to begin! To be continued in *HATCHET MEN REBORN: IMPERIAL LOVE.*

BLUEINK REVIEW

Simmeon Anderson's ambitious novel is a fusion of science fiction, alternate history, post-apocalyptic fiction, and international thriller that ties in Greek, Roman and Egyptian mythology. It spans centuries and follows a group of advanced humans (aka Hatchet Men Shadows) as they attempt to save humankind from their nemeses (the Hatchet Men Ghosts).

The main storyline is set largely in 2050 Baltimore in a radically advanced future. Racism, and any form of hate crime, has been outlawed, and cities float via magnetic levitation, but crimes like homicide, drug dealing and sex trafficking are at an all-time high.

(Reviewed: July, 2021)

FOREWORD REVIEWS

Clarion Review

In Simmeon Anderson's fantasy novel *The Hatchet Men*, an ancient war carries over onto a modern era.

Thousands of years ago, a race of godlike beings, the Watchers, crashed to Earth. They gifted powers to remarkable humans, transforming them into Hatchet Men who were near immortal, vulnerable only to each other. Two factions formed: the Ghosts and Shadows. The two groups waged war across centuries, altering the course of history. Now, the Ghosts are missing, and the Shadows hope to keep humans from destroying themselves or the planet.

In the fantasy novel *The Hatchet Men*, supernatural beings work to protect humanity from looming danger.

John M. Murray (July 23, 2021)

ABOUT THE AUTHOR

Simmeon Anderson a.k.a Fence was born in New York City and raised in Brooklyn. He is the proud father of six children. His mother inspired him to write his first novel Cartel Kings and Gangster Chitty, Chitty, Bang, Bang in 2006. He wrote the book while he was in lock up in the Baltimore City Jail after reading a letter from his mother challenging him to replace all the energy that he used in the streets by converting it into something positive and to become someone great. Simmeon has been enjoying writing fantasy, fiction and non-fiction novels ever since.

Made in the USA
Middletown, DE
19 June 2022